SO-BSN-038

SCAM

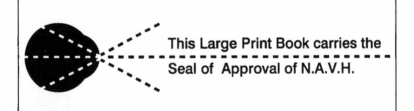

This Large Print Book carries the
Seal of Approval of N.A.V.H.

SCAM

PARNELL HALL

Thorndike Press • Thorndike, Maine

Copyright © 1997 by Parnell Hall

All rights reserved.

Published in 1997 by arrangement with Warner Books, Inc.

Thorndike Large Print ® Americana Series.

The tree indicium is a trademark of Thorndike Press.

The text of this Large Print edition is unabridged.
Other aspects of the book may vary from the original edition.

Set in 16 pt. Plantin.

Printed in the United States on permanent paper.

Library of Congress Cataloging in Publication Data

Hall, Parnell.
    Scam / Parnell Hall.
      p.   cm.
    ISBN 0-7862-1210-1 (lg. print : hc : alk. paper)
    1. Large type books. 2. Hastings, Stanley (Fictitious
character) — Fiction. 3. Private investigators — New
York (State) — New York — Fiction. 4. New York
(N.Y.) — Fiction. I. Title.
    [PS3558.A37327S27   1997b]
    813´.54—dc21   97-23469

For Jim and Franny

1.

"I'm being set up."

I stifled a grin. Cranston Pritchert was six foot six and skinny as a rail, and when he said he was being set up, all I could think of was a candlepin on a bowling lane. Since the gentleman seemed to be upset, I figured grinning would have been an inappropriate reaction, and if questioned I certainly would not have wanted to explain. I bit my lip, tried not to smile.

"Go on," I said.

Cranston Pritchert opened his mouth. Closed it again. "I don't know where to begin."

"Begin at the end."

He looked at me. "Huh?"

"If you're having trouble telling your story, don't bother. Start with the punch line. Why are you here?"

That invitation did not put Cranston Pritchert at his ease. Anything but. His lip curled up slightly. "Yes, that's so clever, isn't it?" he said. "Is that what you tell all your clients?"

It most certainly wasn't. I don't *have* any clients. At least not the kind Cranston Pritchert meant. See, I'm not the kind of private detective people immediately think of. The kind you see on TV. The kind who solve people's problems by having fist fights and car chases and running around with flashy blondes.

No, unfortunately, I'm the kind of private detective that exists in real life. The kind that does largely negligence work. I chase ambulance for the law firm of Rosenberg and Stone. That consists mainly of interviewing accident victims and taking pictures of their broken arms and legs, not to mention the cracks in the sidewalk that tripped them.

I doubt if that would have impressed Cranston Pritchert much.

We were sitting in my office on West 47th Street, the one-room hole-in-the-wall affair with the sign STANLEY HASTINGS DETECTIVE AGENCY on the door. Cranston Pritchert had been waiting outside when I'd come by at nine o'clock to check the answering machine and pick up the mail. If he hadn't been, he'd have missed me. I don't hang out in the office much. By nine oh five I'd have been gone.

"All right, look," I said. "We're off on the wrong foot here. I don't mean to be rude, but I've gotta go out on a case."

Pritchert blinked. "You already *have* a case?"

"I do three or four cases a day."

"You're kidding."

"Not at all. Ninety percent of detective work is routine. My ten o'clock case is a hit-and-run. I'll take down all the pertinent information from the victim, turn it over to the lawyer, and I'm done."

"What about finding the car?"

"That's not my job."

"What if the lawyer asked you to?"

"He won't."

"Why?"

"Because he can file suit without it. They don't need to catch the driver. It's like a no-fault situation. Even if they don't know who did it, they can still sue."

"I see."

"Now, I told you all about my business. You wanna tell me about yours? If not, I gotta run."

Cranston Pritchert stood up. He put up his hands, towered over me. "No, no," he said. "Please. Even if you turn me down. Even if you can't take the case. I gotta talk to somebody. Won't you at least listen?"

"I'm perfectly willing to listen," I said. "You were just having trouble getting started and frankly I'm pressed for time."

"I understand," Pritchert said. "I'm sorry. I promise. I'm not going to waste any more of your time. Just hear me out."

"Fine," I said. "So, tell me. What's your problem?"

Pritchert dropped his hands to his sides. He pulled his chin in and stood there, stiff as a ramrod, as if at attention, looking more than ever like a candlepin.

I looked at him, prayed he wouldn't say it again.

He did.

"I'm being set up."

2.

Eventually I got the story, but not before we'd gone around at least two more times. My query *Who's setting you up?* might have led to promising ground, but merely provoked the response *I don't know.* Similarly, *How are you being set up?* resulted in the deflection *I'm not sure.*

It was a while before I stumbled on the old faithful *Why don't you tell me what happened?* Which merely earned me a second helping of *I don't know where to begin.*

At which point I stood up, snapped shut my briefcase and headed for the door.

He stopped me, apologized, and I finally got the story.

"It's my company," he said, once we had both sat back down.

"Your company?"

"Yes. Philip Greenberg Investments."

"If it's your company, why is it named Philip Greenberg?"

He put up his hands. "No, no. It's not *my* company. It's the company I work for."

"What do you do for them?"

"I'm a vice-president."

"What does that entail?"

"I beg your pardon?"

"What does your company do?"

"Oh. Just what it sounds like. Make investments. Buy and sell."

"On the stock market?"

"No. Not stocks. Properties. Businesses. Real estate. One of our strengths is we're rather diversified. Say we invest in a hotel. We might turn right around and sell it. We might renovate it and then sell it. We might rent it out. We might run it as a business. Or we might develop it as part of a chain. You see?"

Not at all. Business investments and real estate go right over my head. But it was probably not the time to say so.

"And you're the vice-president?" I said.

"Well, I'm *a* vice-president. Actually, there's two others."

"Oh?"

"Yeah. Marty Rothstein and Kevin Dunbar."

"You have three vice-presidents?"

"That's right."

"Who's the president?"

"There is no president."

"Oh? So who runs the company?"

"The board of directors."

"And who is that?"

Cranston Pritchert nodded. "Exactly. That's just it." He ticked them off on his fingers. "There's me. Kevin. Marty. And the treasurer, Jack Jenkins. That's four. The fifth member was the chairman of the board. Philip Greenberg. He died last month."

"Oh?"

"Yes," Pritchert said. "And that's the whole problem. There's a proxy fight going on for control of the company. There's a stockholders meeting coming up. To vote in a new chairman of the board."

"Who are the stockholders?"

"The main ones are me, Kevin, and Marty."

"Didn't Philip Greenberg own stock?"

"Yes, of course. It went to his granddaughter, Amy. Nearest living relative. But she has no interest in the company. She's in her twenties. Playgirl. Could care less about business."

"But she has the stock?"

"Yes."

"A controlling interest?"

He frowned. "Not really controlling. Whoever she voted with would be in a powerful position. Still, it would take more proxies. If everyone ganged up against them —"

I put up my hands. "Fine," I said. "So

you're a stockholder?"

"Yes."

"As well as these other guys?"

"Kevin and Marty. That's right."

"And you all want to be chairman of the board?"

He frowned. "That's putting it a little bluntly. This company is my future. I would like to control my future. I —"

I put up my hands again. Looked at my watch. "Please. I have to be in the Bronx by ten o'clock. The fact is, there's a proxy fight going on, there's a stockholders meeting, and they're gonna vote in a chairman of the board?"

"That's right."

"What has this got to do with you being set up?"

"That's just it. I'm not sure."

Before we went around again, I said, "Fine. Tell me about the incident that makes you think you're being set up."

He took a breath. "It was last week. Thursday night. After work. I went out for a drink."

"With who?"

"Just by myself."

"You usually drink alone?"

"You make it sound like a bad habit."

"I'm sorry. I'm just trying to get the infor-

14

mation. Do you normally go out with people from work?"

"No."

"Then you, Marty, and Kevin aren't close."

"Well, not socially."

"Fine," I said. "I'm sorry I interrupted. Anyway, you went out for a drink?"

"Yeah."

"Where?"

"At a bar."

"I figured that. Where's the bar?"

"On Third Avenue."

"Third Avenue and where?"

"65th Street."

"Where's work?"

"66th and Lex."

"Uh-huh. So you went out to this bar and what happened?"

"Well, there was a girl there."

"Oh?"

"Yeah. Young. Attractive. Anyway, we got to talking. And I wound up buying her a drink."

"I see."

He frowned impatiently. "No, it wasn't like that."

"Like what?"

"Like what you're thinking. It was just very pleasant. We sat there talking and I wound

15

up buying her a drink."

"What were you talking about?"

"Nothing in particular. Just talking."

"So?"

"So, anyway we had a couple of drinks and that's it."

"What do you mean, that's it?"

"That's all I remember."

"Oh?"

"Next thing I know, I'm sitting on the front steps of a brownstone and a guy's prodding me with his foot and telling me to move on."

"Where was this?"

"I'm not exactly sure. But not more than a few blocks away."

"What time was it?"

"About nine-thirty."

"Nine-thirty that night?"

"That's right."

"I take it the girl was gone?"

"Of course."

"I see. Mr. Pritchert, exactly what is it you want?"

"I want you to find the girl."

"Oh?"

"That's the only way I'm going to find out what happened."

"Why does it matter?"

"Are you kidding? With the proxy fight

16

going on? Something like this is all it would take for me to lose everything."

"Uh-huh. So you want me to find this girl?"

"That's right."

"Okay. What's her name?"

"I don't know."

"You don't know?"

"No."

"You didn't ask her name?"

"I did, but she didn't tell me."

"Why not?"

"I don't know why not. But it's one of the reasons I think something happened."

"How did she get away with not telling you her name?"

"She passed it off. Made a joke. Changed the subject. I don't know." He shook his head. Grimaced. "Women. I have trouble with women."

"So it seems."

"No, I mean relating. Even in business, women throw me. They don't think like me. You know?"

I took a breath. "Mr. Pritchert, I have an appointment."

"Right. Sorry." Pritchert blinked. Then he stuck out his chin. "No, I'm *not* sorry. All I said was she didn't tell me her name. Then *you* started arguing about it."

17

I exhaled. "Okay. Guilty. But the fact is, she didn't tell. So you don't know. Which makes her a little harder to find. So tell me. What does she look like?"

"She's about twenty-five. Blond hair. Short. Curly. Little turned-up nose. Blue eyes. Bright smile." He frowned. "I'm not sure how tall she is — she was sitting on a stool. She was wearing a tank top and shorts. Red, the top was. She had large breasts. Very large. And a thin waist. A very attractive girl."

"Uh-huh. Now this was last Thursday night?"

"That's right."

"Why'd you wait till now?"

"I wasn't sure what to do. It took me a while to think it over."

"Nothing happened to prompt your decision?"

"No. What could have?"

"I don't know. That's why I'm asking."

"Well, nothing did."

"Uh-huh. Now the girl — I take it you've never seen her before?"

"No."

"You don't have any idea who she is?"

"No."

"It didn't come up in conversation? You didn't ask her what she did?"

"She didn't talk about herself. It was all kidding. Small talk."

"Uh-huh. What's the name of the bar?"

"I don't know."

"What a surprise."

His jaw came up. "Hey. I don't like your attitude."

"I'm sorry, but it would be nice to have *something* to go on. How am I going to find this bar?"

"It's on the east side of Third Avenue. In the middle of the block. It has a yellow awning. You can't miss it."

"You've been there before?"

"Sure. Many times."

"And you've never seen this girl?"

"How many times do I have to tell you? No."

"Well, that's something."

"What do you mean?"

"It makes it look more like she was there just to meet you."

"Exactly," Pritchert said. "That's exactly right. So you see. That proves it."

He looked at me portentously, and I had the horrible feeling he was about to say it again.

He did.

"I'm being set up."

3.

"It's a scam."

I blinked at Alice. "What?"

"Come on," Alice said. "The whole thing's fishy."

"Fishy?"

"Sure. A guy goes into a bar, starts drinking with a girl, passes out, and wakes up on the street. He immediately concludes this has something to do with a proxy fight."

"Not immediately. This happened last week."

Alice rolled her eyes, turned back to what she was stirring on the stove. "That's irrelevant. Or at least trivial. Never mind the speed at which he arrived at the conclusion, the fact is that he made the connection at all."

"You're saying there's no connection?"

"I'm saying it sounds unlikely."

"I agree. So why do you say it's a scam?"

"That's just the way it strikes me."

I took a breath. "I'm sure it is. Would you mind sharing your thought process? I have no idea what you're talking about."

Alice tasted the sauce she was stirring,

headed for the spice rack. "The proxy fight is bullshit," Alice said. She selected a jar, turned back to the stove. "I'm not saying there isn't one. There probably is. But it probably has nothing to do with the girl in the bar."

"How is that a scam?"

"That's not a scam. It has nothing to do with it."

"Alice, you said it was a scam."

"Yeah. But not that."

"Then what?"

"The guy's story."

"I'm still not following you. Who's pulling a scam on who?"

"He's pulling a scam on you."

"On me?"

"Sure."

"Just how do you figure that?"

"He wants the girl."

"Huh?"

"The guy wants the girl. That's obvious. It's the one thing we know for sure. He wants you to find the girl. All the rest of this stuff is just window dressing."

I blinked. Off the wall as that sounded, I was not about to reject it out of hand.

You see, Alice is often right. Or at least she gives that impression. The truth is, my wife could anchor a national debate team. If she wanted to tell me black was white, I'd be hard pressed to argue.

Just as I was now.

"I'm still not following. What do you mean by window dressing?"

"Just that. The guy wants to find the girl. But he's embarrassed to say so. So he invents a reason."

"That sounds pretty stupid."

"Men are not always totally logical when women are involved."

While I groped for a comeback to that, Alice said, "So you went to this bar?"

"Yeah, but it was a washout."

"Why?"

"The bartender wasn't there."

"The one who was on that night?"

"Right."

"So when will he be on?"

"Tomorrow night."

"You'll go back then?"

"Sure."

"So you figure you worked what today, an hour?"

"What?"

"On this case. You gonna bill him for an hour?"

"I wasn't going to bill him at all."

Alice turned away from the stove. "What, are you nuts? You went to the bar."

"The guy I wanted to see wasn't there."

"So what?"

"So it's not like I did anything."

"You made the effort. What's the guy want, a written guarantee?"

"No, but —"

"You say the guy's not paying you by the day."

"Right. Because I have other cases."

"You could cancel them."

"Huh."

"The guy agreed to fifty bucks an hour, right? Isn't that what you said? Well, Richard's paying you twenty. Please correct me if I'm wrong, but you got a hundred and sixty dollar day working for Richard, or four hundred dollars working for him."

"Your math is fine. I'm just not sure if finding this girl is a full-time job."

"Well, you put in an hour already, right? Going to this bar."

"I'm not sure I should bill him for it."

"Right," Alice said. "And do you know why?"

"I told you. Because I didn't really do anything."

"Don't be silly," Alice said. "That's not why."

I took a breath. "Okay," I said. "Then *you* tell me why."

"You're afraid you won't find her."

"Huh?"

"You're afraid you won't find the girl. You're afraid you can't do it. In which case, you won't want to bill him at all."

"Oh."

"Will you?"

I hated to admit it, but as usual Alice had put her finger right on it. That was *exactly* the case. My main problem with finding this girl for Cranston Pritchert was I wasn't sure I'd be able to do it. Because, aside from talking to the bartender who was unlikely to be any help at all, there wasn't much I could do.

While I hesitated, thinking this, Alice bored in, voicing my doubts. "You think the bartender will be any help?"

"I don't know."

"If he isn't, what will you do?"

"I'm not sure."

"The bartender's your only real lead?"

"More or less."

"So basically this guy hired you to interview the bartender?"

"That's right."

"Why can't he do it himself?"

"Huh?"

"Why does he need you? Why doesn't he go in there and ask the bartender himself?"

"I don't know."

"Did you ask him?"

"Huh?"

"Did you ask him why he didn't want to interview the bartender himself?"

"No."

"Why not?"

"It didn't occur to me."

"Well, it's occurred to you now. It might be a good idea to ask the gentleman."

"It's probably nothing, Alice. He's probably just embarrassed."

"Maybe so. But that in itself would be something. Fifty bucks an hour is pretty embarrassed."

"You know, you're making a lot of deductions from no facts at all."

"Exactly."

"What?"

"No facts at all. Obviously this guy hasn't told you everything." Alice tasted the sauce, nodded her approval, switched off the burner. "Which lets you off the hook. You interview the bartender, report back to your client, and you're done."

Somehow that didn't seem like a solution. "Then what?" I said.

Alice smiled. Shrugged.

"That's up to him."

4.

The bartender seemed young. Of course, everyone I meet these days does. I'm sure to him I seemed old.

He had brown hair, cut short on the top and long in the back, and a scrawny moustache. He twitched his nose, cocked his head at me and said, "You a cop?"

Damn.

In a project in Harlem I'm often taken for a cop because otherwise why would I be there? But in an East Side singles bar? Sure, I'd just come off work, so I was sporting a suit and tie. But why did that say cop rather than ad executive?

Obviously, it was my manner. Which was a bit of a kick in the head. I'd just been contemplating ordering a Diet Coke and wondering how much it would set me back and whether I could charge it to Cranston Pritchert on the grounds I had to order it to maintain my cover, and now I find my cover's blown before I even begin.

I shook my head, flopped open my ID. "No," I said, "I'm private. I got no beef with you. But I could use a little help."

The guy was even younger than I thought, because he grinned. "You're a private detective?"

"That's right."

"You after someone's wife?"

"I beg your pardon?"

"Getting evidence for a divorce?"

"No, no. Nothing like that."

"What, then?"

"I'm looking for someone."

"Who?"

"This last Thursday night. There's a guy in here after work."

"There's lots of guys in here after work."

"Yeah, well this one had to duck to get in the door."

"Oh?"

"Guy looks like he could play guard for the Knicks if he was black and put on weight."

"Oh, him."

"You know who I mean?"

"Hard to miss, isn't he?"

"I would imagine. You happen to see him Thursday night?"

"Yeah. He was in here."

"You know his name?"

"No, I don't. And that's how they like it."

"I beg your pardon?"

"You know the song from the TV show, Sometimes you gotta go where everybody knows your name? That's bullshit. A bar like this, you wanna go where *nobody* knows your name. Now, they all know *my* name. Sandy. Hey, Sandy, get me a beer. But their name?" He shrugged. "I don't ask."

"But he was a regular?"

"Fairly. He popped in every now and then."

"This Thursday night — you see him talking to anyone in particular?"

"Sure. The girl."

"What girl?"

"Excuse me."

It was midafternoon and the bar was nearly empty, but the two business types that were there had just signaled for another round. Sandy moved down the bar to pick up the two empty glasses, then grabbed a cocktail shaker and started mixing another drink.

"What girl?" I persisted.

Sandy leaned in so the businessmen couldn't hear. "Girl with the boobs," he said.

"Could you be more explicit?"

"I could, but that says it all. Girl had big breasts, and wanted you to know it. Wearing a tank top two sizes too small. Eye-popping, she was."

"And he was interested?"

"Oh, yeah. Hitting it off just fine, they were."

"You hear any of the conversation?"

"Not so's you'd notice."

"Would you tell me if you did?"

"Sure. Why not?"

"You didn't hear anything?"

"Nothing worth mentioning. I filled their drinks a couple of times. Seems to me they were talking the usual bullshit. City's going to pot, economy's going to hell." He poured the contents of the shaker into the martini glass. "Hell of a pickup line."

"What were they drinking?"

"Them? He's drinking scotch and soda. She's drinking daiquiris."

"Was that usual?"

"For him, yeah. Her, I wouldn't know."

Sandy opened a beer, set it and the martini in front of the two businessmen, and extracted a bill from the pile on the bar. It appeared to be a ten. I was glad I hadn't ordered that Diet Coke.

"You'd never seen the girl before?" I said when he came back.

"First time."

"You happen to see them leave?"

"No, I didn't. You gotta understand. Right now, no one's here. But five o'clock, this place will be packed. Be hardly room to move."

"Uh-huh," I said. "Tell me. This girl. Is there anyone *else* you saw talking to her? Anyone might be able to help me out?"

"No one in particular. I'm sure half a dozen guys hit on her. But I wouldn't know who they were." He picked up the two empty glasses and dunked them in the sink. "Look. You wanna hang out till five o'clock, start asking people if they saw this girl, do me a favor. Don't. I'm talking to you because I'm a nice guy and I'm the bartender. But to the customers? A private detective in a singles bar is the kiss of death." He shook the glasses, set them on the bar. He shrugged. "Just a hint."

Not exactly the hint I was looking for.

5.

Cranston Pritchert was not pleased.

"You got nothing?" he said.

"It would seem there's nothing to get."

"What about the girl?"

"There's nothing to go on."

"You have a description."

"That I do. And if you want, I can go back tonight and ask around. But the bartender says that will probably do no good."

"Why not?"

"Because private detectives are not particularly popular in singles bars. They tend to make people nervous."

"You don't have to say you're a private detective."

"Of course not. Pardon me, but I'm taking a survey of how many large-busted blondes hang out in singles bars, and have you happened to see one?"

Pritchert frowned. "Don't be ridiculous."

"I'm sorry," I said. "But you see the point. It's very difficult for me to do this job. On the other hand, it would be easy for you. When you get off work tonight why don't you go to the bar, as you often do, have a drink and ask around?"

"I don't want to do that."

"Why not?"

"It would make me seem foolish. I can't afford to appear foolish with this proxy fight going on."

"You think having me asking around doesn't make you seem foolish?"

His eyes widened. "You're not mentioning me."

"Are you kidding? I'm asking about the girl. You think no one's gonna notice she's talking to someone six foot six?"

"Hell."

"Well, that's the situation. So far I've only talked to the bartender. I could go back during happy hour, work some line, start asking customers. But if you think I can describe the girl and leave you out of it, you must be dreaming."

He frowned, thought that over.

"If you don't want me to do that," I said, "there's nothing I can do. Now, I put in two hours already, one last night and one the day before. That's a hundred bucks. You gave me a two hundred dollar retainer. If you like, I'll return a hundred to you now and forget the whole thing. Frankly, that's what I'd prefer to do, because the bartender has already told me he doesn't want me hanging around."

"You're not working for the bartender," Pritchert said.

"No, I'm not. And I'm not working for you either, unless there's something I can actually do. Frankly, this whole thing seems a tempest in a teapot."

Pritchert frowned. "What do you mean?"

"I mean just because a girl tries to pick you up in a bar, there's no reason to assume anything sinister. Now, if the girl showed up, tried to shake you down, that would be something else. But the way things stand, there's no reason to assume anything of the sort. You met a girl, you had a few too many drinks, you don't remember everything that happened. Big deal. If you got nothing more to go on, I don't see how I can help you."

"I tell you, it means something."

"How do you know that? Intuition?"

"You can call it what you like. The fact is, I want something done."

"What?"

"I want you to find this girl."

"And how would you propose I do that?"

He took a breath. "You're the detective. You should be telling me."

"I am telling you. I'm telling you it's a long shot and it's probably a waste of time. If you want me to go through the motions, I'll go through the motions. Right now I got a woman in Queens fell down in a McDonald's and broke her arm. So I gotta be going."

"How can I reach you?"

"Huh?"

"Suppose I need to reach you during business hours."

"Why would you?"

"I don't know. But if I did."

I took out one of Richard Rosenberg's business cards. "This is the attorney I work for. The switchboard can always reach me."

"You going to work now?"

"That's right."

"When do you get off?"

"In the afternoon."

"When?"

"Depends on what cases come in. Some days I'm off by two, some days I work till six."

"What about today?"

"So far I just got the one case. I should knock it off by noon." He frowned. "So in theory I could work for you then. Assuming nothing else came in. And assuming there was something you wanted me to do."

"I want you to find the girl."

"I understand. Can you suggest one line

of inquiry I might pursue at twelve o'clock this afternoon?"

He rubbed his forehead. Exhaled. "All right. Try the bar. Tonight. During happy hour."

"All right," I said. "If that's what you want. But if I don't get a lead, this will eat up your last hundred bucks. At which point I am done. Unless you have more ideas, more money, or preferably both."

"What if you get a lead?"

"Exactly," I said. "That's the point I want to make. If I should get a lead, do you want me to follow it up?"

"Absolutely."

"At fifty bucks an hour plus expenses?"

"Of course. That's what we agreed on."

"I know. What I'm asking is how far do you want me to go?"

"I beg your pardon?"

"I mean, what's the limit? Suppose I get a lead tonight and have to stake out an apartment for ten hours waiting for the woman to come back. You gonna foot the bill?"

"Ten hours?"

"That was an example. *You* tell *me* how many hours."

"I don't know. It would depend on the situation."

"Fine. You want me to call you and ask?"

He put up his hand. "No, no. Don't call me. I'll call you."

"What? You're psychic? You'll know if I need to talk to you?"

"No, no. You're an honest man. I'll trust you. If you get a lead, you follow it up. I'll trust you to use your best judgment. I'm instructing you to follow up anything that seems promising. I'll meet you here tomorrow morning to get your report."

"Suppose I'm sitting on a stakeout?"

"Good point. If you're not here, I'll call the number you gave me. You say they can reach you?"

"Yeah. I have a beeper. They can page me."

"Fine. That's what I'll do."

I frowned. Put up my hand. "Mr. Pritchert. This is all well and good. But I have to tell you, the whole thing's a long shot. My professional opinion is, I'll spend two hours in the bar, learn nothing useful, use up your money, and be done."

Pritchert held up one finger. Looked very much like a high school teacher about to lecture a naughty pupil. "I don't like you going in with that attitude. If you expect to fail, you will fail. If there's nothing to get, fine. But I want you to make an honest effort.

Give it a fair shot."

I sighed. "All right," I said. "I will have a positive attitude and give it a fair shot."

I don't think I sounded very convincing.

6.

Betty Brody broke her leg.

Doo dah. Doo dah.

Betty Brody broke her leg.

All the doo dah day.

Yeah, I know. One shouldn't joke about another one's misfortune. But in my profession, one can't help it.

I handle three or four cases a day, five days a week, fifty-two weeks a year. And they're all the same. At least, they seem that way.

First off, they're all negligence cases. Of these, over half, probably even seventy-five percent, are trip-and-falls. The injury is usually a broken arm or leg. That's how I can always recognize my clients — they're the ones wearing the casts.

For another thing, over fifty percent of my clients are black. That's because the clients all come from TV ads, and the people who call a lawyer they see advertised on television tend to be economically challenged. Rosenberg and Stone compounds the problem by advertising largely on syndicated black sitcoms. So, as door after apartment door swings open to reveal yet another black client on crutches, I can't help thinking it won't be long before there won't be an African-American left standing in all of New York.

Needless to say, I revealed none of that to Betty Brody. I never cracked a smile. I treated her injury with the solemnity it deserved, and I had the nice lady all primed to sign the retainer empowering Richard Rosenberg to act as her attorney, when my beeper went off.

I explained to Betty Brody that I would need to use her phone, but we could complete our transaction first. Richard Rosenberg's prime directive is sign the clients, and I do not take kindly to interruptions at retainer-signing time. I'm not superstitious, still there's always the chance the client's husband, boyfriend, or whatever will come home and say, "Hey, what the hell you signing there?" and the game will be up. Not that it would matter in terms of me getting paid — still and all, I like to do the job.

Anyway, I signed up Betty Brody and her broken leg and called the office.

"Rosenberg and Stone."

"Hi, Mary," I said.

It was a pleasure.

I should explain. Richard Rosenberg employed two switchboard girls, Wendy and Janet. Both were away on summer vacation, and I couldn't have been happier. Wendy and Janet were simple tools at best. Well, that's not fair — they were borderline competent; competent enough to have lasted this long without getting fired. But only because they were incompetent enough to be willing to work for the tiny wages Richard Rosenberg was willing to pay. The fact is, I was never able to depend on them. Any information they gave me was likely to be wrong. More than once I had had to search for a nonexistent client, phone number, or address.

As if that weren't bad enough, they happened to have identical voices, so you never knew which one you were dealing with. Which was a bit of a pain. I could never say, "Hi, Wendy" or, "Hi, Janet." Worse, if god forbid I should have to call them back, I never knew which to call.

Now they were on vacation, and Richard had hired one woman to take their place. Which in a way made sense — one competent woman to do the work of two incompetent ones. Which worked just fine. The woman was crisp, efficient, and right on the button. Moreover, she was only one person, so there was no danger of confusing her with anyone else. Plus, her name was Mary Mason, which rhymed with Perry Mason, so, bad as I am with names, I wasn't likely to forget hers.

"Hi, Mary," I said. "It's Stanley," secure in the knowledge that she was going to give me a case and that the information would be correct.

Wrong again.

The message was to call Cranston Pritchert.

7.

"This better be good."

I wasn't kidding. Having driven all the way back from Queens to meet Cranston Pritchert in my office, I wasn't about to take any shit. I was also billing him for the travel time.

"It's good. Believe me, it's good."

"Oh yeah?"

Pritchert frowned. "Well, actually, it isn't good. What I mean is, it's something. Something concrete."

"Like what?"

Pritchert dropped his briefcase on my desk, popped it open, and pulled out a sheet of paper.

"Like this," he said.

I looked. It was a letter, consisting of words cut from newspaper headlines and pasted on a sheet of paper. There was no date, no greeting, no salutation.

It said, I SAW YOU IN THE SINGLES BAR.

"See?" Pritchert said. "What did I tell you?"

I frowned. "Where did you get this?"

42

"It was in the mail."

"What mail?"

"This morning's mail."

"It came to your house?"

"No. To the office."

"Someone sent this to your office?"

"That's right."

"Where's the envelope?"

"Huh?"

"The envelope it came in."

"Oh. I don't have it."

"What?"

"I threw it out."

"You threw it out?"

"Well, I didn't know."

"How could you throw it out?"

"Hey. I didn't know. I got the morning mail. This was just one of the letters in it. I open it up, throw the envelopes away. Then I get to this."

I put up my hand. "I'm still not following. Where is this happening?"

"I told you. At work."

"Yes, but where at work? In your office?"

"Yes. In my office."

"You're seated at your desk?"

"That's right."

"Where do you throw the envelope?"

"In the wastebasket."

"So it should still be there?"

"I suppose so. Why?"

"You didn't fish it out after you got the letter?"

"No. Why should I?" Pritchert said, irritably. "Look, you're making such a deal about the envelope, what about the message?"

"What about it?"

He stared at me. "What do you mean, what about it? Now we know what's going on."

"We do?"

"Yes, of course. The girl was a setup, just like I said. Someone set me up because of the proxy fight."

"How can you get all of that from this letter?"

"Are you kidding? Just look at it."

"I'm looking at it."

"Well, there you are. *I saw you in the singles bar.* What could be clearer than that?"

"The statement is clear. The implications are not."

"Are you kidding?"

"Not at all. It could be blackmail, extortion, a threat, or a practical joke. The intentions of the person who sent it are not clear."

He frowned. "What are you saying?"

I pointed to the letter. Shrugged. "This is obviously only preliminary. Designed to fluster and upset you, so you'll be ripe for what comes next."

"What comes next?"

"Yes, of course."

"And what would that be?"

"How the hell should I know? Blackmail sounds good to me. How does it sound to you?"

"Blackmail?"

"Sure."

He grimaced, shook his head. "I don't think it's blackmail. I think it has to do with the proxy fight."

"The idea is someone trying to embarrass you?"

"Exactly."

"The problem there," I said, "is if someone were trying to embarrass you, they simply would. I mean, what's the worst-case scenario? Suppose they had compromising pictures of you with this girl — then why threaten you in this manner? Why not simply send a print to each and every stockholder?"

Pritchert nearly gagged. "Good god, do you think they'd do that?"

"Obviously not, or they wouldn't be doing this."

"Why?"

"Because there'd be no need. They

wouldn't need to threaten you. The damage would already be done."

"Uh-huh," Pritchert said. "Now, look. I want you to do something about this."

"What?"

"I want you to find the girl."

"The girl?"

"Yes. She's obviously the key to the whole thing. *I saw you in the singles bar.* That means, whoever it is, they saw me with the girl."

"So?"

"So, we have to find her. It's as simple as that."

"That's one way to go about it," I said. "Meanwhile, let's see what else we can do."

"Else?"

"Yeah. I mean right now. Whaddya say we take a run over to your office."

"My office?"

"Yeah."

"What for?"

"To get the envelope."

Pritchert frowned. "I don't understand. What's so important about the envelope?"

"It could be a lot of things."

"Like what?"

"First off, the address."

"The address?"

"Sure. You say you opened the envelope,

threw it away, and then read the letter. Right?"

"Right."

"The reason you threw it away was because you had no idea there was anything special about it. So obviously the address on the envelope wasn't cut from newspaper headlines. Was it?"

"No. Of course not."

"So how *was* it addressed?"

"I beg your pardon?"

"Was it typed or handwritten?"

"I don't remember."

"You don't remember?"

"I keep telling you, I had no idea it was important."

"Yes, but you know it's important now. You knew it was important as soon as you read the letter. So think. Was the envelope handwritten or typed?"

"I tell you, I don't know."

"So," I said, "there's one thing we can learn from the envelope — whether it was handwritten or typed. Once we know that, it's possible to trace it. To a particular handwriting or a particular machine.

"Then there's the postmark. Where and when was the letter sent? Most likely, right here from New York, but that's something to establish.

"Then there's the return address. Was a phony return address used, or was there simply none?

"You can learn a lot from an envelope."

"I suppose so," Pritchert said.

"So whaddya say we go get it?"

Pritchert held up both hands. "No, no. I don't want you going to the office."

"Why not?"

"Are you kidding? I don't want to explain."

"To who?"

"Kevin and Marty, of course."

"Kevin and Marty?"

"The other vice-presidents. I told you about them," Pritchert said impatiently.

"Right, you did. So, what's the big deal? I could be a potential customer for all they know."

"Then I'd have to explain. I'm no good at explaining. They'd ask questions, I wouldn't know what to say."

"Fine, then I won't go in. I'll drive you to the office, you run up and get the envelope."

"Drive me?"

"Yeah. My car's in the municipal lot."

"There's a municipal lot?"

"Yeah. On 53rd Street. Come on," I said, heading for the door. "Let's get the envelope."

"Now? You mean now?"

"Of course now. This is a solid lead. The first one we got. Let's go nail it down."

That obviously didn't suit Pritchert's plans. But he couldn't seem to think of a reason not to go. He frowned, picked up his briefcase, and followed me out the door.

8.

I hate midtown. In terms of driving, I mean. Not only can't you park in midtown, you can't even stand. I hadn't been waiting more than five minutes outside Cranston Pritchert's office building when a transit cop came by and made me move on.

I drove around the block once, but the son of a bitch was still there. As I slowed down, he gave me the evil eye. I gave him a frozen smile and started around the block again.

Third time's the charm.

Like hell.

My buddy was still there, and as I drove up he jerked his thumb.

It was all I needed. My own personal transit cop.

Only in New York.

When I got around the block again Cranston Pritchert was standing there. So was the transit cop, but the hell with him. I pulled into the curb, rolled down the window.

"Where is it?"

"What?"

"The envelope. Where's the envelope."

"I don't have it."

"What?"

At that moment the transit cop insinuated himself, said, "All right, buddy, move it along."

"Get in the car."

"What?" Pritchert said.

"I can't stand here. Get in the car."

Pritchert got in, and I pulled out and headed around the block again.

"What do you mean, you don't have it?"

"It's gone."

"Gone?"

"It's not there."

"You mean someone took it out of the wastebasket."

"No. They emptied the wastebasket."

"What?"

"Yeah. I went up and looked and they'd dumped the basket."

"Who?"

"What?"

"Who emptied the wastebasket?"

"What do you mean, who? The cleaning people."

"They clean up in the afternoon?"

"I don't know when they clean. The fact is, they did."

"They dump anyone else's basket?"

"How the hell should I know?"

"Well, it's something we should find out. I really should go up there with you."

"No, damn it," Pritchert said. "I told you no."

"Where does the garbage go?"

"Huh?"

"When they dump it, where does it go? Does a guy come through with a bin, they dump the garbage into that? Or a plastic sack?"

"I don't know."

"You never noticed?"

"No. Why would I?"

I turned the corner, pulled up in front of the building again. Believe it or not, the transit cop was still there. I kept going, headed around again.

"All right, here's the thing," I said. "There's two possibilities here. One, the garbage got dumped just as you say, or, two, someone dumped it to get rid of the envelope. I'm trying to pin down which."

"How could you do that?"

"I told you. Go up there and see if they dumped anyone else's."

"I don't want you doing that."

"No, but you could. When you go back upstairs, that's the first thing you should check on."

"I'm going to go around asking people if

their garbage was dumped?"

"Don't be a schmuck. Are you telling me you can't manage to wander around, take a look?"

"I'm not a spy."

"No, you're not. So you do the best you can. If the other baskets haven't been dumped, there's a good chance someone pilfered yours. Which would be interesting as hell. If the others *have* been dumped, then the question is where. If we can find out where, maybe we can get that envelope back."

Pritchert grimaced. "I really think you're making too much of the envelope. The important thing is the girl."

"I'll work on the girl. But that's later tonight. Right now, I'm working on this."

"And you're driving me crazy," Pritchert said. "If I go running around the office trying to find out where the garbage is dumped, you don't think someone's gonna notice?"

"So they do. Say you think you threw out an important paper."

"Oh, that's going to make me look great."

"What do you care how you look? We got a crisis here. We're trying to handle it. Just say you threw something out."

"And they'll want to know what."

"It doesn't matter what."

"If it has to do with the business, it does."

"So say it wasn't. Say it was theater tickets."

"Theater tickets?"

"Sure. You had an envelope of theater tickets in your jacket pocket, you took it out, it got mixed up in the mail."

"Stop the car," Pritchert said.

We'd come around the block again. I pulled up next to the transit cop to let him out.

Pritchert turned to me. "Look," he said. "I'm glad you're such a good liar. But I don't think I could pull it off. Now, I'll go back up there and take a look, but frankly I don't think I'm going to get a thing. The key is the girl. You gotta find her. I want you to go back to the bar tonight during happy hour and turn it upside down. I can't believe someone there didn't see me. You either find someone who knows the girl, or you find someone who saw what she did. But I don't think we're gonna know what she did until we talk to her. So let's get her."

Pritchert nodded in agreement with himself, opened the door and got out. Which was quite a production, him being so tall. He had to jackknife his way out of the seat. He got out, slammed the door.

That sound was echoed by another one,

closer, right in front of my face. I looked up.

The transit cop looked smug.

There was a parking ticket under the wiper blade.

9.

I was in a foul mood driving back to the office. First, because I got a forty-dollar ticket for stopping in a No Stopping zone. Second, because my six-foot-six beanpole client was an asshole who couldn't seem to do anything right, and wouldn't let me do it for him. And third, because competent though she might be, Mary Mason had not beeped me with another case, leaving me with nothing to do.

I drove back to the municipal lot, left the car, and went back up to the office.

The answering machine light was not blinking.

The mail had long since arrived, bearing nothing of note.

Great.

I ran out to the PhotoMat, dropped off the roll of film with the pictures of Betty Brody's broken leg, and picked up the rolls I'd dropped off the day before. I took the pictures back up to the office to ID.

ID'ing film is boring and important. It's boring because the pictures are all the same, and it's important for the same reason. Take a roll of film with pictures of three black men with casts on their legs. If you wanna know which is which, they better be pictures you took yesterday, not sometime last week. That's not racist, by the way — three white men with casts on their legs, you'd have the same problem. You just don't get them that often.

I finished ID'ing the film, which left me with *really* nothing to do. Great. Two in the afternoon and I'm done?

It occurred to me maybe I should take in a movie. That would be one way to get work. Kind of like hopping in the shower when you're waiting for a phone call. The minute I got in the theater my beeper would go off. Hell, the minute I plunked down the nonrefundable seven fifty for the ticket. But it would be worth it. At twenty bucks an hour and seventy-five cents a mile, a three-hour, twenty-mile sign-up would be seventy-five bucks. So if you looked at it that way, it would be a ten to one return on my investment.

I picked up the *New York Post*, tilted back in my desk chair, and turned to the entertainment section.

I couldn't find a damn thing I wanted to see. At least, not in a convenient theater at a convenient time. I mean, Broadway in the forties was where I was. By the time I had expanded my search as far as the Third Avenue and 59th Street theaters I knew I was in trouble.

I flipped to the back for the sports pages. Of course, I'd already seen them early this morning. The Red Sox had lost again, minimal coverage — tough being a Boston fan in New York City. On the other hand, the Yankees had earned a two-page banner headline insinuating they had committed the crime of the century in failing to win.

The Mets had won. That was a rare enough occasion these days to have prompted the headline "You gotta believe!"

I flipped a page. Pete Sampras was the men's singles winner. No surprise there, he'd been winning everything lately.

I flipped another page. "Knicks embarrassed by Nets, still team to beat in playoffs."

I flipped another page.

Something I'd just read bothered me. I had a feeling it was the Knicks headline. At least they'd be making the playoffs. The Celtics, never having recovered from the death of Reggie Lewis and the retirements of Bird and McHale, would not.

But that wasn't it.

I frowned, flipped back a page. There was

the tennis headline, "Sampras men's singles winner." That bothered me too. Sampras was the man, but it wasn't that long ago it was Courier. And how long ago was it Lendl?

How old am I?

I sat there, devastated for the thousandth time by the aging process, the newspaper a blur in front of me.

I focused in again.

Sampras, men's singles winner.

It wasn't just him.

The headline wasn't a banner headline. Being only tennis and not a top tournament, it was relegated to two columns. And the headline wasn't even set in caps. They were upper- and lower-case block italics. I don't know what they call them in the printing trade, but that's what they looked like to me. Anyway, they were block letters slanted slightly to the right.

When I say upper and lower case, only the S in Sampras was capitalized. All the other words were entirely lower-case letters.

What struck me was the word *singles.*

Cranston Pritchert's threatening letter was lying face up on the desk. I picked it up and compared.

Sure enough, the word *singles* in "I saw you in the singles bar" was made of lower-case block italics of exactly the same size. If there was a difference, I couldn't see it.

I looked at the letter again.

The words had been cut with scissors, yes, but not in neat little rectangles. There seemed to be an element of haste about the letter. The cuts were sloppy and not exact.

Particularly the word *bar*. The three letters, *b, a, r,* were all lower-case block letters. But they were bigger than the letters in *singles* and they were not italics, they were straight up and down.

But that wasn't all. As I said, the word had not been neatly cut out. Particularly, the cut in front of the *b* was slanted, and along it you could see the rounded curve of what appeared to be another letter.

I turned the paper back to the basketball page. "Knicks embarrassed by Nets, still team to beat in playoffs" was an upper- and lower-case banner headline spread out over two pages. I held the letter up next to it. Sure enough, the word *embarrassed* could have yielded the word *bar*. The sloppy cut would precede it with a small round piece of the *m*.

I blinked, flipped another page.

"You gotta believe!"

I looked at the letter. Sure enough, capital *Y*, lower-case *o*, lower-case *u*.

Son of a bitch.

You gotta believe, indeed.

10.

Richard Rosenberg looked up from the letter and frowned. "Why did you bring me this?"

"You're a lawyer."

The frown deepened into a wince, seemed to border on a scowl. "I *know* I'm a lawyer. What's that got to do with it?"

"I need your advice."

"Aha!" Richard said. He leaned back in his desk chair and smiled smugly, as if he had just scored a telling point.

I recognized the tactic. It was one of the cross-examination techniques that had made Richard Rosenberg one of New York City's top negligence lawyers. A little man, with a seemingly endless supply of nervous energy, Richard Rosenberg was a human dynamo with a reputation for wearing opposing counsel down. Insurance companies tended to settle with him rather than risk going to court. I couldn't blame them. Talking to Richard always was a challenge. Even for a friend and employee.

In this instance, I wasn't sure of my best response to "Aha!" I decided to wait, and see if Richard intended to amplify it.

He did.

Richard raised one finger in the air, cocked his head, and squinted at me sideways. "You are asking me now for legal advice?"

"That's right."

"And you have no intention of paying me?"

"I couldn't possibly afford you."

"I'll take that for a yes. So, you are here asking for free advice?"

"If you want to look at it that way."

"What other way is there to look at it?"

"I thought it might interest you."

"Interest me?"

"Yes. How often do you get a letter like this in the mail?"

"Someone sent you this?"

"Actually, no."

"I didn't think so. You're not the type to hang out in singles bars. So, this is not your letter?"

"No."

"Whose is it?"

"A client."

"Aha!" Richard said, in a voice that left no doubt that he had scored another telling point. "So you have a client?"

"That's right."

"Is this one of *my* clients?"

"No."

"This is your *own* client?"

"Yes."

"This client is paying you money?"

"What's your point, Richard?"

"You have a client who has hired you to do a job. Part of your job requires legal advice. Any other private detective would hire a lawyer and stick the client with the fee. But you, prince that you are, haven't got the heart to do that. Instead, you decide to do the client a favor by presuming on our friendship to finagle free legal advice. Is that a fairly accurate assessment of the situation?"

"Not at all."

"Oh, really? Where did I go wrong? Would you mind pointing it out to me?"

"I'm not doing this for the client."

"I beg your pardon?"

"I'm not trying to protect the client. I'm trying to protect me. I think the client's pulling a fast one on me and I'm not sure what to do."

"You're telling me you need protection from your own client?"

"That's what I'm trying to find out."

Richard sighed, shook his head. "What a moron. All right, tell me about it."

I gave him the whole spiel, just the way

Cranston Pritchert had given it to me. I must say, repeating it only pointed up how little sense it made.

"So," Richard said when I was finished, "this letter was apparently cut from this morning's paper?"

"To the best I can determine."

"But your client says it came in the morning mail?"

"That's right."

"Your contention is that to be in the morning mail a letter would have to have been mailed yesterday?"

"Well, wouldn't it?"

"I'm not sure," Richard said. "What time does the post office open?"

"I don't know."

"Neither do I, but it's something that could be checked."

"You're saying his story could be true?"

"No, but if you're going to brand it false, you ought to be sure of your terms. Say the post office opens at eight o'clock — I don't know that it does, but make that assumption — would it be possible to get the morning paper at seven, rig the extortion letter, go to the post office at eight, and drop it in the mail slot in time for it to be postmarked and go out with the morning delivery?"

"I don't know."

"Of course you don't. You haven't looked into it. But say you did, and say you found out it was possible — would that corroborate your client's story?"

"I don't know, Richard. Would it?"

"I'm asking you."

I smiled. "Yes, but you're doing it in the way lawyers do in order to make a point. Which means you already know the answer."

"If you know that, you must know the answer too."

"I don't know," I said. "I would assume it doesn't corroborate a thing. The fact that it's possible doesn't make it likely. Unless you can come up with a reason *why* someone would do that, to assume it makes no sense." I looked at Richard. "Am I close?"

"You're dead on. So, we should be able to dismiss that theory."

"Which was yours to begin with."

Richard raised his eyebrows. "Excuse *me*. You think a lawyer shouldn't raise points for fear they might turn out to be inconclusive?"

I put up my hand. "Richard, let's not go off on a tangent. The fact is, we're in agreement. In all probability this letter did not arrive in the morning mail. Right?"

"I think it's a logical assumption."

"So, where did it come from?"

Richard pursed his lips. "I would say there were two possibilities. One, someone prepared it and left it on your client's desk. Most likely in an envelope — you'll notice it's folded to fit one. In that case, the envelope would not have gone through the mail. It might have had your client's name on it, it might have been a plain envelope, and it might not have even been sealed.

"The second possibility is that your client did it himself. In which case he folded it so he could claim it had come in the mail. In either case, that's why he was so reluctant to produce the envelope, and eventually couldn't do so." Richard frowned. "This is all so simplistic, I can't believe you haven't already figured it out yourself."

"Actually, I have."

"Then what are you doing here?"

"I told you. I want your advice."

"On what?"

"What's my legal responsibility here? This man has hired me to do a job. Now I find myself in a position where I can't believe a single word he says."

"So?"

"So, what's my obligation here? What am I supposed to do?"

"You're supposed to carry out your client's wishes."

"If my client's lying to me, I don't know what those wishes are."

"True. In which case, there's probably only one way to find out."

"What's that?"

"Ask him."

11.

The receptionist at Philip Greenberg Investments frowned. "I beg your pardon?"

"I'm Harold Bainbridge," I repeated. "I'm here to see Cranston Pritchert."

"Do you have an appointment, Mr. Bainbridge?"

"No, I don't. But I'm sure he'll see me."

The receptionist, an efficient-looking young woman with curly red hair, scooped up the phone and punched in a number. "Mr. Pritchert? There's a Harold Bainbridge here to see you." She listened a moment, then said, "And what is this in regard to, Mr. Bainbridge?"

"An investment."

She relayed that message, and got another earful from Cranston Pritchert. "What kind of an investment, Mr. Bainbridge?"

"I prefer to keep that confidential. If Mr. Pritchert can give me a moment of his time, I'd appreciate it. Otherwise, I suppose I could come back."

I figured that would work.

It didn't.

"I'm sorry," the receptionist said, after relaying the message, "but Mr. Pritchert would have to know what this is about before he'd be willing to grant you an appointment. Could you tell me generally what it is in which you'd like to invest?"

"Singles bars."

Pritchert was out in fifteen seconds, white as a sheet. If the sight of me was any relief to him, you wouldn't have known it. If anything, it only panicked him more.

"Aha," he said. "Aha. Mr. . . . ?"

"Bainbridge."

"Yes. Bainbridge. You wanted to see me?"

"Yes, I did. Do you suppose we could talk about it in your office?"

"Oh," Pritchert said. He thought a moment, and added, "Oh."

I marched over to him, took his hand, and shook it. I said, "I really appreciate your giving me the time."

Now I had hold of him, I figured I'd just push him in the direction of his office. Before I could, two men came down the hall, one short and stocky, one tall and thin. At least, tall by ordinary standards — he was half a head shorter than Pritchert.

"Hey, Cranston," the tall one said. "You got a live one there?"

"Nice talk," the short, stocky one said. He

was a solid man, with hard eyes and a little black mustache. He extended his hand. "I'm Kevin Dunbar. Mr. . . . ?"

"Bainbridge. Harold Bainbridge."

"Pleased to meet you, Mr. Bainbridge. This is Marty Rothstein. If there's anything our firm can do for you . . ."

"That's very nice of you," I said, "but I just want to talk to Mr. Pritchert."

"About an investment?"

"Of course."

Marty Rothstein smiled. "That's fine, Mr. Bainbridge. But we want you to realize. When you deal with us, you're not just hiring a broker. You're in partnership with the whole firm. Anything we can do for you, you have only to ask."

"That's nice to know," I said.

I grabbed Cranston Pritchert by the elbow, practically dragged him down the hall, where he recovered his wits enough to at least guide me into the proper office. He slammed the door, then wheeled around and towered over me.

The color had returned to his cheeks. Now they were progressing toward red. "Just what the hell do you think you're doing?" he demanded.

"Trying to help you."

"Help me? What, are you nuts? Help me?"

70

"You hired me to do a job. I'm trying to do it."

"I hired you to find the girl. That's what you should be doing. I told you not to come here."

"Yes, you did."

"And you came here anyway. Which was the last thing I wanted. And then you ran into them. Do you know who those guys were? Do you know who you were talking to?"

"Sure. The other two vice-presidents. You told me all about them."

"Did I tell you we're in a proxy fight and there's an election coming up? Did I tell you that? Did I tell you I can't bear a hint of scandal? And then you come walking in here and blow the whole thing."

"Give me a break. I didn't blow anything. I'm just another investor. All you gotta do is play along."

"I told you I couldn't do that."

"Yeah, well, you got no choice. It turned out I had to see you."

"Why?"

"I found out who sent the letter."

"What?"

"The extortion letter. I found out who sent it."

He stared at me. "What?"

"I found out who sent the extortion letter."

He blinked. "How did you do that?"

"Actually, it was rather easy."

"Oh yeah. So who sent it?"

"You did."

"What?"

"I don't know why you did, but you did. I don't like being played for a patsy, and that's why I'm here."

"That's ridiculous."

"I agree. It's totally ridiculous. If you want to pay me good money to find out why you sent yourself an extortion letter, well, that's your business. But when the clues lead back to you, that's mine. Now, you wanna keep playing games, or you wanna sit down and talk this over?"

"I have no idea what you're talking about."

"Yeah, sure. Well, there's a parking ticket on your expense account."

He frowned. "What?"

"The parking ticket I got while you were up here searching for the envelope that didn't exist. Pretending someone dumped your wastebasket."

When I said that, his eyes flicked.

I glanced in that direction, saw the wastebasket next to his desk. I took a step between him and it.

"My, my. If this was dumped, you sure

filled it up again fast."

I reached in the wastebasket, pulled something out.

"Well, well, what have we here?"

What we had was a cut-up copy of today's *Post*. The dumb boob hadn't even gotten rid of it.

I looked at him, shook my head. "I cannot believe you left this here for anyone to find."

Pritchert glared at me a moment. I could see his mind going, trying to figure if there was any way at all to keep up the pretense.

Apparently, he couldn't come up with one. He exhaled, said, "Damn."

I spread my arms. "So there you are. That's why I'm here. I don't like being played for a sucker. If you'd like to clue me in, I'd be glad to listen. Otherwise, I believe my services to you are over."

Pritchert put up his hands. "No, no. Please. You've gotta help me."

"Under the circumstances, that's a little difficult."

"No, no. I can explain."

"You sent the letter?"

"I didn't send it."

"I understand. No one sent the letter. But you made it up."

"Yeah."

"You mind telling me why?"

"It was your attitude."

I blinked. "My attitude?"

"Yeah. I told you my story. I told you I needed help. I told you what I wanted you to do. But you talked to the bartender, and you let him talk you out of it. You came back, told me looking for the girl was a lost cause. But you're wrong. I've gotta find her."

"Yeah. So?"

"So, I could tell you weren't taking this seriously. I felt I had to do something to get your attention."

I looked at him. "You rigged the phony extortion letter to make me more diligent in my pursuit of this girl?"

"I know it sounds bad when you say it like that."

"No kidding. But that's the fact?"

He took a breath. Exhaled. "That's the fact. You saw my partners out there. You see what they're like? They thought you were a client of mine and they dived right in. You know what they're looking for? A loophole to steal you away."

"I thought you were all working together. I'm not just hiring a broker, I'm taking on a whole firm."

"Yeah, yeah, sure," Pritchert said. "But you could be a major investor. And you know what a major investor is?"

"What?"

"A potential stockholder. A lot of our clients, they start investing with our firm, eventually they wind up investing in the firm itself. Sure, the money the clients bring in is all partnership assets. But if you become a stockholder, it suddenly makes a huge difference which one of us your allegiance is with."

"Yeah, fine," I said. "But the point is, you lied to me, you tricked me, and as a result I spent a lot of time and energy running around after a false scent. If you're not happy with the current situation, well, I'm not happy with it either. So, if you want to fire me, fine. The way things stand, it would probably be a relief."

Pritchert set his chin, glared at me. Made me wait.

"I don't want to fire you," he said.

I exhaled. Shook my head.

"Too bad."

12.

Sandy the bartender gave me the fisheye when I walked in. I ignored him, elbowed my way through the happy hour throng to the far end of the bar. The place was packed. The clientele on the whole seemed well-dressed and young. The men outnumbered the women by about two to one. The women were generally attractive, though none seemed exotic. The spectacularly endowed young blonde obviously wasn't there.

On the other hand, it occurred to me, if she had been she would have stood out, especially in a tight tank top. So anyone who'd been there that night ought to re-member her.

I'm sure there were a lot of ways to play it, and a TV detective would have had no trouble coming up with one bullshit line or another. But I couldn't think of a thing to say that wasn't likely to get me punched right in the nose. I mean, this wasn't a gay bar — a guy wasn't apt to appreciate another guy asking him if he came here often.

Which is why I fell back on that old

standby, the truth. I took out my ID, flopped it open in front of a guy at the end of the bar, and said, "Excuse me, I'm a private detective. I'm trying to locate a witness. I wonder if you could help me."

The guy, a young salesman type in a gray suit, didn't appear too thrilled, but the woman sitting next to him said, "Ooh, a private eye. What's this all about?"

"I'm trying to find someone. I'm looking for people who were here around this same time last Thursday night."

The woman was young, relatively attractive, and wore a lime-green something or other — I'm terrible with clothes — but I think it was a pants suit with a sort of half jacket, half vest thing on top. Anyway, she frowned, which made her look younger, gave her an almost schoolgirl pout, and said, "I wasn't here Thursday. Were you?"

The young man hesitated, and I immediately knew his dilemma. He hadn't been here, but hated to say so and lose importance in her eyes, and was toying with the idea of claiming to have been here and trying to bluff it through.

I wasn't about to let him. "No big deal," I said. "I'm just trying to find someone who was here that night." I turned and flopped the ID in front of the guy to my left. "How about you — you happen to be here Thursday night?"

The guy, a broad-shouldered macho type, regarded me with hostile eyes. "What's it to you?"

"No big deal," I said. "Just trying to locate a witness. I'm looking for people who were here last Thursday night."

"He's a private eye," the lime-green woman said.

Macho man looked at her. I could see his mind going. Maybe he could ace out the guy she was sitting with. "Were you here Thursday night?" he said.

The salesman type put up his hands defensively, which gave him a petulant look. "Hey," he said. "This is nothing to do with us. None of us were here that night. Let's let it alone."

"Yeah, but someone must have been here that night," the lime-green lady said.

Macho man picked up on it. "Absolutely," he said. He pointed to her. "Maybe we should ask around."

"Yeah, but ask what?" she said. She turned to me. "Who are you looking for, and what do you want with him?"

"Actually, it's a her," I said.

"A woman?" Macho man said. "You're looking for a woman?"

"Of course he's looking for a woman," the salesman said. "He just has a new approach. Look, this happened Thursday night. I wasn't here. He wasn't here. Why don't you ask someone else?"

"Not till he tells us what this is all about," the lime-green lady said. "You can't just ask the question and leave it like that. Suppose we'd been here Thursday night — what then?"

"I would ask you if you'd seen a particular woman." I smiled. "Since you weren't here, I can't ask."

"But why do you want to know?" she persisted.

"He can't tell you that," the salesman said. He looked at me. "Right? You're working for a client, it's confidential, you can't tell us a thing."

That was exactly the case, but wasn't about to win me any popularity contests. I smiled again. "It's not as bad as all that."

A hand clamped down on my shoulder.

I turned around, looked up into the eyes of my buddy, Sandy the bartender. Without the bar between us, he looked bigger, broader, more imposing. Macho man might have taken him, but I sure couldn't. Things did not look good.

"You bothering these folks?" Sandy said.

Macho man got up from his bar stool. I had the sickening realization he was going to defend me, a humiliation I could have done without.

Sandy forestalled it. He put up his hand. "No trouble, folks. No trouble at all. You and this gentleman can discuss anything you like. I just need to have a few words with him first." He smiled. "Bartender's prerogative, right?"

With his hand on my shoulder, he piloted me away from the bar and into an alcove near the telephone. In that particular establishment, it was as secluded as you could get.

"All right," he said. "You're here looking for the girl?"

"Yes, I am."

"You recall me telling you not to do that?"

"I believe you made that suggestion, yes."

"And you came back anyway."

"I have a job to do." I took a breath. "Believe me, I don't like it any more than you do."

"Uh-huh," Sandy said. "So your client made you come back here, huh?"

"That's right."

"He's not going to quit till he finds this girl?"

"So he says."

80

"And you gotta listen to him, that's why you won't listen to me?"

I exhaled. "I told you how it is. I'm trying not to make trouble. Just between you and me, those people I was talking to didn't seem threatened at all. They thought it was great fun."

"Oh, they did, huh?" Sandy said.

"Well, actually, only two out of three. The guy in the middle's trying to hit on the girl. He thinks I'm a pain in the ass. But the other two think it's fun."

The bartender's eyes were hard. "It's not fun. It's business. You got your business, I got mine. Unfortunately, they conflict."

I shrugged. "What can I say?"

"You're telling me you won't quit?"

"I can't."

"You mean your client won't let you."

"Something like that."

"Because he wants to find this girl?"

"Right."

Sandy frowned, pursed his lips.

"What's it worth to him?"

13.

I sat across the table from Darren Carter and watched him drink his incredibly expensive beer.

Darren Carter was Sandy the bartender. The beer was incredibly expensive because we were in a topless bar.

It was a fairly grungy affair around 20th Street and Eighth Avenue. Don't get me wrong — I don't hang out in topless bars, so I couldn't tell you what an *upscale* one was like. But even with no means of comparison, this one was the pits.

It was a second-floor walkup over a fish store, and the odor had a tendency to seep up. That was for starters. The place was also filthy. The floor was strewn with sawdust. In some bars that's classy. Not here. Here it replaced sweeping. I didn't even want to think what must be under it.

The bar was poorly lit, except for the stage, where harsh lights glared. That's where the girls performed. They wore high heels and garters and not much else. The high heels were so you could look up their crotch. The garters were so you could stuff money in. That's what the guys next to the stage were doing.

Sandy and I were not next to the stage. I told him if he wanted to sit there he was sitting alone, and any money he stuffed would be his own. Sandy didn't seem to mind. In point of fact, he seemed somewhat embarrassed to be there.

"I wouldn't want you to get the wrong idea," he said.

"Oh?"

"You know, like I hang out in these places all the time. It's not like that."

"I'm sure it isn't."

He looked at me sharply. "What's that supposed to mean?"

I exhaled. Shook my head. "It doesn't mean anything. I'm not here to judge you. Frankly, I couldn't care less. Like I said, I'm just trying to do my job."

"Well, I wouldn't want you to get the wrong idea. I just broke up with my girl-friend, see. Almost two months now. The thing is, I'm a bartender. People get the idea, bartender in a singles bar, the women are all over him. They see Tom Cruise mixing drinks in a movie, so that's the expectation, right?"

"I'm with you there," I said. "When I tell

people I'm a detective, all they know is what they see on TV."

"Exactly," Sandy said. "So you know. There's this image to live up to. Unrealistic, you know. So I'm a bartender in a singles bar, what does that mean? I bust my ass mixing drinks. By the time I get off work, the girls that are looking for action have been hit on and are long gone."

"I never thought of it that way," I said.

The reason we were discussing Sandy's sex life was we had already exhausted the more pertinent topics. Such as how come he hadn't owned up to knowing the girl before. His answer, though somewhat incomplete and unsatisfactory, was probably true: a natural reluctance to divulge where he knew her from coupled with a disinclination to get involved in a customer's personal life.

His reason for aiding me now was also twofold: if I wasn't going to let the matter drop, the quickest way to get rid of me was to give me what I wanted. And if anyone was going to profit from that, it might as well be him. Per agreement, Sandy stood to pick up a hundred bucks of Cranston Pritchert's expense money if I scored.

As for me, I was making fifty bucks an hour for looking at women's breasts. Ordinarily, my favorite occupation. But there are breasts, and there are breasts.

The way I understand it, the reason for the recent proliferation of topless bars was partly in response to the AIDS epidemic. As actual sex had become too risky, it had been replaced by the fantasy. Trust to the American entrepreneur to give the customer what he wanted. Topless bars answered the burning question *Where can I see a naked woman without having to actually sleep with one?*

The only thing was, as soon as topless bars became big business, show biz took over. If big breasts were nice, huge breasts must be truly wonderful. So break out the silicone and full speed ahead.

I don't know if that's universally true, but it was certainly true here. Big was the main selling point. The bartender had a microphone hooked up to a scratchy PA system, and as each new girl hit the stage he would announce, "Here she is, Wendy Whoppers," or, "Here she is, Jessica Jugs." And each new girl was bigger than the last.

As soon as the novelty wore off, there was little joy in looking at what I knew was basically plastic.

As I sat there, watching woman after woman parade by with beach balls on her chest, it occurred to me, that would be the ultimate torture. To be forced to sit and watch until one was conditioned to hate breasts.

Which seemed a distinct possibility. "Here she is, Marla Melons," the bartender said, and here came another young blonde down the runway. Nice face, decent figure, but breasts that stuck out like torpedoes. They didn't hang down like flesh, they jutted out like styrofoam.

I shook my head, wondered what could induce an attractive young woman to disfigure herself like that.

Sandy nudged me and pointed.

"That's her."

14.

It was eleven-thirty when she came out the front door. Sandy was long gone, having sauntered off with a hundred bucks in his pocket and a smile on his lips. Shortly after which, it occurred to me what a great scam that would be — the guy takes me to a topless bar, points to any large-busted blonde at random, and walks out with the cash. While I didn't think the guy would really do that, on the other hand I didn't know him well enough to be sure he wouldn't. It was an unsettling thought.

Another was whether I'd recognize her when she came out.

I did, but just barely. She was wearing a full-length yellow rain slicker, a felt hat, and dark glasses. As I have indicated, I am not particularly fashion-conscious. Still, I wondered why one would combine a rain slicker with a felt hat.

The dark glasses I understood. It was the cultivated incognito, or I-am-a-celebrity look. Slightly pathetic under the circumstances.

87

I observed all this from across the street behind a parked car. Hopelessly theatrical, to be sure, but the strip joint had a bouncer out front, and I'd been doing my best not to let him know I was staking the place out. So far so good, and I didn't want to blow it now. I wasn't going near the girl until she was safely down the block.

Unfortunately, she stepped out in the street and hailed a cab.

I hailed one too and lucked out. The driver didn't bat an eye when I said, "Follow that cab," just pulled out and tailed along. The driver, who was a Pakistani or some such nationality — when it comes to pigeon-holing people I am ethnically challenged — was totally cooperative, but wanted to talk to me, and his accent was so thick I couldn't understand what he said. We were all the way uptown before I realized what he was asking me was if this was a stunt for the Letterman show.

Good lord. Not at eleven-thirty at night, mister. But let him think what he wanted as long as he played along.

We followed the girl's cab up the West Side, through the park at 86th Street, then across 84th Street to Third Avenue and up Third to the corner of East 85th. She paid off her cab and got out just as I got out of mine.

I walked up, put on my most engaging smile. "Excuse me, miss."

Her response was immediate. "Fuck off, mister! You get the fuck away from me!"

To a New Yorker, that's practically an endearment. I put up my hands, said, "Please. I just want to talk. I saw you at the bar."

"Yeah, well, you got the wrong idea. You keep away or I'll scream."

"Don't scream. I'm a private detective. Look. Here's my ID."

"I don't care who you are, you keep away."

My cab had driven off. Hers hadn't. Now the driver got out. He was one of the largest black men I'd ever seen. As he strode around the cab and got between her and me, my first thought was, he's her pimp. My second was that that was a horribly racist perception.

My third was that he was going to kill me.

"You botherin' her?" he said.

"Absolutely not," I said. "I'm a private detective, as you can see." I held the ID in front of me like a shield. "I have a few questions for the young lady. She's under absolutely no obligation to answer them unless she sees fit. But if she doesn't let me ask them, she won't know what they are."

The cabbie jerked his thumb in my direction. "You want me to bust his head?"

She frowned, looked at me. "What's this all about?"

"I'm a private detective. I was hired to find you." She recoiled slightly. I put up my hand, said, "Not by your parents, if that's what you're worried about."

"My parents!"

"No, no. Scratch that. I don't know your parents, I know nothing about your parents, this has nothing to do with your parents. I'm just saying, if that was your thought, forget it. The fact is, there's a guy wanted me to find you and ask you some questions. If you happen to know the answers, it might be worth some money to you. No one's trying to hassle you at all."

If I'd won the black cabbie's heart, you wouldn't have known it. "You want me to bust his head?" he repeated.

She put up her hand. "No. Thank you, no."

I blinked. Thank you? The mind boggled. Did she really say thank you?

"Please," I said. "If you'd be willing to just talk."

She pursed her lips. "What's this all about?"

I jerked my thumb. "Does a singles bar downtown ring a bell?"

She thought that over. Cocked her head.

"Buy me a cup of coffee?"

15.

"I don't want you to get the wrong idea."

Hmm. Almost exactly what Sandy the bartender said. I wondered what it was about topless bars that made people afraid other people would get the wrong idea. I also wondered what the right idea was.

But I merely said, "Oh." A time-honored private detective interrogative technique.

"Yeah," she said. "Just because I work in a place like that. That's not who I am."

"Who are you?"

She frowned, set her cup of coffee down, and looked out the diner window at the traffic going by on 86th Street. After a moment she turned back, said, almost defiantly, "I'm an actress. That's what I came to New York for. That's what I want to be. There's just too damn many of us. I can't get any work."

"Tell me about it."

She looked at me in surprise. "You're an actor?"

"I used to be."

"Then you know. It's a killer. I got talent

too. I mean, real talent. Legit. I did the classics in school. Shaw. Chekhov. Hell, I've done Shakespeare. So the dancing — it's not me. It's to pay the rent."

"I see."

She shook her head. "No, you don't. You're looking down your nose, you're thinking I should wait tables or some such shit. You happen to know what that pays?"

I didn't, but it occurred to me it was probably about what I was making.

Fortunately, a comment was not called for. She forged right ahead. "So, before you're so quick to judge me, you ought to look at the facts. Ten to one, your apartment's rent stabilized, you've been in it for a while, the rent's not so bad. But try renting one now. Try living in New York. Try making it as an actor."

"Hey, I'm on your side. I know it's tough."

"Yeah, but you still disapprove. And you can't know. I mean, if you were young and you had a chance to make the money dancing, are you telling me there's no way you would?"

The thought *No, but I wouldn't put plastic in my chest either,* sprang to mind.

She read it, averted her eyes. At least I *assume* she averted her eyes — she was still wearing the dark glasses. "Yeah," she said.

"I know. I had the operation. But I needed the job. So there you are. It is tough. I go for legit auditions, I have to strap myself down."

I got the feeling I was hearing a spiel that had been repeated time and time again. I wasn't unsympathetic. Still . . .

"Uh-huh," I said. "Now, about the singles bar."

"Oh, that."

"Yeah, that. You know what I'm talking about? Then let's pin it down. Thursday night. Third Avenue and 65th. You and the walking telephone pole."

"Uh-huh."

"Well?"

She cocked her head. "You mentioned something about money?"

"If you are forthcoming, and tell me what I need to know, there's a hundred bucks in it for you."

"Oh, whoopie gee."

"So whaddya expect for ten minutes' work?"

"You'd be surprised." She put up her hand. "No, scratch that. I'm not like that. You say ten minutes?"

"Well, you tell me. Will this take more than that?"

She sipped her coffee, thought a bit.

"Okay," she said.

"Fine. Let's have it."

"Huh-uh," she said. "You first."

I counted the bills under the table, trying to look like I was just being cautious. Actually, I didn't want her to see how little I had.

I slapped five twenties on the table. "Here's a hundred. Talk and it's yours."

She shook her head. "Huh-uh. Hand it over."

"What's the matter? Don't you trust me?"

"Sure I do. But you're the one who wants the information, you're the one who has to trust me."

I slid the bills across the table. They disappeared into the pocket of the yellow slicker.

"Okay," I said. "What's the story?"

She shrugged. "Perfectly simple. That guy — I was hired to have drinks with him."

"Hired?"

"That's right."

"By who?"

"I don't know."

"You don't know?"

She stuck out her chin. "That's right. I don't know. I'm sorry if you don't like that, but that's the fact."

"How does it happen that you don't know?"

"I wasn't told."

I put up my hand. "Please. Start from the beginning. Assume I know nothing. Which is a pretty good assumption. How were you hired? How did you hear about this? How did you know what to do?"

"Actually, it was my agent."

"Your agent?"

"Yeah. Well, not my theatrical agent. The other one."

"The other one?"

"Yeah. You know. For dancing."

"I see. So that agent called?"

"Right."

"What did he say?"

"It's a she."

"What did *she* say?"

"Said a man called, wanted to hire me."

"What did you say?"

"I said, no way. You gotta understand, I don't do that sort of thing. I'm not a hooker. I dance."

"Uh-huh. So what then?"

"She said it wasn't like that. I'd get paid for my time, but all I'd have to do is have drinks with some guy."

"So?"

"So, frankly, that didn't sound any better. But Shelly said, no, she thought it was legit."

"Shelly?"

"My agent. She said it was a legitimate job, it was just for two hours, and all I'd have to do would be to drink in this bar."

"I don't understand."

"I didn't either. But Shelly said it was perfectly simple. There was a man this guy wanted kept occupied for two hours."

"What?"

"That's right. All I had to do was go to this bar and drink with this guy for two hours. After that, I was free to do anything I wanted. I could stay there, I could walk out, I could ditch him, whatever. But for that two hours I didn't let him out of my sight."

"And you agreed to that?"

"I agreed to listen."

"What do you mean?"

"Well, the guy didn't tell me that. My agent did. Anyway, she talked me into listening to him."

"The guy?"

"Right."

"So then you met him?"

"No, I didn't."

"Oh? I thought you said . . . ?"

"Yeah, but I didn't meet him. He called me on the phone. That's what I agreed to. To let him call me, tell me what he wanted."

"So he did?"

"Yeah."

"What did he say?"

"I was to go to this singles bar. I'd meet a man there. I couldn't miss him because he was tall and thin. I was to have drinks with him, kid him along, keep him there for two hours. In return for which I would get five hundred bucks."

"Less agent fees?"

"No, free and clear. What Shelly got was her business. The five hundred was mine."

"And that's all?"

"That's it."

"There was nothing special you were supposed to do?"

"No, just keep the guy there."

"The guy on the phone — did he tell you anything else?"

"No, that was it."

"And you never met him — the guy on the phone?"

"No, I didn't."

"And that's all you know about him?"

"Yeah. Except . . ."

"Except what?"

"He had a funny voice."

"Oh?"

"Yeah. Kind of low and strained. Like he was disguising it."

"Oh, yeah?"

"Yeah."

"Was it someone you knew?"

"No, of course not."

"Well, why would he do that if you didn't know him?"

"I have no idea."

"He didn't sound like anyone?"

"I told you. No."

"And what did he say?"

"Just what I said. I should go to the bar, five o'clock. When the guy came in I should talk to him, keep him there till seven."

"That's all he told you to do?"

"That's all."

"How did he describe this guy?"

"Said he was tall and thin, I couldn't miss him."

"That was the whole description, tall and thin?"

"And white. Tall, thin, and white. There's a lot of tall black men. Not so many white."

"Did he tell you his name?"

She shook her head. "No names."

"No names?"

"Right."

"Why do you say names?"

"Because I wasn't given any."

"No, why do you use the plural? Names. Who else's name weren't you given?"

"Oh. Well, the guy in the bar and the guy on the phone."

"So you weren't given his name either."

"Right."

"You had no idea who you were talking to?"

"No, but it didn't matter."

"What do you mean by that?"

"He'd already talked to Shelly. We already had a deal. So long as I said yes."

"Which you did?"

"That's right."

I took a sip of coffee. "There wasn't any other way you were supposed to know this guy? I mean, what if you'd gotten into the singles bar and there were two tall, thin white guys there?"

"I don't know. But it didn't happen. You really expect something like that to happen?"

I certainly did. From personal experience, had I been given that assignment, there would not have been two tall, thin white guys in the bar, there'd have been three.

Of course, in her case, everything had been fine.

"Okay, so what happened?"

"What do you mean?"

"You went to the bar, you met the guy, and then what?"

"What do you think? I sat down next to him, said hello, and he offered to buy me a drink."

"As easy as that?"

"What, am I so unattractive? You can't imagine someone buying me a drink?"

"No, I'm sure he did. So what did you talk about?"

"Nothing much. Just bullshit. What's a nice girl like you doing in a place like this? Do you come here often? You know, the same old corny, cliché lines. Guys say 'em in a joking manner, goof on 'em. You know?"

"Actually, I don't. But go on. What else did you talk about?"

"He told a few jokes — not very good, as I recall — and I laughed at 'em and he kept buying drinks."

"How many did he buy?"

"More than he should. He must have had three or four, and he didn't hold them well. You know, once he stumbled off to the men's room, took his time coming back. In fact, I wasn't sure he *was* coming back."

"Did he?"

"Yeah. Eventually. But after that he wasn't too coherent."

"But he came back to you?"

"He came back to the bar, yeah."

"And you kept on drinking with him."

"Yeah, sure. That was the deal."

"And he kept talking to you?"

She shrugged her shoulders, wrinkled her nose. "Like I say, he'd had too much to drink, wasn't relating really well. I sat there with him, trying to make small talk, kid him along. I don't think he was really interested at that point."

"How long did you stay with him?"

"Until seven. Like I was supposed to."

"What happened then?"

"I left."

"With him?"

"Don't be silly. Why would I leave with him?"

"I don't know why. I'm just asking if you did."

"Of course not. Seven o'clock, I got up and went."

"So anyone who says the two of you left together would be wrong?"

She pulled back, cocked her head. "Who said that?"

"I didn't say anyone said that. I'm just saying if they did."

"They'd be wrong." She frowned, looked at her coffee cup. "I suppose someone might have got the wrong idea."

"Oh? How is that?"

"Well, he got up when I left, and I think he followed me out. Not that I waited for him — I got the hell out of there fast as I could. But someone who saw him follow me might think we left together."

"But you didn't?"

"No, we didn't. I left by myself and went on home."

"And what happened to the guy?"

"I have no idea."

"The guy who paid you to do this — you ever hear from him again?"

"No, I didn't."

"What about your agent?"

"What about her?"

"She hear from him? Was there any feedback on the job?"

"Not that I know of."

"Did you ask?"

"No. Why would I ask?"

"I don't know. Just curiosity."

"Yeah, well, the answer is no. In something like that, you wouldn't expect to hear from the client unless there was a problem. Since I did the job, there wouldn't be any problem. So I wouldn't expect to hear." She looked at me. "Is that it? Can I go now?"

I put up my hand. "Just a couple more things."

"A couple?"

"Yeah. First off, what's your name?"

"Oh," she said. She blushed somewhat. I assumed it was the realization I knew her only as Marla Melons. "It's Lucy. Lucy Blaine."

"And your address?"

She held up one finger. "Huh-uh. That you don't get. I may be dumb, but I'm not stupid. I don't give out my address or my phone number. You want me, you call my agent."

"Actually, that was the other question," I said. "How do I reach your agent?"

"Her name's Shelly Daniels. She has an office on Eighth Avenue. I'll give you the phone number."

She didn't have to look it up. She had it memorized. Her dancing agent. I wondered if I'd asked for the number of her legitimate agent, if she'd have had to look it up.

It occurred to me, Christ, was I getting old and cynical.

I pushed back my coffee cup, picked up the bill. "Well," I said, "shall we go?"

She shook her head. "Huh-uh. *We* don't do anything. I sit here and you go."

"Is that really necessary?"

She grinned. "You think you're the first guy tried to follow me home? Forget about it. You go out there, you hail a cab, and you go. I'm no dummy. You leave first."

She was no dummy.

I left first.

16.

Cranston Pritchert sounded peeved. "I told you not to call me here."

"I know, but I got something for you. Can you talk?"

"What do you mean, can I talk?"

"Is it safe to talk on the phone? If not, can you come to my office?"

"Not this morning. I'm up to my ears in work. Can't this wait?"

"Sure. I'm sorry I bothered you. Just wanted to tell you I found the girl."

I hung up.

I suppose I shouldn't have done it, but I couldn't resist. The guy was being such a prick.

The phone rang ten seconds later. I picked it up, said, "Hastings Detective Agency."

"God damn it," Pritchert said. "You hung up on me."

"I thought you didn't have time to talk."

"Don't be an asshole. You say you found the girl?"

"Yes, I did."

"Who is she? What's her story?"

"You want this over the phone?"

"Not really, but I don't have time to run over there. So give it to me fast. If I start talking business, it means someone walked in."

"Okay," I said. "The girl's name is Lucy Blaine. She works as a topless dancer under the stage name Marla Melons."

"What!"

"That's right. If you'd like to catch her act, I can take you to the bar. Anyway, you're absolutely right about it being a setup. She was paid five hundred dollars to have drinks with you."

"She was *what?*"

"She was paid to have drinks with you in the bar. Her instructions were to keep you there until seven o'clock that night."

"Keep me there?"

"So she says. She was to hang out in the bar, meet you, get you to buy her drinks, and keep you busy until seven o'clock. After which she simply left."

"Wait a minute, wait a minute," Pritchert said. "That isn't what happened at all. I told you. One moment I'm drinking with this girl, the next I wake up on someone's front steps."

"She said you might have followed her out."

"Followed her out?"

"Yeah. When she left. She said you were pretty drunk, but she thinks you might have followed her out of the bar."

"She doesn't know?"

"No. According to her, seven o'clock she went out the front door, never looked back."

"What about pictures?"

"Pictures?"

"Yeah, pictures. Did anyone take any pictures?"

"Wait a minute. What are you getting at, pictures?"

"Don't be a jerk. I mean compromising pictures. While I was so drunk I don't remember, did anyone take pictures of me with the girl?"

"Not that I know of."

"You didn't ask her?"

"Why the hell would I ask her that?"

"Are you kidding? I told you I was being set up. A compromising picture would be the icing on the cake. Hell, you were the one who brought it up, for Christ's sake. Saying if someone wanted to embarrass me, that's how they'd do it. Send a picture to all the stockholders. Isn't that what you said?"

"Yeah, but I meant racy pictures. Pictures with your pants down. Compromising stuff.

Just sitting in the bar with the girl isn't going to do it."

"Oh, really? I happen to be a married man."

"Is that right?"

"Yeah, that's right. So how does it look like then?"

"That's the first time you brought up the point."

"So?"

"So, you don't seem too concerned about it. You're scared to death someone might send a picture to the stockholders. How come you're not worried they might send one to your wife?"

"Are you kidding me? There's a proxy fight going on."

"Even so."

"Look, schmuck," Pritchert said. "It's none of your damn business. But the fact is I can tell my wife someone's trying to frame me because of the proxy fight. I can't tell a stockholder that."

"Uh-huh," I said. "Well, the subject of pictures never came up, and the way the girl tells it, there probably weren't any."

"Then what was the big idea?"

"Your guess is as good as mine."

"Well, what does the girl say?"

"Just what I told you. She was hired to

keep you in the bar until seven o'clock. That's all she knows."

"Does she know who hired her?"

"She never met him. Just talked to him on the phone."

"Oh, yeah?"

"Yeah. She says the guy's voice was low and strained and she figured he was disguising it."

"What did he say?"

"Just what I told you. She'd go to the bar, hang out, pick you up, and keep you buying drinks until seven o'clock. She wasn't given your name, you were described to her simply as a tall, thin white guy. Which leaves open the possibility this could have been a mistake."

"A mistake?"

"Sure. There's always the chance you're the *wrong* tall, thin white guy, and the guy she was waiting for never showed up."

"That's really far-fetched."

"Is it? In my experience, fuckups of that nature happen all the time."

"You might have told me that before I hired you," Pritchert said dryly. Before I could think of a comeback, he went on. "I don't think that merits consideration. I'm the guy, all right. I want to know what happened, and I want to know why. What's the girl's name again?"

"Lucy Blaine."

"Lucy Blaine."

"I wouldn't write it down where anyone can find it."

"Oh, thanks so much. Whaddya think I am, stupid?"

I let that lie there.

"What's her address?" he said.

"I don't have it."

"You don't have it?"

"No."

"Or her phone number?"

"I don't have that either."

"You didn't get her address or phone number?"

"That's right."

"Why the hell not?"

"She wouldn't give it to me."

"Give it to you? What are you, nuts? Give it to you? You found this girl, you talked to her, and then you let her walk away from you?"

"It was either that or have her call the cops."

"So *let her* call the cops. Let her explain to the cops what she's doing setting guys up in singles bars."

"Yeah, fine," I said. "Then your story gets written up in the *New York Post*. I thought you had a proxy fight going on

110

and wanted to hush this up."

"I do, but —"

"Well, you can't have it both ways. You're either discreet or you start yelling you've been framed, and you keep yelling until someone believes you."

"All right, all right," Pritchert said. "I don't have time for that now. The point is, if you didn't get her address or phone number, how are we going to reach her again?"

"For one thing, we know where she works. For another, I got the name of her agent."

"Oh?"

"Name's Shelly Daniels. Got an office on Eighth Avenue. I got the phone number."

"How do you know it's legit?"

"She's listed in the yellow pages."

"Uh-huh. You talk to her yet?"

"No, but according to the girl, she actually met the guy. He came to her office, made all the preliminary arrangements. Which makes her a more important lead than the girl. Now, you want me to chase her down, I can, but it will have to be later in the day."

"What do you mean?"

"I'm working this morning. I have two cases lined up for Rosenberg and Stone. I'll knock 'em off as fast as I can, but it's possible another case will come in. I'll get to the agent

111

quick as I can, I just can't tell you when."

"Fine," Pritchert said. "But I think your premise is wrong. The woman's not important. The important thing is the girl. I need to know what happened during the time I blacked out."

"She says she doesn't know."

"Yeah, but she's probably lying. Okay, so this agent is our contact to the girl. And her name is . . . what was it again?"

"Shelly Daniels."

"Shelly Daniels. And the phone number?"

I gave it to him. Waited while he wrote it down.

"Now then," I said. "Before we go any further, you owe me some money."

"How much?"

"Quite a bit. The two hundred you gave me I paid out in bribes."

"Bribes?"

"A hundred bucks to the bartender, and a hundred to the girl. That wipes that out. So you owe me for my time and expenses so far. I put in eight hours yesterday, I had two hours before. That's five hundred dollars so far."

"Eight hours?"

"You can't just walk up on the runway of a topless bar and start talking to the dancers. I had to wait for her to leave."

"Of course. Okay, you'll get the money."

"So you want me to go ahead with this? Interview the agent?"

There was a pause. Then, "I don't see the need. The agent's only important to contact the girl. I can do that. All right, fine. So you'll be working. What if I need to reach you?"

"I'll be on the beeper. Same as before. You can call the office, have them page me. You still have the number?"

"Yeah, I got it. Okay. Good work. I'll talk to you later."

And he hung up.

I blinked.

Good work?

I wondered what the guy sounded like when he *wasn't* happy about something.

17.

Mary Mason beeped me twice.

Doo dah. Doo dah.

Mary Mason beeped me twice.

All the doo dah day.

The first beep was for a boy who fell off a playground swing in Brooklyn.

The second was for a girl who was hit by a car in Queens.

The girl in Queens was dead.

Which was a hell of a sobering note.

I'd had a trip-and-fall in Harlem and a trip-and-fall in the Bronx. Those were the two cases I'd told Cranston Pritchert about. I'd gotten beeped on my way to the second appointment, called in and been given the case in Brooklyn. I was on my way back from that when I was beeped off the Interboro Parkway and given the one in Queens.

So the fact is, I'd had the jingle *Mary Mason beeped me twice* in my head when I called in.

And then she tells me the kid's dead.

Jesus.

Of course, you get them sometimes.

You're dealing with personal injury, and the most extreme personal injury is death.

A case like that is always rough.

It's rougher when it's a kid.

At least there'd been the passage of time. It wasn't like it had happened today. The hit-and-run had taken place last week. So the family would have had time to adjust.

But still.

I was not a happy camper as I rang the doorbell.

Or while I listened to the mother's story.

Maria Perez was twenty-four years of age. Divorced. The mother of two.

Now the mother of one.

She would have been attractive if she hadn't been distraught. She cried telling the story. I'd known she would.

Maria Perez had been crossing Jamaica Avenue with her children to buy a shaved ice. Her one-year-old boy was in a stroller.

Her four-year-old girl was not.

A gypsy cab had run the light and run her daughter down.

"I yelled at her to look out, but she just stood there, she didn't move," the mother said, before dissolving into sobs.

It killed me.

And what really tore me up was, bad as I felt for this woman with her tragic loss, I couldn't help thinking *why?*

Why did you yell at her? Why did you *have* to yell at her? Why was she walking by *herself?* Why weren't you holding her *hand?*

I was bummed as hell driving back to Manhattan. As you might expect. But it wasn't just the sign-up I'd been through. It was also the fact that Mary Mason had beeped me twice, and each time I'd reacted like Pavlov's dog, salivating at the expectation that the call would be from Cranston Pritchert, relenting and telling me, yes, of course, go interview the agent, he should have said so in the first place.

Only it hadn't been.

And by the time I got back to Manhattan at three-thirty that afternoon, I had come to the unhappy realization it wasn't going to be.

I parked in the midtown parking garage and went back up to the office just on the off chance he'd left a message on the answering machine. But of course he hadn't.

So, there I was, three-thirty in the afternoon in midtown Manhattan with nothing to do.

Except.

My office was on 47th Street, just off Seventh Avenue.

Shelly Daniels' office was on Eighth.

I wondered how close.

I got out the phone book, turned to the street conversion page, which tells you where the addresses on the avenues are located. To get the cross street for an address on Eighth Avenue, the instructions were to take the building number, knock off the last digit, divide by two and add ten.

I did, with an unexpected result.

Shelly Daniels' office was only three blocks away.

How about that?

Three blocks.

And Cranston Pritchert wasn't going to interview the woman. He only cared about her as a source to find the girl. Which was really narrow-minded thinking. Who *cared* what the girl had to say? I'd already heard her story, and there was nothing there. But this woman had actually met the guy. Talked to him face to face. She could describe who he was. Hell, she might even have a name. She'd at least know what the guy wanted and what the guy said. Not interview her? It simply made no sense.

I mean, if Cranston Pritchert was going to be that much of a jerk.

The thing was, I'd asked him if he wanted me to interview the woman, and he'd said not to bother. Which meant he wasn't going to pay me for it. That was simple enough. If

I did it, I wouldn't get paid. Nobody works for nothing. That's a given in this business. A guy would have to be a total schmuck.

Still.

Three-thirty in the afternoon. With no job to do. And the office just three blocks away.

I shook my head to clear it.

Snap out of it. You're not thinking rationally. There's no point going over there.

You'd have to be a total schmuck.

18.

It was exactly what I expected. Which surprised me. But I guess even I can't always be wrong. Anyway, Shelly Daniels might have had a luxurious suite of offices with a front desk manned by a grim but efficient-looking receptionist, but she didn't. She had a hole in the wall on the second floor over an all-male movie theater.

The sign on the door said SHELLY DANIELS TALENT AGENCY. The sign was hanging on a hook, which did not exactly inspire confidence, instead gave the impression the office was being rented by the hour.

I pushed open the door and went in.

The office was smaller than mine, and about as poorly furnished: one desk, one chair, a bookcase, and a couple of file cabinets.

The woman at the desk looked tough as nails, a remarkable accomplishment for someone that short and thin. Her emaciated, sharp, angular face was topped by a beehive of teased red hair. She had wing-tipped glasses on her nose, a pencil behind her ear, and a cigarette dangling from her mouth.

The cigarette was not her first. A full ashtray, a pack of cigarettes, and a lighter were on the desk in front of her. The stench of stale tobacco permeated the office, and a smoggy haze hung in the air.

The woman was on the phone when I walked in.

"You heard me," she said. "You want a hooker, you call somewhere else. You want dancers, you want models, you want show girls, that's fine. This is not an escort service. We're not selling sex. You call up and bitch the girl didn't come across, you're talking to my deaf ear." She slammed down the phone, scowled up at me. "What can I do for you?"

It occurred to me there were a number of approaches I could take with the woman, and most of them weren't going to fly.

I pulled out my ID, opened it.

She put up her hand, scowled again. "Hey, hey, didn't you hear me on the phone? I run a legitimate operation here, no funny business."

"Relax," I said. "I'm not a cop."

She frowned. "Huh?"

"It's not a badge, just an ID. I'm a private detective. I need some information."

She frowned, squinted at the ID. "Then why the hell didn't you say so? You come in here, flip that open, all dramatic like some detective on TV." She cocked her head. "You an actor?"

"Actually, I used to be."

She pointed her finger. "See? I can tell. It's the eye. I can always spot 'em. You lookin' for work? No, of course not. You're a detective. What was it you say you wanted?"

"I need some information."

"Why would you want information from me?"

"Are you Shelly Daniels?"

"Is that the information you want?"

"It's a start. Actually, it's about your business."

"What about it?"

"You book dancers, don't you?"

"I book dancers, actors, singers, mimes, jugglers, and clowns. What was it you were interested in?"

"Actually, what you said on the phone just now."

She drew back slightly, and her eyes were wary. "What do you mean?"

"You were talking about the fact you were a talent agent and your bookings were professional, not personal."

"Hey, I like that. That's a nice way of putting it."

"Thank you. I'm wondering just what would happen if someone did want to book one of your girls for a private gig."

"I have men too."

"I beg your pardon?"

"I have both actors and actresses here. You said *girls* as if I were running a meat market."

"No offense meant. At any rate, would you happen to be handling the bookings for a woman by the name of Lucy Blaine?"

Her eyes narrowed. "Why do you ask?"

"Well, she said you were, and she wouldn't give me her phone number, but she gave me yours."

"Is this with regard to a booking?"

"Yes, it is."

"You want to book her?"

"No."

She frowned. "You want to explain?"

"According to Lucy Blaine, she was hired through your agency to hang out in a singles bar and have cocktails with a gentleman." I put up my hand. "Please understand, there is no contention that there was anything wrong with this. No one's claiming the girl was solicited for prostitution, or anything of the kind. It was, as far as we know, a perfectly straightforward, legal business arrangement. The girl was hired for a specific function, which she performed."

The woman's eyes were hard. "So?"

"I've been hired to find out why. Toward that end I tracked down the woman, Lucy Blaine. I spoke with her last night." I looked at her. "Perhaps she's contacted you?"

Her eyes betrayed nothing. "Go on."

"According to her, she never met the gentleman who hired her, she was merely given instructions on the phone. The only one who actually met the man was you."

"So?" she said again.

"That's why I've come to you."

"You expect me to divulge information about a client?"

"A regular client, no. But I have a feeling this wasn't like that. I have a feeling this was some guy off the street you'd never seen before and will probably never see again. I would say one of the *reasons* this guy came to your agency was because you didn't know him from Adam."

"What difference would that make?"

I shrugged. "Well, think it over. When it's time to stand up and be counted, a lot will depend on which side you're on."

"And just what do you mean by that?"

"This transaction was somewhat unusual.

It is entirely possible that the intent behind it was also illegal." As she started to flare up, I put up my hand. "Please. I'm not saying *you* did anything illegal. In fact, that's the whole point. But, from what the girl said, there's every indication she was paid to take part in some sort of scam. Should that turn out to be true, it would be helpful if you could establish you were an innocent bystander rather than an active participant."

As words went, I figured *innocent bystander* a far more tactful choice than *unwitting dupe*. Still, I wasn't sure if I was getting anywhere.

Turned out I was.

"So," the woman said, mulling it over out loud. "You're saying if I tell you what I know, it would be considered a show of good faith in the event it turned out the deal wasn't kosher?"

"That's the idea, yes."

"You're saying I would not be selling out a client, merely explaining an irregular booking?"

"Exactly."

She frowned. "I don't think I could do that."

"Why not?"

"You come to me as a client, I treat you as a client."

"Excuse me?"

"You'll pardon me, but who are you? Some man off the street comes in, wants to ask me some questions. Why should I answer? What's in it for me?"

Now I was *sure* Lucy Blaine'd called her.

"What *should* be in it for you?" I said.

"Two hundred dollars."

I shook my head. "Sorry."

"Take it or leave it."

"Then I'll have to leave it, 'cause I ain't got it."

"What have you got?"

I had a hundred dollars. I'd taken it out of the cash machine on the way over, on the off chance it came to that. That Lucy Blaine had called her. Had told her what had happened. Had told her what I'd paid *her.* Just on the off chance it came down to a hundred bucks would get me what I needed to know.

Damn.

Turned out it would.

And Cranston Pritchert hadn't authorized it.

Which made it *my* hundred bucks.

Damn.

Just how bad did I want to know?

Okay, so I'm stupid. But sitting there in the poker game of life, I just couldn't bear to fold. There was too much at stake. If I had to throw a hundred bucks in the pot, it seemed no way I wasn't going to make it back threefold.

I reached in my pocket, pulled out the five twenties that had popped out of the cash machine.

"A hundred bucks," I said, "if you tell me what I need to know."

I pushed it toward the center of the desk and stood there.

She didn't move, just sat there eyeing it.

And I felt great. I got you, babe. There's my bet. Call, raise, or fold.

She called.

A bony hand snaked out, grabbed the bills, folded them up.

"Okay," she said. "What do you want to know?"

"You met the guy who hired Lucy Blaine?"

"Yes, I did."

"How did you meet him?"

"He walked in the door, just like you did."

"He call first?"

"Not that I know of."

"What do you mean?"

"I get calls all day long. Inquiries." She shrugged. "Any one of them might have been him."

"Like the phone call when I came in?"

She grinned, stubbed out the cigarette.

"What phone call? You're paying for it, so what the hell." She lit another cigarette, blew out the smoke, and jerked her thumb. "I hear someone come to the door, I'm on the phone. It looks like a sucker, I'm talking hot babes. It looks like a cop, I'm into the my-girls-don't-do-that-stuff routine."

"I look like a cop?"

"No offense, but you could have been."

"Great," I said. "Now, what about this guy?"

"He comes in like I said, and wants to hire a girl." She shrugged. "Well, I'm cagy, of course — *he* could be a cop. But we talk it over, and he sounds legit."

"What did he say?"

"Most of it you already know. He wants a girl to hang out in a singles bar and have drinks with a guy Thursday night, five to seven."

"That's the whole thing?"

"That's it. She's to keep him there, and under no circumstances is she to let him go."

"What if he tries to leave?"

"She's to stop him. Whatever it takes."

"What if she can't?"

"She's to go with him, try to steer him somewhere else."

"Where?"

"It doesn't matter, just so long as she

doesn't let him get out of her sight."

"Any other instructions? Anything special she was supposed to do?"

"No. That's it."

Damn.

"And the guy she was supposed to have drinks with — did he tell you who he was?"

"No. He said that was something he'd take up with her."

"And you agreed to that?"

She cocked her head. Pointed. "You makin' a judgment here?"

I put up my hand. "No, no. I'm just asking for the information. The fact is, the client didn't tell you about the bar or the guy or anything of the sort? None of the specifics?"

"Like I say, no. All we discussed was the deal."

"What *was* the deal?"

She paused a moment. Then, almost defiantly, "The deal was a thousand dollars. Five hundred to the girl, five hundred to me."

"A thousand dollars?"

"That's right."

"How did he pay?"

"How do you think? He paid in cash."

I exhaled. "Uh-huh. And the client — did he happen to give you his name?"

"No, he did not."

"What a surprise," I said. "But you did meet this guy. Talk to him in person."

"That's right."

"Would you recognize him if you saw him again?"

"Are you kidding?" she said. "I couldn't miss him."

"Oh yeah? How's that?"

"That string bean?" She snorted. "Hell, he had to be six six."

19.

Sergeant MacAullif cocked his head.

"To what do I owe this pleasure?"

Hmm. Ten times more cordial a greeting than I might have expected. Sergeant MacAullif was a homicide officer with whom I'd been associated on several occasions. Those associations had ranged from the cordial to the less than cordial, such as the time he'd slammed me up against the side of a car while my arm was in a sling. Not that he hadn't had provocation. Still, in dealing with MacAullif, one was never sure quite what to expect. So a neutral greeting was fine.

"I was just in the neighborhood, thought I'd drop in."

MacAullif's eyes narrowed. He leaned back in his desk chair, cocked his head. "Don't put me in a bad mood. I'm having a perfectly good day, no reason to spoil it by acting cute."

"You don't buy the just-in-the-neighborhood bit?"

"Give me a break. What kind of case are you on?"

"A totally frustrating one."

"You done anything illegal yet?"

"Absolutely not."

"What's the matter? Sudden attack of ethics?"

"Now that you mention it."

"What?"

"Ethics really is the problem."

"Oh, you got a problem?"

"Well, now that you mention it."

"Don't piss me off," MacAullif said. "I'm in too good a mood. You know *why* I'm in a good mood? I cleared two cases yesterday. I got a lead on a third. Plus, the turn-'em-loose judge scheduled to try the repeat offender I nailed dead to rights just came down with the flu, and the case has been reassigned to a hard-nose jurist who'll put the creep away. Now, that may not sound like much to you, but frankly I don't have days like this often. So, you wanna spoil it for me, you're gonna have to work overtime."

"Why would I do a thing like that?"

" 'Cause you're a total pain in the ass can't handle the simplest thing without makin' it worse than it is. Now, you say you got an ethical problem?"

"In a way."

"In what way would that be?"

"A private detective's got a duty to his client, right?"

"Yeah. So?"

"What if the client isn't shooting square?"

MacAullif shrugged. "Most clients are gonna lie. That's a fact of life. If that was enough to relieve you of your obligations, there wouldn't be any."

"Clients?"

"Obligations."

"Suppose it's worse than that?"

"What do you mean?"

"Suppose the client's playing you for a sucker?"

"In your case, that's no surprise. Though I *am* surprised that you noticed."

"Want to hear the story or not?"

"The story of how you got duped? Go ahead. Make my day."

I gave him the whole spiel from top to bottom, including the phony extortion letter, the topless dancer, and the chain-smoking talent agent.

As he listened, MacAullif's smile grew broader and broader. By the time I was finished, he was grinning like a zany.

"I love it," he said. "I absolutely love it. You're like one of those hamsters that runs around on a wheel — no matter how fast you go, you never get anyplace."

"Thank you. That's exactly what I was hoping to hear."

"So, what's the punch line? How much are you being paid to do this?"

"How does fifty bucks an hour sound?"

"For bein' a patsy? Barely adequate. How much of it have you actually seen?"

"Oh, well there . . ."

"Oh, well there? I love it. Could you translate that, please?"

"I got a two hundred buck retainer."

"And?"

"I laid out three hundred in expenses."

MacAullif nodded. "Perfect. Just perfect. You should write this up for *Detective Monthly*. Hell, you might even get the centerfold."

"I told you it was a mess, MacAullif."

"That you did. And you didn't lie. Tell me, why are you bringing this to *me*? Isn't this the kind of thing you should lay on Rosenberg?"

"He's gone home for the day."

"Ah, better and better," MacAullif said. "You're telling me I wasn't even your first choice."

"You were third."

"Third?"

"My wife's at a PTA meeting."

"I can't even tell if that's true or a wise-crack. Listen, just what is it you're after here?"

"Like I said, what's my obligation? I think I'm being used as part of some elaborate scam. Ethically, how am I bound?"

"Don't be a jackass. You aren't bound at all."

"Yeah, but do I have a right to take action against the best interests of my own client?"

"Such as?"

"Okay. Let's assume my client set this up. Say he's the six foot six individual who showed up at the talent agency and arranged to hire this girl."

"Which has yet to be proven," MacAullif pointed out.

"Yeah, but take it as a premise. My client's one of three vice-presidents in a company about to elect a new chairman of the board. It's hotly contested, and there's a proxy fight going on. My client claims he's being set up, and hires me to investigate. Lo and behold, I discover someone *did* hire a girl to try to pick him up in a bar. My client cries foul, drags me to the stockholders meeting, and asks me to tell what I know."

"Would that work?"

"I'm not sure. Frankly, I'm not that sharp

at business matters."

"No shit."

"But the way I understand it, aside from three vice-presidents, the largest stockholder is the granddaughter of the late chairman of the board. She would be at the meeting, and might be influenced by what I had to say."

"You mean whoever she votes for is in?"

"Not necessarily. The holdings aren't that big. In the end, the proxies will decide it."

MacAullif frowned. "When's the meeting?"

"Next week."

"Then the proxies must already be in."

"True, but if my client's doing what I think he's doing, then his next move would be to call the larger stockholders and get them to come to the meeting in person. A proxy is superseded when the stockholder's actually there. So, he'd get enough stockholders at the meeting to gain a controlling interest, and then have me do my stuff."

"How do you know all that — about proxies, I mean?"

"Actually, I read it in a book."

"A detective novel?"

"That doesn't make it wrong."

"It doesn't make it right, either."

"No, but it's logical. Everything points to it. I locate this talent agent and my client tells me not to interview her. I can't understand why, but the answer is simple. He's the one who hired her, and he doesn't want me to uncover that."

"I got all that," MacAullif said. "You don't have to spell it out. Listen, all ethical considerations aside, why should it ever come to that? Why don't you just confront your client with this?"

"Can't reach him. I called him at home, his wife said he was working late. I called him at work, and the office is closed."

"So you decided to lay it on me."

"I thought you'd get a kick out of it."

"Actually, I did," MacAullif said. "You made a total fool of yourself. But you didn't do anything illegal. You didn't make me an accessory to a crime. And you didn't present me with anything I have to act on. All you did was expose yourself to humiliation and ridicule." He shrugged, shook his head. "Hell, it's the best of all possible worlds."

"Yeah, fine," I said. "Suppose I talk to my client, and he denies being the guy who hired the girl, claims he was set up and demands I go to the stockholders meeting and tell what I know — what the hell do I do then?"

MacAullif grinned, nodded in agreement with himself.

"The best of all possible worlds."

20.

I came out of One Police Plaza, walked down to City Hall, and caught the Lexington Avenue Express uptown. I had my car, but I'd left it uptown in the municipal lot. You can't fight City Hall, and you can't park near it either. When visiting MacAullif, I often took the subway. Just another glamorous, strap-hanging New York PI.

I came up for air at Lexington Avenue and 59th Street, and walked uptown to 66th. There was a pay phone on the corner that appeared to be both unoccupied and working, a long-shot parlay in New York City. I considered investing a quarter to see if Cranston Pritchert was there. I decided against it. I didn't really want to warn him I was coming. No, I'd only call upstairs if I couldn't get in.

Turned out I could. The lobby was wide open. Which was a bit unusual. Manhattan office buildings often lock the doors at night, have security guards, make visitors sign a register to get in, or some combination of the three. Cranston Pritchert's building had none of them. The employees of Philip Greenberg Investments could come and go as they pleased.

Of course, so could various assorted derelicts, winos, muggers, rapists, and murderers, but hey, it wasn't my building.

I went in, rang for the elevator, took it up to the eighth floor.

As I came out of the elevator and walked down the hall, it occurred to me I'd done exactly the same thing the day before, when I'd barged in to confront Cranston Pritchert with faking the extortion letter. And here I was, not much more than twenty-four hours later, confronting him with yet another perfidious act. It occurred to me my client and I did not have the best possible working relationship.

The massive oak door guarding the offices of Philip Greenberg Investments looked formidable, but proved to be unlocked. I slipped in, closing it gently behind me — no need to warn my prey. Lights were on, but there was no one there. I cocked my head, listened, couldn't hear a sound. If Pritchert was there, he must be in his office.

He wasn't, though. When I walked down the hall and poked my head in, there was no one there. Then it occurred to me, was this really his office? I mean, how much attention had I been paying yesterday? He'd led me in here, talking all the time. My only real concern had been the wastebasket. Yes, there was one there, but it was standard office furniture, and who was to say every office didn't have one just like it? I mean, was that really his desk?

I walked around it, surveyed the top. A telephone, an appointment book, a memo pad.

And a letter addressed to Cranston Pritchert.

Yes, this was his office.

So, where the hell was he?

Well, more than likely, out to dinner.

And, cynical son of a bitch that I am, it occurred to me he was probably out to dinner with Lucy Blaine, Marla Melons, or whatever the hell her name was, and the two of them were laughing their ass off over this scam they pulled on the poor dipshit PI.

It also occurred to me, *I* hadn't had dinner at all.

Suffice it to say, I was not a happy camper.

So, what did I do now? Go home, or wait for my client to come back?

Well, after my talk with MacAullif, I was too pissed to go home. It wasn't just that the guy had lied to me. Hell, I wanted to get paid.

While I waited, I checked out the other offices.

The one at the end of the hall was twice the size of Cranston Pritchert's, and boasted a portable bar. Obviously the office of the late Philip Greenberg. I wondered if Cranston would get it, if he succeeded in being elected chairman of the board.

Across the hall was an office identical to Pritchert's. The letters on that desk were addressed to a Mr. Kevin Dunbar.

I tried to stem the growing sense of pride over the ease with which my efficient detective work was identifying the occupants of the offices.

Next to Dunbar's was an office dominated by file cabinets, calculators, and ledger books. I didn't want to get cocky, but I had a feeling it might belong to the accountant.

The office next to it was identical to Kevin Dunbar and Cranston Pritchert's.

With one small exception.

The body of Cranston Pritchert lay stretched out on the floor.

21.

The cop didn't know me from Adam. Which was a bit of a surprise. I've been involved in enough homicide investigations by now that I've got to know a few cops. But he wasn't one of them.

His name was Belcher. Sergeant Timothy Belcher. One might imagine a kid by the name of Belcher would take a lot of ribbing and become tough as nails. It would certainly have accounted for the expression on the guy's face.

Sergeant Belcher was medium height, medium build, but looked solid as a rock. The image started with his jaw, which appeared permanently set. I swear it didn't move when he talked.

The eyes didn't either. They bored right through you. And the single expression on the deadpan face, or so it seemed to me, was, *You lying sack of shit, I don't believe a single word you say.*

"All right," Belcher said. "Let's go over it again."

I had already told him everything. Belcher

had advised me that I had the right to remain silent, but had managed to convey the impression that if I chose to exercise that right, I would be the unhappiest private detective that ever lived.

He needn't have bothered. With my client dead, I had no one left to protect. Except me. And I didn't happen to be guilty, so I had nothing to worry about. I mean, that's the way the system works, isn't it?

At any rate, I had already talked, and Belcher had liked it so much he wanted to hear it again. In fact, he must have really liked it, because this time he had a stenographer brought in to take it down so he could go over it to his heart's content.

"Okay," I said. "I came up here tonight to look for my client."

"The client is Cranston Pritchert?"

"That's right."

"The dead man?"

"Yes. The dead man."

"You've seen the dead man and you identify him as Cranston Pritchert, your client, the man who employed you?"

"That's right."

"When did he employ you, and when did the two of you first meet?"

"He came to my office Monday morning."

"This past Monday morning?"

"That's right."

"At what time?"

"Around nine o'clock."

"And what happened then?"

I went through it all again. The whole shmear. Just as I told it to MacAullif, and just as I'd already told it to him. Everything I'd done up to and including finding the body and calling the cops.

"So," Belcher said, when I was done. "This extortion letter you refer to — the one you say your client rigged himself — do you still have that?"

"Actually, no, I don't."

"And why is that?"

"After he admitted making it, it wasn't important anymore."

"So, what did you do with it?"

"I think I left it on his desk."

"You think?"

"Like I say, it wasn't important. I brought it to his office, confronted him with it. When he admitted it was his, it didn't matter anymore. I remember sticking it in front of his face. To the best of my recollection, I left it on his desk."

"It's not there now."

"No, I would assume he threw it out."

"And the paper you say he cut this out

from — that was in his wastebasket?"

"Yes, it was."

"Is it there now?"

"I didn't look, but I would assume that it's been dumped."

"Why would you assume that?"

"Because it was yesterday. I would assume the offices are cleaned."

"Every day?"

"As to that, I have no idea. Maybe it's there, maybe it's gone. But this is silly." I jerked my thumb. "The office is right next door. We could take a look."

"We can and will take a look," Belcher said. "But I assure you this is not silly. The questions matter, and your answers matter. Your opinion is what's important here."

Oh, boy.

I said nothing. Sat. Waited.

"At any rate," Belcher said, "it is your statement that Cranston Pritchert admitted to you that he, himself, had fashioned the extortion letter out of headlines cut from the newspaper?"

"That's right."

"And what exactly did the letter say?"

"I saw you in the singles bar."

"That's all?"

"That's all."

"Was the letter signed?"

"It was not."

"And the reason your client gave you for fabricating this letter?"

"He wanted me to find this girl. He thought I wasn't taking it seriously enough. He wanted to give me added incentive."

"Those were his exact words?"

"That's the gist of it, yes."

"And when you say that's the gist of it . . . ?"

"That is an entirely accurate assessment of his stated intent."

"Uh-huh. Now then. You did as your client asked and tracked down this girl?"

"Yes, I did."

"You communicated this to him?"

"That's right."

"At the same time you informed him that you had located the girl's agent, and that *she* was the only one who had had contact with the man who hired her?"

"That's right."

"And he instructed you to ignore this agent?"

"Yes, he did."

"But you called on her anyway?"

"That's right."

"Why?"

I frowned. "That's a tough question. The

thing is, I'd been working on this for days. And I finally got a lead. A good, solid lead. More than a lead. A break. I not only found the girl, I found someone who actually met the guy who hired the girl. Which had to be the payoff. I mean, how can you not follow that up?"

"I see," Belcher said. "You found that frustrating?"

"I beg your pardon?"

"It was frustrating that your client didn't want to follow up the lead?"

"Yes, it was."

"So much so that you followed it up on your own initiative?"

"Yes, I did."

"And then when you follow it up, you find out the girl was employed by a man who looks exactly like your client."

"That's a generalization."

"But an accurate one. The man was described as looking like your client."

"It was a very general description."

"Granted. But in your own mind, when you heard that description, who was the first person you thought it might be?"

"My client."

"Isn't that the reason you came here tonight? Isn't that what you said? To ask your client if he was the man who went to the talent agency to hire the girl?"

"That's right."

"You had reason to be very angry with your client, didn't you?"

"Not angry enough to shoot him."

"Shoot him? Are you making a confession here?"

"I just said I *didn't* shoot him."

"I heard what you said. That's a self-serving declaration, and means very little, but your denial is now on record. You claim you did not shoot your client, Cranston Pritchert?"

"I did not."

"You were angry with him?"

"Yes."

"You came here tonight to confront him?"

"In a way."

"Did you come here to confront him?"

"Yes, I did."

"You were angry with him, and you came here to confront him?"

"Yes."

"But you didn't kill him?"

What a sorry state of affairs.

22.

The cop in the lobby never stood a chance. MacAullif steamrolled him as if he wasn't even there. He never even broke stride. He whipped his shield out as he came in the front door, leveled his finger at the cop, and said, "Don't give me any shit, I happen to be a sergeant, you're supposed to guard this suspect, fine, you guard him from the front door, you do a good job and you keep people away from me, got it?"

The cop who'd been assigned to ride herd over me was young, impressionable, and overwhelmed. He got it. "Yes, sir," he said. I swear he almost saluted. He turned and marched to the front door of the lobby, probably hoping someone would come in it so he could hassle *them*.

MacAullif wheeled on me, leveled a finger. "All right, fuckface, you're on."

I put up my hands. "Hey, don't blame me."

"Don't blame you?" MacAullif said. "That's a good one. Don't blame you? I'm drivin' home over the Manhattan Bridge at

148

the end of an absolutely fabulous day. Spoke to the wife, and she's got steaks ready to throw on the fire, and I can't wait 'cause I'm starving 'cause I got hung up in the office listening to some asshole tell me a fairy tale."

"Everything I said was true."

"Oh, I'm sure it was. With a few minor omissions."

"MacAullif —"

"So, what happens? I'm cruisin' over the bridge, when what should come over the police band but a homicide: male, Caucasian, six-six, tentative ID one Cranston Pritchert."

"MacAullif —"

"And if that wasn't enough to ruin my dinner, they got a suspect in custody, apprehended at the scene, ID'd as one private detective by the name of Stanley Hastings."

"I wasn't apprehended."

"Right, right. And you're not in custody, you and that cop were just havin' a little chat."

"Bullshit, MacAullif. I'm the one called it in, for Christ's sake."

"Of course you are. What a schmuck. You think I'm upset about the suspect bit? Big fuckin' deal. Everyone's a suspect. I'm a little perturbed by the fact you phoned it in."

"I should have just left things as they were and skipped out?"

"Don't get cute. Is the ME up there now?"

"I think so."

"You think so?"

"I think the guy who came up when I was going down is the medical examiner. They hustled me into the elevator, so I can't be sure."

"Yeah, well, I'd be very interested in the time of death."

"So would I."

MacAullif shook his head, waved his hands. "No, no. You're not reading me, schmuck. I'd be interested to know if this guy was dead when you were in my office telling me the fairy story."

"He probably was."

"Oh, is that right?"

"Like I said, I tried to call and got no answer before I came to you."

"And when you got no answer, you went up to the office, looked to see what was going on, and found your client dead."

"No, I didn't."

"Yes, you did. That's how you called it in."

"Right. But after I talked to you."

"And that was the first time you'd been up there?"

"I was up there yesterday."

"I mean tonight."

"MacAullif —"

"The timing's bad. Real bad. You come to my office, tell me everything about your client's case. Including the fact you don't trust him. Which is a little out of the ordinary."

"I had cause."

"If your client was dead, you had *real* cause."

"I didn't *know* he was dead."

"The timing stinks. Look what you've done." MacAullif pointed to himself, spread his hands. "*I'm* a fucking witness. They make a case against you, you gotta call me to the stand. I'm a witness twice over. I'm an alibi witness for the time you were in my office. Plus you'll try to bring out what you told me about the case. You know how that would endear me to an ADA?"

"Give me a break. You said yourself no one really thinks I did it."

"Did it, no. Knew about it, that's something else entirely."

"I didn't know about it."

"So you say. But what else *could* you say? If you found the body, didn't dare call the cops till you laid the foundation. Rushed down to my office, fed me the bullshit line.

151

Rushed back up here and called the cops. Well, guess what — we'd be right where we are now, wouldn't we?"

"That's not what happened."

"When you were in my office you had no idea this guy was dead?"

"None at all."

"It was just coincidence?"

"It was just bad luck."

"Oh, no. You don't *know* from bad luck. But you're *gonna* know from bad luck, 'cause your bad luck is just starting. Your first bit of bad luck is the fact I'm here talkin' to you instead of sitting home in Bay Ridge eating a fucking steak. Your second bit of bad luck is the fact I'm now on the hook to talk to the cops and tell 'em what I know. Not that I want to do that, but I happen to be a cop, and it happens to be my fuckin' duty. And if I didn't do that, they would have my fuckin' shield. So I gotta tell everything you told me. Which, aside from being a royal pain in the ass, if it doesn't jibe with everything you told them — and why should it? — like I'm taking notes on your fucking story, like it might be important, like I actually give a damn — well, then, there's gonna be hell to pay. Now, who do you think is gonna be payin' it, you or me?"

"I know it's a mess. You don't have to rub it in."

"Oh, right. Like I'm to blame. Like I'm the one makin' your life miserable."

"You wanna stop using me for a punching bag and take a look at the evidence here?"

"What evidence? You got a six foot six stiff, what else you got?"

"He was shot."

"So I hear."

"Once."

"Once is enough."

"In the heart."

"Figures. Probably couldn't reach his head. You got anything else useful?"

"He wasn't shot in his own office. He was shot in some other guy's."

"What other guy?"

"One of the other vice-presidents."

"What's his name?"

"Oh."

"You know his name or don't you?"

"Give me a break. I'm bad with names."

"No shit."

"You shoot the questions at me that fast, of course I'm gonna blank. One of them's Kevin Dunbar, and it wasn't him. So it's the other one. Whose name is . . ."

"Christ."

"It's not Greenberg, he's the deceased chairman of the board."

"If I shot you now, it would be justifiable homicide."

"Oh yeah. Marty Rothstein. That's the other vice-president. It was in his office."

"Ah. Major clue. This case is almost cracked."

"Hey, there's a lot of leads. On account of the work I did."

"Give yourself a gold star. In everything you told me, there's only one thing's really key."

"What's that?"

"If it's true, of course. If you didn't find the body before and make the whole thing up."

"So help me. What did I say that's key?"

"You called his wife. Isn't that what you said? You called him at home and his wife said he was working late."

"Yeah. So?"

"Where's home?"

"I don't know."

"You don't know."

"No, I don't know. I have his phone number and his business address. I don't have his home address. I mean, it's not like I have a form that clients fill out. I don't send out monthly statements."

"You don't keep files?"

"Most of my work is for Rosenberg and Stone. This wasn't."

"So you don't keep a file?"

"Hey, MacAullif, screw the file. What's so fucking important?"

"The fact you called his wife. A guy gets killed, the wife is usually suspect number one. The ME puts the time of death around the time you made that call, the call becomes important as hell."

"Right."

"Depending on where the guy lives. Turns out he lives next door, she could have run over and killed him just fine."

"It's a two one two number."

"Narrows it down. A lot more, now the Bronx is seven one eight. Still, Manhattan's a pretty big place."

That was a relief. Not that Cranston Pritchert's wife might be out of it — I never met the woman, *someone* killed him, and it might as well have been her. No, it was a relief MacAullif was talking about it. Discussing the crime like a crime, instead of a personal affront against him. If I could keep him focused in that direction, on an analytical examination of the evidence, I might just luck out. I might be able to get out of this thing with our friendship, such as it

155

was, virtually intact.

It was not my day. Because at that moment the elevator doors opened, and out walked Sergeant Belcher.

Actually, I had my back to the elevator, so I didn't see him.

MacAullif did.

His mouth fell open, his eyes narrowed, his face darkened.

Under his breath he murmured, "Oh, shit."

23.

"How bad is it?"

"I'm not sure."

I wasn't, either. It was much later that evening and I'd just gotten home.

First, I'd been held in the office building lobby for what seemed like hours. Then I'd been dragged downtown. The good news was I hadn't been booked. The bad news was I'd been fingerprinted. That, I was told, was just so the cops could tell which fingerprints at the crime scene happened to be mine. The implication was so they could eliminate them, not so they could prove me guilty.

Whatever the reason, the fingerprinting was unnecessary, because if the cops had checked they would have found they had my fingerprints on file from my previous encounters with the law. That didn't seem like a great thing to mention, somehow, so I kept quiet and let them print me again.

After that, I was held for interrogation. I pointed out that I had already given a signed statement, but no one was listening to me.

The end result was I was held downtown for no reason whatsoever, and didn't get home till close to midnight.

I had managed a phone call to Alice, so she wasn't hysterical, merely concerned.

"Uh-huh," Alice said. She zapped some milk in the microwave, added coffee, set it in front of me. "Here."

"At midnight? It'll keep me up."

"It's decaf."

"If it's decaf, what's the point?"

"It's hot. Drink it. So what happened?"

"Someone shot my client."

"So you said. That leaves a few gaps in the story. You wanna fill me in?"

I brought Alice up to speed. Which took a bit of doing. It had been a long day. Including my conversation with Cranston Pritchert. Him telling me not to call on the talent agent. Me doing it anyway. My talk with MacAullif. My discovery of the body. My ensuing adventures with the NYPD.

"Good lord," Alice said.

"Yeah. And that's not the worst of it."

"Oh?"

"Apparently there's no love lost between the investigating officer and MacAullif."

"Why?"

"I have no idea. It was really weird. Mac-Aullif's there bawling me out, Belcher comes down in the elevator. They see each other, they just stand there, glaring. Neither one says a word. Then they walk out to the street. Belcher's back about ten minutes later. Mac-Aullif never came back."

"He ask you about him?"

"Who?"

"The cop. What's-his-name. Belcher. When he came back, did he ask you about MacAullif?"

"No."

"Had you already told him?"

"Sure. In my signed statement. I told him after I called on the talent agent. I went to MacAullif and told him the whole thing."

"Before you found the body."

"Right."

"He didn't suggest you might have found the body first, then called on MacAullif?"

"*He* didn't, no."

"What do you mean, *he* didn't?"

"MacAullif did. When he came charging down there. That's why he came. He thought I'd done exactly that."

"And you hadn't?"

"Alice. Don't make me prove an alibi to you."

"Well, it seems like a logical move."

"Good god, if it looks that good to you, think how it looks to the cops."

"Yeah," Alice said. "Anyway, you told this cop about MacAullif in your statement?"

"Right."

"How'd he react?"

"Huh?"

"The cop — you say he and MacAullif have a problem — so how'd he react when you mentioned his name?"

"I didn't notice."

"You didn't notice?"

"No. Why would I? I just found a dead body. I'm making a statement."

"Yeah, but if there was a big reaction. Like the cop said *him!* Or *you're kidding!* Or started bearing down and cross-examining you the minute you mentioned MacAullif's name."

"Yeah, but he didn't. He was perfectly cool about it."

"But you weren't looking for a reaction."

"No."

"So how do you know he was perfectly cool?"

"I don't. All I mean is there was no reaction that I noticed."

"But you're not that observant."

"Thanks a lot."

"Well, you're not. You see the things you want to see. Other things go right by you."

I took a sip of coffee. "I don't want to

debate it, Alice. The fact is, I didn't notice."

"Uh-huh. So where does this leave you?"

"It leaves me without a client."

"And without a fee. We're lucky you broke even."

I grimaced.

"What is it?"

"I had to pay off the agent."

"What?"

"She wanted a hundred bucks just like the other two."

"Wait a minute, wait a minute," Alice said. "You said your client told you not to bother with the woman. But you did it anyway."

"That's right."

"Are you telling me you gave her a hundred dollars of our money?"

"That's unfair."

"What?"

"Calling it *our money.*"

"Well, it *is* our money, isn't it?"

"Yes, it is. But saying it like that — it's like I had no right."

"Are you saying you *had* a right?"

"I'm saying I made a bad guess. How was I to know the guy was dead."

Alice shook her head. "Stanley."

"Alice, if my client's not dead —"

"You would have paid a hundred bucks to find out *he* was the one who hired her. Which

161

was what he was trying to keep you from finding out."

"Right."

"Think he would have reimbursed you for doing that?"

"No, I don't. But I think it would have been worth a hundred bucks to find out I was being set up."

"Why? What could you have done?"

"I don't know. The problem is, it makes no sense. Even before he's dead. I paid a hundred bucks to find an answer. Turns out *he's* the answer. But it's the *wrong* answer. And it doesn't make sense.

"Okay, that was a little unlucky. Now I go and ask him to explain it for me and he's dead. This is very unlucky. And makes even *less* sense. Yes, I'm a hundred bucks down at this point, but that would seem to be the least of my worries."

"Have you seen our bank balance lately?"

"Alice."

She put up her hand. "Okay, I'll drop it. But answer me this. Say the guy *wasn't* dead when you went up there to talk to him. To tell him what you found out, that he was the guy."

"Yeah?"

Alice shrugged. "What could he possibly have said?"

Exactly.

24.

Richard wasn't any more sympathetic than Alice. Of course, he also had an ax to grind.

I'd stopped by the office to explain I was involved in a murder investigation, which might make it necessary for me to pass on some of his cases.

Naturally, this did not thrill Richard. His position was I was working for him, and the police could go fuck themselves. This was not, by the way, my impression of his opinion — those happen to be his exact words.

"Richard," I said. "This is a little more complicated than you might think."

"Complicated? How is it complicated? You had a client, the client's dead, now you have no obligation at all."

"I'm a witness."

"Big deal. So you get on the stand and you tell what you know. And you don't have to hold anything back because you're not protecting anyone."

"I'm protecting myself."

"From what? You didn't do anything wrong."

"Well . . ."

"Did you?"

"No."

"There you are."

I took a breath. "There are complications, Richard."

"What sort of complications?"

"For one thing, MacAullif."

"What about him?"

"I went to see him before I found the body."

"So you said. Would you mind telling me why you did that?"

"Actually, because you'd gone home."

"What?"

"I wanted to talk to you about it. MacAullif was a second choice."

Richard cocked his head. "Should I take that as a put-down, or am I supposed to be thrilled to be first?"

"You can take it any way you like. I'm just telling you how it was."

"So what's the big deal with MacAullif?"

"He has a problem with the officer in charge."

"A problem?"

"They don't seem to like each other."

"Why not?"

"I have no idea. I didn't have a chance to talk to him. They ran into each other at the crime scene, it was like MacAullif was banging his wife."

"Oh, come on."

"I tell you, the two guys don't like each other. What it does to me, I can't begin to sort out. Same thing with MacAullif. Who might wind up as my alibi witness, if it turns out the guy was killed while I was talking to him."

"That could be sticky."

"Sure could. And imagine if I'd been able to get a hold of you."

Richard thought that over. "Well, thank goodness for small favors. So, what were you going to ask me if you'd managed to reach me yesterday and made me your alibi witness?"

"I was gonna ask you for advice."

"Advice?"

"Yes."

Richard put up his hand. "Pardon me, but weren't you just in here asking me for advice?"

"That was different."

"Different? It's exactly the same. You thought your client was bamboozling you with a phony extortion letter."

"Which he was."

"Right. And I advised you to call him on it."

"Which I did."

"And the guy caved in and admitted it was his letter."

"Right."

"And here's round two. Second verse, same as the first."

"Not exactly."

"You want to point out a difference?"

"Sure. When I called him on the extortion letter, he had an explanation. It wasn't a *great* one, but it was an explanation. He was trying to motivate me to find this girl. Pretty stupid, but say it's true. At least he's got a reason. But this other thing — the idea he was the one who hired the girl in the first place — well, give me a reason for that."

"You got one?"

"I haven't got one I *like*. The only one I can come up with is, he's trying to win the proxy fight, he wants to make it appear like the other vice-presidents are playing dirty tricks against him, so he sets this up, has me uncover it, and plans to spring it at the stockholders meeting."

Richard frowned. "I can't say I like that theory."

"I hate it like hell."

"No, no," Richard said. "I don't mean the

implications, the emotional baggage, all the crap you bring to it. I mean, as a theory, it's not very good."

"What's wrong with it?"

"Well, the way it plays out, your client goes to the talent agent to hire the girl, right?"

"Right."

"He goes there in person, up to her office, meets with the talent agent, arranges with her to hire the girl?"

"Yeah. So?"

"He calls the girl on the phone, disguises his voice, tells her what he wants her to do in the bar. The reason he does that — uses the phone and disguises his voice — is so she won't know he's the one hiring her. Am I right so far?"

"Absolutely."

"He goes out to the bar and plays the scene with the girl. Then shows up at your office and hires you to find her. Which shouldn't be that hard to do, which is why he's deliberately chosen a girl everyone will be sure to notice." Richard spread his arms, rolled his eyes. "But, lo and behold, he's chosen the one detective in the world who can't find a girl with boobs the size of battleships. The man is absolutely astounded, and decides he needs to force the issue with a phony extortion letter."

"I'm losing the thread here, Richard. You were saying why this was a *bad* theory."

"Oh, it is. Don't be thrown by the fact that my assessment of your competence sounds logical."

"Thanks a lot."

"Anyway, despite seeing through the extortion letter, you redouble your efforts to find the girl and happen to achieve success. She tells you about the phone call, and about being hired through her agent. Your client commends you on your work, and instructs you to disregard the agent."

"So I won't find out he hired her."

"Right. But how effective is that? I mean, the guy's six six. If you question the agent at all, it's the first thing she's going to say, and you'll know that it's him."

"Unless he told her not to talk."

"Yeah, but she did. And he can't count on the fact that she won't. Then there's the girl — what if *she* talks to the agent? Which is entirely likely. 'How'd your date go?' 'The guy was a telephone pole.' 'You're kidding.' If they start comparing notes, you think they don't figure it out?"

I frowned. "I see what you mean. But . . ."

"But what?"

"Well, the guy wasn't that bright. I mean, look at the extortion letter bit. It didn't take a rocket scientist to crack that one. So if this was his plan, I'm not surprised it was full of holes."

"Fine," Richard said. "So how does he wind up dead?"

"I have no idea."

"Me either. But if this is his plan, which he set in motion, there's gotta be a place where it went wrong."

"Why?"

"Because he's dead. Unless he planned his own death, which I cannot credit, this was not the result he wanted. Therefore we must assume something went wrong. The only thing we know that was diametrically opposed to this plan was your calling on this agent."

"Shit."

"Sorry about that, but it happens to be the case. You weren't supposed to call on the agent. You were told not to call on the agent. Once again, ninety-nine private detectives out of a hundred, if they weren't being paid for it, wouldn't do it of their own accord. But you, a prince among men, in the pursuit of truth, justice, and the American way, do it anyway. And what did you tell her?"

"What?"

"When you talked to the agent. I know

what you got out of her. What did she get out of you?"

"I'm not following you, Richard."

"You asked her questions about the guy who hired the girl. Why did you tell her you were interested? Why did you want to know?"

"I'd been hired to find out."

"By who?"

"I didn't tell her that."

"No, but she can figure it out. At any rate, it gets her thinking. And, as I said before, she can compare notes with the girl. If she hasn't already, after you leave, that's the first thing she'll do. She'll call the girl up, say, Hey, what's with the guy in the singles bar? Then they'll start talking it over, and before you know it they'll make the connection both guys were six six."

"So they rush out and kill him?"

"Hey," Richard said. "Give me a break. Of course it sounds stupid when you say it like that. But say they make the connection and the agent decides to contact the guy. Well, that meeting is not necessarily an amicable one."

"So she shoots him."

Richard grimaced. Exhaled. "Any statement in the absence of fact is going to sound stupid. But it's not illogical to assume that the actions of this agent or the girl or both resulted in your client's death. Whether they actually shot him or not."

"Can you give me one good reason why they would?"

"Shoot him?"

"Yeah."

Richard shrugged. "I can give you several."

"Really?"

"Sure. One: your client and the agent are in cahoots. He's paid her a pile of money, but after talking to you she wants more. He won't give it to her so she kills him."

"Oh, come on."

"Two: your client and the agent are lovers. When she finds out he has the hots for this topless dancer, she shoots him."

"Richard."

"Three: the bimbo is smuggling drugs in her hollowed-out silicone boobs. Your client stumbles upon this, becomes a liability and has to be eliminated."

"Richard," I said. "Are you telling me we don't have enough information?"

Richard shook his head. "Boy. Talk about rocket scientists."

25.

I got beeped in Queens at eleven-thirty that morning while photographing a pothole on Parson's Boulevard. When I called in, Mary Mason told me the cops were looking for me. That did not bode well. Nor did the address she gave me, which I recognized as Shelly Daniels' talent agency. This was not going to be my day.

There were two cop cars parked outside. I pulled up behind them and got out. Two cops on the sidewalk, who appeared to be joking about the all-male movie theater whose marquee they were standing under, turned their attention to me. One pointed at my car and jerked his thumb — I had pulled up next to a hydrant.

"I'm Stanley Hastings," I said. "I was ordered to report to this address."

I couldn't tell if that meant anything to the cops or not, but the taller of the two said, "Wait here," and went into the building.

"What's up?" I asked the other cop.

He just shrugged, but I could figure it out. I had ever since Mary Mason gave me the address. Why anyone would want to kill a poor, second-rate talent agent was beyond me, but apparently someone had. No wonder the cops wanted to see me. I was probably the last person to see her alive.

The front door opened and Sergeant Belcher came out. Without any amenities he strode up to me and jerked his thumb. "You know whose place this is?"

"Yes, of course."

"Why of course?"

"I was here yesterday. I gave you the address."

"You were in the office yesterday?"

"That's right."

"Shelly Daniels' office?"

"Yeah. Shelly Daniels' office. What happened to her?"

Belcher's eyes narrowed. "What makes you think something happened to her?"

"Are you kidding me? You pull me off the job in Queens and drag me in here. There's cops all over the place. I'd be a damn fool if I didn't think something had happened to her."

"Is that right?" Belcher said.

"Yeah, that's right. You want to play guessing games hoping I'll crack, or you want to fill me in."

"Interesting," Belcher said. "It's your

opinion that Shelly Daniels has met with foul play?"

"Foul play?"

"Huh?"

"You really say foul play?"

"What are you, a comedian? You really give a damn what we say? I'm asking you some questions here, and I expect some co-operation."

"Fine. I'm here to cooperate. Just tell me what you want."

"I want you to answer questions without kidding around. What makes you think this person has met with foul play?"

"I told you. The fact you dragged me in here."

"That's it?"

"That's not enough? What, are you telling me she's alive? You want me to talk to the woman?"

"I've had enough of your lip."

I shut up. That was not a question and required no answer, and if the man had had enough of my lip, anything I said was only going to make it worse. I stood there, waited for him to make his move.

"Let's go over it again," Belcher said. "What time were you in here last night?"

"It must have been close to four o'clock."

"You were in here talking to the agent

about the topless dancer?"

"That's right."

"She wouldn't give you a phone number or address?"

"No, she wouldn't."

"Did she show you a picture?"

"Picture?"

"Yeah."

"No, she didn't. Why?"

"Did she offer to get in touch with the girl for you?"

"No, she didn't."

"You paid this woman a hundred bucks?"

"Yes, I did."

"What for?"

"For information."

"To tell you what she knew?"

"Right."

"You paid her a hundred bucks to tell what she knew, and she wouldn't tell you the girl's phone number or address?"

"Sounds like hell when you put it like that."

"Is that a fact?"

"Yeah, that's a fact."

"What time was it when you left here last night?"

"Around four-fifteen, four-thirty. Somewhere in there."

"That's the last time you saw this woman?"

"That's right."

Belcher nodded, jerked his thumb. "Okay. Let's go."

I followed Belcher upstairs to Shelly Daniels' talent agency, steeling myself for the sight of her dead body.

Only it wasn't there.

Shelly Daniels was not in the room.

Darren "Sandy" Carter was. The bartender was seated at the desk, leafing through a stack of eight-by-ten photos.

When he saw me, he stopped and said, "You."

"What are you doing here?"

"What does it look like?" he said. "And hey, thanks a lot."

"What?"

"For siccin' the cops on me. I mean, thanks a heap."

"Wait a minute," I said. "Where's Shelly Daniels?"

"Ah," Belcher said. "Very good question. I was hoping you could help me out with that."

"What?"

"Well, you gave me this address, but not her home address. And we can't find it."

"Huh?"

"Which is a little unusual. I mean, the woman has to live *somewhere*. You'd expect *some* record to exist."

I put up my hands. "Wait a minute. You're telling me she's not dead?"

"Dead? Why did you think she was dead?"

I took a breath. "Maybe I read too many murder mysteries. I'm sorry, but I thought that was why you called me in here."

"No, we called you in here 'cause we're lookin' for the woman. We can't find her." He shrugged. "Now, a business of this sort, it doesn't necessarily have to open nine o'clock. When she didn't show up then, we weren't concerned. At ten we're beginning to wonder. By eleven it's a little much." He looked at his watch. "It is now after twelve. Maybe the woman keeps strange hours, she could come walking in that door any minute. But as far as I'm concerned, she's missing, and I'd like to know why."

"You expect me to tell you?"

"Not at all." He jerked his thumb. "I expect you to help your friend out with his task."

"What's that?"

"The dancer. You gave us two names. Marla Melons and Lucy Blaine. Neither are on the Rolodex. Which is not surprising — those listings appear to be mainly busi-

177

nesses. Unfortunately, if this agent has an address book she has it with her. Which leaves the files. They're crammed with pictures. Resume photos. They're somewhat in alphabetical order, but, again, there is no Marla Melons or Lucy Blaine. Of course, the girl might have worked under another name."

"Oh, no."

"Oh, yes." Belcher nodded. "I would suggest you pull up a chair." He jerked his thumb toward the file cabinets, which were bulging. "Could be a long afternoon."

26.

MacAullif wasn't surprised to see me.

"So," he said, "what kept you?"

I flopped into the chair next to his desk, ran my hand over my face. "You wouldn't believe."

"I'm very gullible. I'll believe anything."

"Oh, yeah? Well, I happen to have spent the last four hours looking at pictures of girls with big tits."

MacAullif shrugged. "So? I would imagine you do that almost every day. What's so special this time? Someone *pay* you to do it?"

"Not so's you could notice."

"It have something to do with the case?"

"What case?"

"There was a murder yesterday. Tall drink of water. Went about six six."

"That seems to ring a bell. As a matter of fact, I think I may have found the body."

"Yeah, well don't expect a lot of credit. A six six corpse is kind of hard to miss."

"Even so. It's all a matter of knowing where to look."

"Yeah. But that's not exactly the sort of

thing one should be admitting now, is it?"

"Gee, MacAullif," I said. "I'm surprised to find you got the time to fool around."

"Oh, loads of time," MacAullif said. "I'm stuck here another half hour waiting for a ballistics report, and I'm caught up on my paperwork. One of the perks of bein' a sergeant is I can more or less do what I please."

"I'm happy for you."

"Yeah. You want to elaborate on your big tit comment, or was that merely a joke?"

"That's the straight goods. The talent agent's skipped out, and no one can find the topless dancer. The bartender and I spent the afternoon going through her files."

"See anything you liked?"

"I didn't see the girl. Which doesn't mean she wasn't there. I'm not great on faces. She puts a wig on, dyes her hair, or maybe even combs it different, I could have looked right at her and never had a clue."

"Kind of tough for a private detective," MacAullif said. "It's lucky you have so many qualities to compensate."

"I was wondering how long it would take to get around to a discussion of my qualifications."

"You're the one brought the matter up."

"Guilty as charged. Anyway, I had no luck at all. And neither did the bartender."

"What about the place where she works?"

"They hired her through the agent. Paid her through there."

"The agent must have a bank account — what about that?"

"It's a business account with a business address."

"Tough luck."

"Yeah," I said. "You fuck his wife?"

"Huh?"

"The cop. Belcher. You two don't look like best of friends."

"You might say."

"Care to fill me in?"

MacAullif leaned back in his chair, exhaled. "You know, I can't win with you. I'm not involved with this case. I've done no work on this case. Aside from what you told me, I don't know a thing about it. If I wasn't your damn alibi witness, I'd be out of it altogether."

"At least you seem to have gotten over being angry about that."

"Well, you say you didn't do it. Didn't know he was dead when you came to me. While I wouldn't put it past you, I wouldn't expect you to flat out lie about it. So you tell me it didn't happen, I gotta believe."

"Uh-huh. Well," I said, "we've talked

181

about everything else. You wanna talk about the cop?"

"Patty Devlin."

"Huh?"

"It happened over Patty Devlin."

"You fought over a woman?"

MacAullif made a face. "Don't be dumb. Patty Devlin was a hooker sold crack."

"What?"

"Hell of a combination, huh? Anyway, Patty Devlin was a white broad hookin' without a pimp. Not a particularly secure position for a young woman to find herself in. She got beat up a lot. She got busted a lot. Not that she wouldn't have if she'd *had* a pimp. Still, there would have been a sense of stability in her life. She'd have known *who* was beating her up."

"You're a cynical son of a bitch, aren't you?"

"Wait'll you hear the story. Anyway, she's a hooker getting busted on a regular basis. Turns out she's getting knocked down for drugs as often as she is for sex. Anyway, she gets busted with two johns for a sex and drugs party. They're smokin' crack, and bangin' her six ways from Sunday. Free for all, both at once, get high, pick a hole, and hop on.

"Well, the cops bust it up and drag everyone downtown. And who should one of the johns be but Eddie Martinez."

"Who's Eddie Martinez?"

"Eddie Martinez is the son of Alberto Martinez, and Alberto Martinez is a cop."

"Aha," I said.

"Yeah. Aha."

"Would there be any connection between Alberto Martinez and Sergeant Belcher?"

"Good guess. At the time, Sergeant Belcher happened to be partnered with Alberto Martinez."

"So what happened to the kid?"

"The charges were dropped. No big deal. Charges were often dropped. They were dropped against the other john, and the hooker too. The whole thing was thrown out."

"How do you know this?"

"It got around. Story like that gets around. Cop's son busted. Case disappears. Juicy bit of gossip."

"I take it there's more?"

"Oh, yeah. Kid gets busted again. Eddie Martinez. This time it's a little worse. Catch him with a kilo of coke."

"A kilo?"

"Sure. Just your average weekend toot, right? But that's not the big problem. The big problem is, the guys making the bust aren't your average everyday street cops; they're narcs. And they're not going to faint just 'cause Al Martinez says boo. They don't, and Eddie Martinez gets arraigned."

"So?"

"So now the kid's on the hook for felony possession with intent to sell, and lookin' at some hard time. Of course Alberto gets the kid an attorney, and the mouthpiece cuts the kid a deal."

"What kind of deal?"

"What kind of deal do you think? He talks. He rolls over. He rats out his friends."

"Yeah. So?"

"So guess who he rats out?"

"Patty Devlin?"

"Bingo, right on the button. So the cops drag Patty Devlin in, charge her with trafficking. She freaks. What, are they nuts? She's a hooker. She don't move weight. She didn't sell to Eddie Martinez. Hell, he was selling to *her.*"

"The cops believe her?"

"Thing is, they did. 'Cause it made sense. A lot more sense than a penny ante hooker's movin' kilos. If she's movin' kilos, why's she hookin' and sellin' hits of crack? So the narcs cut *her* a deal to testify against *him.*"

"Uh-oh."

"Yeah. Only now she's on the horns of a

dilemma." He cocked his head. "You ever have a horny dilemma?"

"Constantly."

"Yeah, well, the minute she's released, Patty Devlin comes to the realization the deal she's just made is not exactly conducive to good health. She goes back to her apartment on West 45th Street, and what should she see but an unmarked car hanging out down the block. The girl is streetwise on the one hand, paranoid on the other — and with what's comin' down she's got good reason — so she checks it out on the sly, and who should be waiting for her in the car but officers Belcher and Martinez, just about the last people on earth she would like to see."

"So?"

"So, she is now in fear for her life. She hightails it out of there, and over on Eighth Avenue she spots a regular marked police car in front of a doughnut shop."

"You?"

"No. Just couple of cops on radio patrol. But she don't care who they are, just as long as they're not Alberto Martinez. She goes to the cops, says take me downtown."

"They do?"

"Yeah. She's askin' for the narcs. She's askin' for the ADA. The one who cut the deal. Of course, these people are not readily available, you cannot get to them just like that. So, who's catchin' at the time but yours truly."

"They dump her with you?"

"Right. And she tells her story. Most of which I already know, because it's common gossip. But I listen, and I don't like what I hear. So I try to contact the ADA. Who is still not available."

"Martinez and Belcher show up?"

"Sure do. Demanding the girl. Insisting I hand her over."

"But you don't."

"Of course not. I'm holdin' her for the ADA." MacAullif shrugged. "They say, no, no. She's a suspect, she's a fugitive from justice, they're taking her into custody."

"You don't budge."

"No. Well, Martinez flips out. He damn near pulls his gun. If there are not other cops here at the time, they probably overpower me and take her away. But as it happens, they don't. I got backup and I use it. And they wind up outside, and I wind up holding the girl for the ADA."

"So the kid went down?"

MacAullif made a face. "Yeah, sure. Like in a storybook. The good guys win. Justice triumphs." He snorted. "The minute the girl's alone with the ADA, she says she's sorry she lied, but she was scared she'd go to jail, so she made the whole thing up. Of course she wasn't buyin' from the kid, it was her kilo all along, she just gave it to him to hold."

"Are you shitting me?"

"No, I'm not. And the end result is the motherfucker walks."

"You're kidding."

"Not at all. All I've accomplished through my moral stand is to make two enemies for life. And the one thing a cop does not need is enemies on the force."

"But, if the kid walked —"

"Hey," MacAullif said. "And there's the irony for you. I'm the one got the broad to the ADA so she could make that happen. But does that matter to them? Not at all. I turn the girl over to them, they beat the shit out of her till she changes her story, with the same result. Either way, the kid walks. All I did was keep them from beating her up. But to them, that's enough. It's us against them, pick a side. I'm the bad guy, didn't go along."

"When did all this happen?"

"Long time ago. Before I ever met you. But an officer never forgets. Cops and elephants. Long-term memory's just fine."

"I think the bit about elephants is a myth."

"The point is, I can't think of an officer I'd like less in charge of this investigation."

"I see what you mean."

"Do you? I was kidding before about being your alibi witness. Then I see who's in charge, and suddenly it's no joke." MacAullif pointed. "This one's right up your street. Your TV mentality. Good cops and bad cops. Belcher is what you would call a bad cop. A sadistic, rotten son of a bitch who harbors a grudge. How's he been with you so far?"

"Pretty above board."

"Not overtly hostile?"

"Nothing I could point to, no."

"Well, it's early on. The problem is, the guy would love nothing better than to get me. If he thinks you're a friend of mine, he'll be out to get you."

"I stand warned."

"Do you? Then let me give you a little advice. Your client's dead. You got no stake in this no more. There's no need for you to be messin' around with this."

"Yeah, well it's a two-edged sword."

"What do you mean?"

"If the guy's out to get me, I gotta protect myself. And how can I do that if I don't know the score?"

MacAullif winced, put up his hands. "No,

no, no. You got it all screwed around. You're not involved in this. You did a job, it's done. And you told the cops everything you know. End of story. You leave it alone, and they leave it alone."

I frowned. "Maybe. But you're making a big assumption."

"What's that?"

"They leave it alone."

27.

It was a two-story house in Scarsdale on a pleasant, tree-lined lot. I pulled into the driveway, went up to the front door, and rang the bell.

And got no answer. Which was strange. It was nine o'clock in the morning, the garage door was closed, and I would have expected a young woman of independent means to be at home.

Of course, she might well be asleep. I rang the doorbell again.

A red sports car pulled into the driveway, parked behind mine. A knockout of a young blonde got out. She was dressed in a white tennis outfit and had obviously just come from the court. She confirmed this by retrieving a racket and a can of balls from the back seat. She had a slim athletic figure and a light graceful step, and as she came up the path it occurred to me she was one of those young women who was able to appear hot and sweaty and at the same time fresh and clean.

I gave her my best smile, said, "Amy Greenberg?"

She stopped about ten feet from me, held the tennis racket in front of her, not like a weapon, but definitely at the ready.

"Who are you?"

"I'm Stanley Hastings. I'm a private detective. I was hired by Cranston Pritchert."

"Oh," she said. "Then you're the one."

"Who found him? Yes, that's right."

"What do you want with me?"

"I have a few questions to ask you, if you wouldn't mind."

"I don't mind, but, like, I don't know anything."

"Perhaps you'd be willing to listen to what I have to say."

"I already spoke to the police."

"I'm sure you did."

"They were all like, How well did you know what's-his-name? And I was all like, Who the hell is that?"

"Uh-huh. If you could give me a few minutes of your time."

She frowned. Thought a moment. "Okay. Come on in."

Amy Greenberg's living room gave off the same signals as the sports car — it boasted a bar and a projection TV.

"Sit down," she said. She gestured to the bar. "Can I get you anything?"

"Not this early."

She smiled. "Hey, I didn't mean, like, you're a detective, you must drink first thing in the morning. I just played two sets of tennis, I'm all, Give me a Gatorade. You want a soft drink or something?"

"No, I'm fine."

Amy bent over and opened the mini refrigerator, which gave me a good idea of just how well she fit into her shorts. She took out a quart of Gatorade, poured some into a glass, and chugged it down. "Now," she said. "What's this all about?"

I took a breath. "I'm wondering how much you know."

She shrugged. "I know what happened. One of the vice-presidents is dead."

"Cranston Pritchert."

"Yeah. And he hired you and you found the body." She shivered. "That must have been something. You're on the phone with the cops and you're like, Hey, there's a body here."

"Uh-huh," I said. "Do you know *why* he hired me?"

"Not for sure. Why don't you fill me in."

"He was concerned about the stockholders meeting. In particular, the election of the new chairman of the board. He and the other vice-presidents were vying for it, and he thought someone was trying to ace him out."

"Like, how?"

"By making him appear foolish. And thereby costing him votes."

She frowned. "I'm not sure I follow you."

I wasn't either. Whether it was the way she looked, the way she dressed, the way she talked, the way she lived, or all of the above, Amy Greenberg struck me as terribly young, and I had no idea how much of what I was saying was getting through.

"Well," I said, "why don't I start at the beginning."

Amy poured another glass of Gatorade. "Well," she said. "Like, okay."

I told her the whole thing. Just as I'd done for Alice. Just as I'd done for Richard. Just as I'd done for MacAullif. Just as I'd done for the cops. It occurred to me, a few more times, I might get pretty good at it.

Amy Greenberg sat there drinking Gatorade and listened without interrupting until I was done. Then she frowned and said, "I don't understand."

Actually, she had gotten more than I thought.

"I mean," she said, "you're saying like, this guy set the whole thing up himself? To use at the stockholders meeting?"

"That's how it appeared."

"You don't think that anymore?"

"I didn't say that."

"Yeah, but you're like, That's how it *appeared*. Why appeared?"

"Because he's dead. It makes no sense once he's dead."

"Yeah, but, like, what if that's *why* he's dead?"

I frowned. "What do you mean?"

"I dunno." She shrugged. "I mean, I don't really *know* anything. But, like, what you say. If he was trying to ace the other guys out, and they find out about it, and they're like, Hey, set *me* up, buddy, and they kill him."

"That's a thought. Only . . ."

"Only what?"

"It seems a little extreme."

"Hey, the guy's dead. *Someone* killed him."

"All right. Say that were true. Who do you think it would be?"

"Hey, how should I know? I don't know these guys. I don't know the business. I'm a stockholder, sure, and Grandpa was chairman of the board. But that's it. I never, like, worked there."

"But you've been to the office?"

"I used to see Gramps."

"How about since he died?"

"I went like once. Looked in his office for, you know, personal things. The accountant showed me around. He's all, Sorry about your grandfather, and I'm like, Hey, you gotta go, you gotta go."

"Uh-huh. Is that the only time you were ever up there?"

"Since he died. Yeah."

"Okay, look," I said. "You're not active in the business, but you do have a considerable amount of stock."

"Right. From Gramps."

"Are you going to the stockholders meeting?"

"I guess I have to."

"Why?"

"To vote." She smiled. "You wouldn't believe how I'm a very popular girl. All the guys are calling me up, wanting to talk."

"You mean members of the board?"

"Right."

"Even Cranston Pritchert?"

"Him too."

"Did you talk to them?"

"Are you kidding? They're like, Let me tell you how to vote, and I'm like, Down, boy, I'll vote how I please. I may not know business, but I know what I like."

"Uh-huh," I said. "So the point is, you're

going to the meeting because you have a financial interest at stake."

"Sure."

"Well, that's why I'm here. Cranston Pritchert hired me to make an investigation. He was killed before I could complete it. Which is too bad, because I had some very promising leads. Now, this is your company. At least, one in which you have a large investment because you hold a good deal of stock. It would be to your advantage to make sure that no one within your company was doing anything which might undermine its best interests."

She looked at me a long moment, exhaled, ran her hand over her forehead, and said, "Whew. You mind trying that again? Like, what are you trying to say?"

"I'm suggesting I complete my investigation. I'm wondering if you'd like to hire me to do so."

She frowned. "I'm not sure I understand."

Damn.

She understood just fine. She just didn't want to *do* it. Which wasn't that much of a surprise. Still, with that much money at stake, I had hoped at least to have appealed to her curiosity.

While I was trying to think of another approach, my beeper went off.

"Damn," I said. "That will be the office calling me."

"The office?"

"The law firm I work for. I gotta call in."

"You can use the phone in the kitchen," she said.

I went in the kitchen, called Rosenberg and Stone. Mary Mason gave me a sign-up at Jacoby Hospital in the Bronx. That was convenient — it was right on my way home. I took down the information, went to look for Amy Greenberg.

She was out front in her car. She had backed out of the driveway so I could get out, and now she was sitting in the convertible and talking on the car phone.

Damn.

I had hoped to have one last crack at talking her into hiring me. But it was not to be. I waved to her, got in my car, backed out of the driveway, and drove off.

In the rear-view mirror I could see her talking animatedly on the car phone, her smile wide, her eyes bright.

She was probably talking about me.

I could imagine her saying, "He was all, Why don't you hire me? And I was all, Like, why?"

Why indeed.

28.

What a humiliating position to find oneself in. But the thing is, I needed the money. Well, that's just part of it. The other part is, I just couldn't let it alone. Couldn't walk away. I mean, it's easy to say, not being involved, hey, give it up, it's got nothing to do with you.

But the guy was my client. In a strange way, I owed him.

Plus, he owed me.

Which is where the humiliation comes in.

Miriam Pritchert lived on East 78th Street in a modern high-rise apartment building, where the doorman in the lobby was mighty reluctant to let me in. The guy thought I was a cop, and figured the cops had bothered her enough.

I persisted with the doorman, got the grieving widow on the phone, and talked my way upstairs.

Miriam Pritchert was a bit of a surprise. I guess perversely I had expected someone four foot two. But, no, she was almost as tall as he was. I mean, proportionally. She wasn't six six, but she was damn near six feet.

She was also a knockout. A lean, attractive woman with straight brown hair that hung almost to her waist, she wore a pale blue sunsuit, a pair of running shoes, and a puzzled frown.

"Mr. Hastings?" she said. Her tone indicated she didn't believe it.

"That's right."

"You're the one who called me on the phone."

The night of the murder. Right. At least she'd made the connection.

"That's right," I said.

"Well, come in, I guess. But just for a moment. I'm going out."

"I don't want to keep you," I said. "There are just a couple of matters to clear up."

"I don't understand," she said. But she ushered me into the living room, indicated a chair, and sat opposite me on the couch. "Now, what's this all about?"

"I'm sorry to intrude on you at a time like this. But your husband's death left certain matters unresolved."

"What matters?"

"I'm wondering how much you know?"

"I know what the police told me. My husband was found in his office." She looked at me. "In fact, you're the one who found him. Isn't that right?"

"Yes, it is."

"Because he hired you to find some girl?"

"That's right."

"That's really all I know. But what else is there?"

"Well, I actually located the girl. She —"

"Yes, yes, I know. She's a topless dancer, she met my husband in a bar. I know all that. What I mean is, I don't know why. It simply makes no sense."

"Your husband thought it might have something to do with the proxy fight."

"In what way?"

"An attempt to embarrass him and lose him votes."

"That seems somewhat far-fetched."

"Perhaps. But that's what he thought. I take it he never mentioned this to you?"

"Getting picked up in a bar? I should think not." She shifted position on the couch. "Mr. . . . ?"

"Hastings."

"Hastings. As I said, I'm going out. What you've told me is nothing new. And I don't like going over it again. Was there anything else?"

"Actually there was."

"Oh?"

"As I said, your husband hired me to do

a job. I've made considerable progress so far, locating not only the girl, but also her agent. Now both have disappeared. Leaving the job undone. I'm wondering if you'd like me to complete it."

"I beg your pardon?"

"It appears someone was attempting to take advantage of your husband. As his heir, I'd think you'd want to find out why."

She blinked. Frowned. "You're asking me to hire you?"

"I'm asking you if you'd like me to complete my work."

She blinked again. "Thank you, no. Whatever my husband may have been involved in, I can't see how it has anything to do with me. It disturbs me to think he was trying to pick up girls in bars. But as it is, I see no point in going into all that now."

"What if it was more sinister than that?"

"How could it be?"

I took a breath. "You'll pardon me, but your husband is dead."

"Which is a matter for the police. I'm sure they're capable of handling it."

What could I say to that? Tell her that might be true, if the officer in charge didn't happen to be swayed by personal grudges? Somehow that seemed a little much to lay on a grieving widow.

Only she wasn't exactly grieving, this grieving widow. She wasn't wearing black, and as I said, she looked damn good. It occurred to me, perhaps I should set my sights on her a few notches higher.

Particularly if getting her to hire me was out.

"Fine," I said. "If you'd like to leave the investigation to the police, that's perfectly understandable. There's only one other small matter."

"Oh? And what is that?"

"The work I've already done. The money your husband advanced me, I used up in expenses."

She shrugged her shoulders, spread her arms. "Again, I don't see what that has to do with me."

"I would presume you were the executor of your husband's estate."

"As to that, I wouldn't know. I really can't deal with it now. If you feel you have a claim against my husband's estate, I suggest you put it in writing and I'll forward it to his attorneys."

See what I mean about humiliating? I'd practically been reduced to groveling.

Miriam Pritchert had stood up. I stood too and, cowed, allowed myself to be shown out the door.

My car was right outside. What can I say? Some days you get lucky. I hadn't gotten hired, but I had found a parking space in front of her building. I unlocked the car, got in, and switched off the code alarm.

Just as a familiar face went in the front door.

I slipped out of the car and gave chase. Surreptitiously, to be sure. I didn't want to be spotted and recognized, either by the doorman or by the visitor. Just inside the door was a bank of mailboxes. I turned my back, pretended to inspect them. I was maybe twenty feet away from the reception desk, but I was still close enough to hear what was going on.

The gentleman in question was indeed calling on Miriam Pritchert.

I'm not good at putting names to faces, and I couldn't do so now, but that didn't matter. One thing I knew for sure.

The young gentleman who had just called on the young, attractive, and none too grieving Miriam Pritchert was one of the two other vice-presidents from her husband's firm.

29.

He took her out to lunch. I know, because I tagged along. They ate at some trendy little restaurant in the East 60s where the drinks probably cost more than my average meal.

I would have loved to have listened in, but it was not to be. The dining room was small and wide open. There was no way to get close to them without being seen.

Oh, well, having a poor memory left me with other fish to fry. I walked down the block to a pay phone, took out my notebook, checked the number, and made a call.

"Philip Greenberg Investments," the receptionist said.

"Marty Rothstein, please."

"I'm sorry. Mr. Rothstein is out to lunch. Could I take a message?"

"How about Kevin Dunbar?"

"One moment, please."

There was a ring and a click and a voice said, "Hello?"

I hung up.

And that was that. There were two vice-presidents, the tall, thin one and the short, stocky one with the mustache. Tall, thin Marty Rothstein was having lunch with Miriam Pritchert. Short, stocky Kevin Dunbar had answered the phone. The ace detective strikes again.

I was just patting myself on the back when my beeper went off. It occurred to me it was just as well. While I would have liked to have stuck around and seen if Miriam Pritchert and her late husband's rival had gone back to her place after lunch, no one was paying me for it. I could use some hours on the clock.

I fished a quarter out of my pocket, called Rosenberg and Stone.

Mary Mason absolutely blew my mind. Not that she meant to, it just worked out that way.

I was standing on the corner of Third Avenue and 68th. The assignment she gave me was 68th Street between Second and Third.

Half a block away.

The location was a rarity in itself, because the East 60s are an affluent neighborhood, and affluent clients are infrequent at Rosenberg and Stone.

But that was the least of it.

My car was still parked in front of Miriam Pritchert's on East 78th Street. And my briefcase was in it — naturally, I hadn't taken

it with me to go tailing Pritchert's wife. Ordinarily, I could not call on a client without
my briefcase. All the forms they need to sign
are in it, including the retainer.

But this wasn't a sign-up. It was a photo
assignment. The client had just gotten home
from the hospital, and Richard wanted me
to take injury photos of the surgical scars.

Even so, ordinarily my camera would be
in my briefcase.

But —

This was my second assignment of the day.
On my way back from Amy Greenberg's, I'd
stopped at Jacoby Hospital in the Bronx to
sign up a guy who'd broken his neck. I kid
you not. The guy'd been hanging upside
down from a defective chinning bar, which
had collapsed, causing him to fall on his
head. The client, one Jaspar T. Baines, was
a thin, muscular black man whom I found
stretched out full-length in bed with his head
in traction.

It was a situation that cried out for a photo,
and I'd smuggled my camera in. I do that by
wearing it on a cord around my neck and
under my arm, so it hangs down under my
jacket as if in a shoulder holster. This was
necessary, because most hospitals won't al-
low you to take pictures.

I'd gotten mine, thank you very much, and

what a fine picture it was.

And because of that I had my camera with me.

What a fantastic stroke of luck.

I hied it down the street to take pictures of Susan Franklyn's reconstructed knee.

Only it wasn't quite that easy. First off, there was a security problem. Susan Franklyn's building was harder to get into than Miriam Pritchert's. The guard in the lobby must have asked me half a dozen questions before he was even willing to call upstairs. Even then he wasn't happy — I swear I thought he was going to ask me for a photo ID.

Then there was the client herself. Susan Franklyn was young, attractive, and modest. Most of Richard Rosenberg's clients couldn't give a damn about modesty — for an injury photo, they'd happily strip to the buff. Not Susan Franklyn. Her injury was only her knee, but she was wearing pants, and she wasn't willing to drop them for the shot. A trifle coy, since she was presumably wearing underwear, not to mention a fairly long shirt. But what the hey, I'd gotten enough breaks on the assignment, I could afford to wait while she changed.

Which she did. Into a bikini bathing suit. Go figure. Ten times more revealing than dropping her pants in the first place.

On the other hand, it made a great shot. The girl was a dish. In a skimpy bikini, she was a delectable dish. Except for the ugly, red, raw, surgical scars criss-crossing her left knee.

Wow. Talk about your daily double. On one roll of film, I had a guy with his neck in traction, and a mutilated pinup model.

Richard would come in his pants.

I finished my photo session, thanked the young woman — whose scars would quickly fade and who would have a nice day at the beach on the money Richard was going to get her — and went out.

I was tempted to spread my arms wide, show the guard in the lobby I hadn't absconded with the family silver, but I stifled the impulse, contented myself with a superior smirk as I went by.

Outside, I checked my watch. Even with the costume change, the whole assignment had only taken a half hour since I'd been beeped. I wondered if Miriam Pritchert and Marty Rothstein were still having lunch.

They weren't. One glance through the window showed the table was vacant.

I wondered if they'd gone up to her place.

Or up to his.

Or if he'd simply gone back to work.

Well, I knew how to check on that.

I went to the pay phone, called his firm.

The receptionist assured me he was still out to lunch.

I dropped another quarter, called Miriam Pritchert. It rang four times and an answering machine came on.

I hung up, dialed four one one, asked for a listing for Martin Rothstein.

There were four. I called them all and none were home. Of course, he didn't have to live in Manhattan. Or he could be listed as M. Rothstein. Or he could have an unlisted number.

On the other hand, he could be on his way back to the office, rather than shacking up with his deceased colleague's wife.

Ah, well, enough idle speculation. I headed back to Miriam Pritchert's apartment to pick up my car.

When I got there, it occurred to me there was one other possibility to check out.

I went in the lobby, asked the doorman for Miriam Pritchert.

The guy gave me a look. "Weren't you just up there?"

"Yes, I was. Now I'm back."

He shook his head. "Lady's had a tough time. Why don't you leave her alone."

Evidently, the guy still took me for a cop.

It occurred to me, if he did, I didn't have to bother to explain a damn thing.

"Yeah," I said. "But you know how it is."

The guy did. He stepped to the house phone, buzzed upstairs. After a few moments he said, "Sorry, there's no answer."

"Maybe she went out."

"Yeah. Maybe."

I didn't like the way he said that. I had the idea he'd seen her go in, knew she was there, and knew she wasn't answering the phone.

I wondered if he also knew she wasn't alone.

Assuming she wasn't.

My train of thought was interrupted by my beeper going off. That brought the doorman up short — he knew cops didn't wear beepers. Which meant my welcome was worn out. The look he gave me told me, whoever I was, I had better call in, and I could damn well do it from somewhere else.

I went to the pay phone to see what Mary Mason had for me. If she had another assignment half a block away, it was going to flip me out.

Not quite.

This time I was wanted by the cops.

30.

It was a small, two-story frame house on a block of similar structures in Forest Hills, Queens. There were cop cars all around the place. I pulled in to the curb and got out.

A uniformed officer on the front steps tried to give me the heave-ho.

"Belcher wants me," I said.

His eyes narrowed. "Who are you?"

"Stanley Hastings."

"Oh, yeah," the cop said. The look he gave me was not kind. But he jerked his thumb and said, "Come on."

I followed him up the steps and in the front door. There was a living room to the left, and a kitchen straight ahead, but we weren't heading there. Instead, the cop led me upstairs.

The top floor apparently consisted of two bedrooms and a bath. The front bedroom was empty. The back bedroom was full of cops. I walked in the door, stopped, and stared.

The bedroom had been set up as an office, with file cabinets, bookshelves, and a desk.

The body of the talent agent was stretched out on the floor. I knew her name, but blanked on it the minute I saw her lying there. Which was not surprising — I'm bad on names to begin with, and the whole scene was surreal. I mean, I'd played this scene before at the woman's Manhattan office. Been dragged in by the cops and expected to see her there. This time I'd been summoned by the cops and not told a thing. I had no idea whose house it was or why I was there. Then I walk into what I think is a bedroom, but, no, it's an office. What's more, it's just like the office I was in before when I expected to find a dead body, and here's the dead body I expected to find lying right where I thought it should be. Somehow, it was as if the whole thing were a stage set, mocked up especially for my benefit.

And before I even have a chance to get my wits together, there's Sergeant Belcher, malevolence itself, snapping questions at me, as if the whole thing was somehow my fault.

"Is it her?" Belcher demanded.

The question was so abrupt it startled me. "Her?"

"Yes, her. The woman you told us about. Is it her?"

"Yes, it is."

"You identify her?"

"Yes, I do."

"Who do you identify her to be?"

"The talent agent. I'm blanking her name."

"Shelly Daniels?"

"That's right."

"This is the woman you called on in her office?"

"Yes, it is."

"This is the woman you paid a hundred dollars to for information?"

"That's right."

"You claim she wouldn't give you the address and phone number of the topless dancer who set up your client?"

"I don't claim anything. The fact is, she didn't."

"You needn't qualify your answers with me. You see a stenographer taking anything down?"

"I like to be accurate."

"Well," Belcher said. "What a commendable trait. How did you get here?"

"I beg your pardon?"

"Are you deaf? How did you get here? Bus? Taxi? Helicopter?"

"I drove."

"You came in your car?"

"That's right."

"How did you find the place?"

"I had the address."

Belcher glowered at me. "I *know* that. I gave the girl the address to give you. How did you *locate* the address?"

"I have a Hagstrom map."

"Oh?"

"I use it in my work. I'm always getting beeped, sent to addresses like this. I look them up on the map."

"You're telling me you looked this address up on your map?"

"Yes, I did."

"This address did not ring a bell?"

"Not offhand."

"You're saying you've never been here before?"

"Not this exact address. I've been in the neighborhood."

"Why is that?"

"For my job. This is Forest Hills. I know I've done cases in Forest Hills."

"Then why didn't the address ring a bell?"

" 'Cause Mary didn't say Forest Hills."

"Mary?"

"Switchboard girl at Rosenberg and Stone. The one who beeped me and sent me here. She didn't say Forest Hills, just gave me a street address in Queens. I didn't know it was Forest Hills until I looked it up on the map."

"That's your story?"

I blinked. "Story? What story? I'm telling you exactly what happened."

"So you say. You drove here in your car?"

"Yes, I did."

"What kind of car you drive?"

"Toyota Corolla."

"What year?"

" '84."

"Color?"

"Tan."

"What's the license number?"

"Why?"

"You wanna give me the license number?"

I gave it to him. He wrote it in his notebook, glared at me, stalked out of the room and down the stairs.

Leaving me alone with three cops and a medical examiner, none of whom had been told what to do with me. Which was kind of bizarre. After a moment, they ignored me and went about their business, while I just stood and watched.

Shelly Daniels had apparently been shot. She was lying on her back, and bleeding from a chest wound in the approximate vicinity of her heart. Her head was lolled back and to the side. Her mouth was open but her eyes were closed. Her glasses had slid up on her forehead. In an incredibly grotesque touch, the medical examiner had hiked up her skirt, and appeared to be sexually molesting her. I realized he must be taking the body temperature. I wondered what it was. If it was at all significant. I figured probably not. Most likely the woman had been dead for days, and the body had completely cooled.

That started another train of thought. Had she been killed the same night as Cranston Pritchert? Who had been killed first? And had they been shot with the same gun? There was no weapon on the scene that I could see. If there had been, it would have answered the first question — the killer had shot Pritchert, then shot Daniels and dropped the gun. Unless the crime-scene unit had already bagged the weapon, nothing that convenient had happened.

I wondered what had.

I heard a clomping on the stairs, and Sergeant Belcher came back into the room. He ignored me, spoke to the medical examiner. "You finished up here?"

"More or less."

"Can we move her out?"

"Sure thing. Just need the stretcher."

"They're down there waiting for your say-so." He took a step to the door. "All right. Let's pack her up."

Two medics appeared with the stretcher, slipped Shelly Daniels into a body bag, and strapped her down. They were very efficient. Within minutes she was gone.

And Belcher's attention turned to me. "All right," he said. "We have a situation here and I think you know what it is."

"Yeah," I said. "I would classify it as a homicide myself."

Belcher scowled. "Don't be cute. You've been through this before, so you know the drill. The name of the game is find the top-less dancer." He jerked his thumb at the crime-scene cops. "As soon as these boys here are through, you're on." He turned to one of the cops, who was dusting the desk for fingerprints. "How much longer?"

The guy shrugged. "Ten, fifteen minutes."

Belcher turned back to me. "Okay. Down-stairs."

He led me downstairs, parked me in the living room. It was a modestly furnished affair, with a couch and coffee table that were either antiques or just old — my grasp on the distinction is vague. I sat on the couch and pondered my fate.

When who should walk in but Darren "Sandy" Carter.

So. Belcher wasn't kidding. We were going through the whole routine again.

The bartender did not look happy. Of course, you couldn't expect him to, but even so. He saw me, said, "What's going on?"

"You mean they didn't tell you?"

He shook his head. "Not a thing."

"It's the talent agent's house. She's dead. They just took the body away."

"Hey, motor mouth!" Belcher snapped from the doorway. He stepped in, insinuated himself between us, glared at me. "I kind of wanted to be the one to tell him that, if you know what I mean." He turned to Sandy. "Now look here, you. You ever see this agent before?"

"I told you, no."

"People tell me lots of things, and some I believe. That don't mean I won't ask 'em again. You say you've never seen the agent before. Well, if you've never *seen* her, you don't know what she looks like, so how would you know?"

Sandy frowned. "What?"

"Too tough a concept for you? If you don't know who the woman is, don't know what she looks like, it is possible you've seen her and did not know it was her. Can you follow that all right?"

"I see what you're saying, yeah."

"Good. Now, as your buddy here points out, the woman's on her way to the morgue.

Which means you'll have to go there to take a look. But first we have other business to attend to."

"What's that?"

"There's an office upstairs. Full of resume photos."

"You gotta be kidding."

"I assure you I'm not. You and your buddy gonna play find the bimbo. Just as soon as the crime-scene boys are done." He jerked his thumb. "In fact, here they come now."

The crime-scene unit came lugging their cameras and equipment down the stairs and out the front door.

"All done?" Belcher called to them.

"It's all yours."

"Okay, guys," Belcher said. "You're on."

I don't know how long we were up there, but it seemed like forever. I sat at the desk and Sandy sat in a chair. Bagging the desk was a coup — I could have the pictures in front of me, turn 'em one at a time. Sandy had to balance his on his lap.

The pictures were pretty much the same as they had been in her Manhattan office. With one exception. One file cabinet was filled with explicit, X-rated shots. Some were just women posing holding their vaginas and ass cheeks open. Others were couples engaging in every conceivable sexual act.

None of the explicit pictures featured our topless dancer, Marla Melons, and from my conversation with her it seemed unlikely any of them would. Still, Sandy and I were in complete agreement that in the interests of justice we should take no chances and examine them anyway.

It was nearly two hours later when Sergeant Belcher came stomping in.

"Any luck?"

We shook our heads.

"You keep at it," Belcher said, pointing at Sandy. He turned to me. "You come with me."

He led me into the other bedroom.

And closed the door.

Uh-oh.

I'd been waiting for it to happen. Up till now, Sergeant Belcher had been perfectly civil. Gruff and brusk, sure. But not unnaturally so. Nothing to indicate he had a personal grudge. Then, suddenly for the first time I'm face to face with him all alone. No need for any pretense now. So what was the deal? Was the guy going to beat me up?

He wasn't.

When he turned to me, Belcher's manner was still formal and official. And I noticed he was holding a paper in his hand.

"Stanley Hastings," he said. "I have here

a search warrant duly obtained on this day, empowering me to search both your person and your car. Do you intend to comply with this warrant?"

My mouth fell open. "What?"

"Don't you understand the concept?" Belcher said. "You were the last person to see the Daniels woman alive. You are to all intents and purposes a suspect. Therefore to be searched. I have the warrant here. You can examine it if you like. May I have the keys to your car?"

"You got a search warrant?"

"Are you having trouble with the English language?" Belcher unfolded the paper, thrust it out at me.

It was just exactly what he said it was. A judge Sidney Moncrieff, based on allegation and belief, had empowered Sergeant Timothy Belcher to search my person and my car.

Belcher extended his hand. "May I have your car keys, please?"

"I don't believe this."

"Believe it or not, do you intend to comply?"

It occurred to me, Belcher was hoping I wouldn't. He was looking for anything to get me on. I dug my keys out of my pocket, passed them over.

Belcher opened the door, called one of the cops, gave him the keys. He closed the door, turned back to me. "Now, you."

Oh, Jesus. This was it. How bad could he rough me up under the guise of a search? Pretty bad, I'll bet.

A shudder passed over me. Was he going to strip me to the skin?

"Take off your jacket, pass it over," Belcher said.

I did, and he went through the pockets, placing the contents on the bed. From one inside pocket, my notebook and pen. From the other, my ID.

Belcher jerked his thumb. "What's with the camera?"

With my jacket off, the camera was now exposed, hanging down at my side.

"It's for my job," I said. "Negligence work. I take injury and accident photos."

"Is there film in there now?"

Sure was. The broken neck and the ugly kneecap. Good god! If he were to expose the film . . .

"What's the matter?" Belcher said.

"Huh?"

"You went white. What is it about the film?"

"Nothing. It's just pictures I took for my job."

"Yeah, well, it sure upset you. Let's have the camera."

"Sure," I said. "If you expose that film . . ."

"Expose it? Are you nuts? I'm gonna develop it, see what you're so afraid of. Come on, let's have it."

Reluctantly, I took the camera from around my neck, handed it to him. It was a relief when he merely laid it on the bed.

"All right, empty your pants pockets," Belcher said.

Well, that was something. He hadn't asked me to take off my pants. With a feeling of relief, I took out change, Chapstick, bills, wallet, and passed them over.

Belcher went through the wallet, inspecting the various cards. He stopped on one.

"Writers Guild of America East," he said. "What's that?"

"Screenwriters union."

"You belong to that?"

"I had a movie produced."

He looked at me. "And you still do this shit?"

That whole sequence had seemed so natural that in that moment I had doubts. Maybe this guy didn't know who I was. That I was a friend of MacAullif. The man he hated. The man against whom he had a personal grudge. Maybe he *wasn't* out to get me, as I had thought. Maybe he was just another cop doing his job.

There was a knock on the door and the cop came in. The one Belcher had sent to search my car.

"Found something," the cop said. He was young, eager, and, it seemed to me, a trifle apprehensive.

"Yeah?" Belcher said. "What is it?"

"You gotta understand, I wasn't expecting to find anything," the cop said, "so I may have touched it. I mean, if my fingerprints should be on it. I just put my hand under the front seat, and there it was."

"There *what* was?" Belcher said. "What did you find?"

"This," the cop said.

He held up a plastic evidence bag.

There was a gun in it.

31.

"You know why you never made it as an actor?" Richard said.

I exhaled into the phone and looked at him with exasperation through the Plexiglas shield in the visitors room in the lockup. "Richard," I said. "I'm in jail charged with murder. I've been waiting for you for three hours. That is not a great opening line."

"I got tied up in court," Richard said. "The city of New York had the stupidity to suggest that a pregnant woman might have fallen down, not due to uneven pavement, but due rather to her increased size." He shook his head. "Big mistake. Probably double the damages. Not only did I ridicule the position, I even hit 'em with the old sexist joke, you know, where the truck driver almost runs over the pregnant woman, shouts out, Hey, lady, you don't watch where you're going, you'll get knocked *down* too."

"Richard —"

"You should have seen the jury. I score both ways. I score with the joke because it's funny. And I score off opposing counsel because I'm attributing it to him."

"Richard —"

"Sorry. I just want to point out, I was having a real good day before you called."

"I'm sorry to spoil it for you."

"Are you? Well, you know why you never made it as an actor?"

Good lord. There was no deflecting him. "No, Richard. Why did I never make it as an actor?"

"Timing."

"Huh?"

"It's your timing. That's what actors need, right? Good timing."

"That's comedians."

"Same difference. You need timing. And yours is bad."

Good lord. Richard must have rehearsed this routine in the car driving out. And knowing Richard, I wasn't going to get a word in till I heard it. "My timing's bad?" I said.

"The worst. Look, here you are, charged with murder. Ordinarily, a murder case, I'd jump at it. But, guess what? I just finished a murder trial. And it wasn't nearly as much fun as I thought it would be. Now you offer me another? Your timing is the pits."

"That's real funny, Richard. You really cheer me up."

"Hey, don't be such a grouse," Richard

said. "You know why I'm kidding around? You're in here charged with killing that talent agent. Well, guess what? I happen to know you didn't do it. So, whatever the case, it's a minor problem, and one that will go away."

"You happen to talk to the cops on your way in?"

"No. Why do you ask?"

"I was caught with the murder weapon."

Richard made a face. "Usually, a bad move. What possessed you to do that?"

"What do you think?"

"Someone planted it on you?"

"Bingo, right on the button."

"Any idea who?"

"I happen to *know* who."

"Care to share that thought?"

"How does the investigating officer grab you?"

Richard made a face again. "Well, now we'll know if this room's bugged."

"Huh?"

"If it is, you'll get a nice roommate shoves a shiv in your gut."

"Richard —"

"What makes you think what you just said? And try to be nonspecific in your answer."

"Remember what I told you — about the personality clash involved?"

"Yes, I do. You think that's it?"

"Why don't I just tell you what happened."

"That might be a good idea."

"The cops had Mary beep me, sent me to an address in Queens. Turned out to be the agent's house, she turned out to be dead. Turns out she's got a second office in her home with file cabinets full of resume photos, and the cop sets me to work going through them looking for the topless dancer. While I'm at it, he goes out and gets a search warrant for my person and my car. The good news is there's nothing on my person. The bad news is, there's a gun in my car."

"And it must be the murder weapon, otherwise they wouldn't have charged you," Richard said. "Well, that seems simple enough."

"Simple?"

"Sure. They'll arraign you for murder and I'll get you out on bail. Piece of cake."

"Richard —"

"Only problem is, if the same gun killed what's-his-name — your dead client — you'll be charged with that too." Richard frowned. "Two counts is bad. Plus, it's a different county, so it's a separate arraignment. With each judge looking at the other one."

"What do you mean, looking at the other one?"

Richard shrugged. Chuckled. "Well, I'm

arguing before this judge, Hey, my client's no flight risk, let him out on bail. And the prosecutor's pointing out you're also wanted for murder in Manhattan — oh, sure, please do release him, Your Honor, because the cops are waiting to arrest him all over again on another murder count."

"Yeah, I know. So, what can you do?"

"Hey, did I say I couldn't do it? Relax. I'll get you out. I just want you to understand. At an arraignment hearing, we're not trying the case. The only points I'll be making are what a swell guy you are and how you pose no flight risk."

"Not the fact that I might be innocent?"

"Oh, no one cares about that. In the eyes of the law, you're innocent until proven guilty. In the eyes of the public, you're guilty the minute you're charged. Who cares? In point of fact, you've been framed, but that's incidental now. Even if I *could* prove it, I wouldn't. It would be bad form, and it's not what anyone wants to hear. No, you'll be arraigned, you'll be bailed, you'll be back on the street, and if the case is as bullshit as it seems, eventually the charges will be dismissed."

Richard shrugged. "In the unlikely event this ever came to trial, then we'd have to take a look at the merits of the case. Of which there appear to be none. The frame's clumsy as hell and it isn't going to stick. I wouldn't let it worry me."

"Why not?"

"Because I'm not in jail." He pointed. "You, now maybe you should worry."

I groaned. "Hey, Richard."

"What?"

"Better work on your timing."

32.

MacAullif made a face when I walked in. "You shouldn't be here."

I shrugged and dropped into the chair next to his desk. "Where else can I go?"

"Indeed," MacAullif said. "I suppose you're lucky to be anywhere at all."

"Richard was eloquent."

"I'm sure he was. Even so. I'm surprised they set bail."

"Bail isn't punitive. It's only to make sure you show up for court. Richard educated the judge on that point."

"I'm sure he did. So what's the disposition of the case?"

"It's cases. As in two. I've been arraigned on two counts of murder, one in Manhattan, one in Queens."

MacAullif nodded. "Some days are worse than others." He shrugged. "I'm not havin' a great day myself."

"You been charged with murder?"

"Not yet."

"Well, just wait. I don't think this guy Belcher likes you much."

"No shit," MacAullif said. He leaned back in his chair, cocked his head. "Weren't you just in the other day? Didn't I tell you a long story about this cop Belcher — how he's poison, he's the kiss of death, you leave him alone?"

"Hey, he sent for me."

"Maybe so, but what were you doin' before that?"

"What do you mean?"

"I mean the case does not stand on the murder weapon alone. At your arraignment, maybe that's all they told the judge, because it's only an arraignment, so that's all they need. But you think they leave it at that? You think there's no investigation going on? You think no one cares what you did?"

"Hey, MacAullif. I haven't had much sleep in the last twenty-four hours, and frankly I'm not focusing very well. What the hell do you mean?"

"Yesterday. Before the arrest. What did you do with your day?"

"Oh."

"Yeah. Oh," MacAullif said. It was amazing how much irony he was able to invest in such a short word. "According to what the police have been able to dig up, you spent the morning calling on Amy Greenberg and Miriam Pritchert. Now, correct me if I'm wrong, but don't those two broads have something to do with the late Cranston Pritchert?"

"MacAullif —"

"One would think so, since it seems that you tried to get both of them to hire you to investigate his death."

"MacAullif —"

"No. Talking to you is like talking to a two-year-old. You hear what I say and do the opposite."

"Oh, bullshit."

"Bullshit? You sit there, framed for murder, and tell me bullshit?"

"Give me a break. The cops didn't know I called on those women. Not when they set me up. That had nothing to do with it."

"Oh, no? Guess what? Miriam Pritchert, I couldn't say, you could be right. But Amy Greenberg is another story. You call on her, give her the song and dance, and, guess what? She calls up and reports it to the cops."

"You're kidding."

MacAullif shook his head. "It's in the file. And it's in there before your arrest. When he calls you to that house, Belcher knows you're nosing around."

"So he sets me up?"

"Doesn't play for you?"

"No, it plays just fine."

"Sure it does." MacAullif held up one finger. "He sets you up for knowing me — that's for starters. I told you he would if you led with your chin. Which, of course, you did."

"Wait a minute, wait a minute," I said. "What has calling on Amy Greenberg got to do with it?"

"Absolutely nothing," MacAullif said. He held up his finger again. "But. It connects you with the case. Again. The cops have gotta fashion a theory for the frame. He's workin' on it now. He may not have it set yet, but he's collecting all the elements he can. You nosing around is a break."

"So he frames me?"

MacAullif put up his hand. "Hey, did I say that? I certainly wouldn't want to accuse a fellow officer of such a thing."

"I'm sure you wouldn't. But that's the case. So how does it happen?"

"What do you mean?"

"I mean the mechanics of it. If Belcher gets the gun and frames me with it, how does that come to pass?"

"Come again."

"Where does he get the gun?"

"He finds it at the crime scene."

"*Which* crime scene?"

MacAullif raised his eyebrows. "Oh. So that's how you're thinking. Good point. The Cranston Pritchert killing." He frowned. "But you found that body. You were there ahead of the cops. So is it possible that there was a gun that you missed that he found?"

"I wouldn't think so, but I can't rule it out."

"Hmm," MacAullif said. "In that case, Belcher finds the gun, decides to appropriate it before he even knows I'm involved."

"Unless he finds it after he came down in the elevator and saw you."

"Yeah," MacAullif said. "I'm not keen on the theory."

"Me either. Odds are he found the gun at the agent's house."

"I should think so," MacAullif said.

"So he finds the gun, conceals it, doesn't tell anyone, and sends for me."

"You arriving in your car, as he might expect." MacAullif looked at me. "How does he know which car is yours?"

"He asked me."

"Oh?"

"He asked me for everything, even the license plate. Presumably so he could get the warrant. But actually, so he could find the car and plant the gun."

"He plant the gun before or after he got the warrant?"

"Before."

"How do you know?"

"Because he didn't do it himself. Search the car, I mean. When he got the warrant, he asked me for the keys, gave them to a cop, and sent him out to search the car. The cop came back with the gun."

"Wait a minute. He asked you for the keys?"

"Yeah."

"So the car was locked. That would make it harder to plant the gun."

I frowned. "Yeah."

"But not impossible," MacAullif said. "He's a cop, he can get in a car door just fine. He could have a jimmy or a set of keys."

"That's not it," I said.

"Oh?"

"It just occurred to me."

"What?"

"I'm not sure I locked the door."

"You're kidding."

"No. It's a crime scene. There's cops all around. I drove up, stopped the car, and got out. I know I didn't set my code alarm. I may not have even locked the door."

"Jesus Christ."

"Well, how the hell was I to know?"

"Because I *told* you, putz," MacAullif said. "I told you not to mess around with this. I told you to be on your guard."

"MacAullif. I know I fucked up. The question is, what do I do now?"

"You shouldn't *do* anything. That's the whole problem. Everything you do, you just get in deeper."

"I'm charged with two murders. How deep can you get?"

"How does convicted grab you?"

"Don't even joke."

"Who's joking? You think Belcher will stand pat? Planting a weapon makes for a strong case, but not necessarily a convicting one. The prosecutor needs more evidence, you can bet Belcher's gonna get it for him."

"How?"

"He'll make it up, just like he did with the gun. The thing is, every step you take gives him that much more to play with."

"So what the hell do I do?"

"I'll tell you what you *don't* do."

"What's that?"

"You don't try to prove Belcher framed you."

I frowned. "Why not?"

"For starters, you can't do it. And that's just for starters."

"Why can't I do it?"

"Because you're a moron."

"MacAullif —"

"You're a moron to even think you could. Have you stopped to consider what you're up against?"

"I know it's tough."

"You don't know shit. You're dealing with a cop. Believe me, this one isn't dumb. How do I know? I know because he's *still* a cop. And to pull the type of shit he pulls and keep his shield, the guy is on the ball."

"So he's smart. So what?"

"So he's smart enough to know what you can prove and what you can't. He plants a gun on you, it's a crude obvious frame, but try to prove it. What argument can you make?"

"Argument?"

"Yeah. Sell me. How do you know the guy planted the gun?"

"I know he did because I didn't put it there."

MacAullif made a noise like a buzzer. "Blah. Sorry. Self-serving declaration. Of no evidentiary value in court. You have to remember we're not trying to convince you, we're trying to convince an ordinary human being who doesn't happen to *be* you. So let's start again. How do you know the guy planted the gun?"

"He had the opportunity. He asked me to describe my car."

"That was so he could get a warrant."

"Fine, but it gave him the opportunity."

"Okay, say he had the opportunity. Why would he do it? What's his motive?"

"To get me."

"Why does he want to get you?"

"You know why."

"Sure I do," MacAullif said. "But you wanna start proving it in court? You wanna try to prove the guy has a grudge against me, you're a friend of mine, and therefore he's out to get you? Even if you could prove that — and that's a big if — you think that's the type of thing I'd like to hear aired in court?"

"Oh, so I'm supposed to take a murder rap so as not to hurt your feelings?"

"Don't be a schmuck," MacAullif said. "I'm just trying to tell you, trying to prove he framed you isn't gonna fly. The guy'll just sit back and laugh at you, and who could blame him?"

"Yeah, but that's what Richard has to do — create reasonable doubt."

"Yeah, and the operative word is *reasonable*. I hate to break it to you, but, Hey, I was framed, is not that original an idea. Hell, every other punk we pick up claims he was framed."

"That doesn't mean it doesn't happen."

"Hey, you don't have to sell me. But you have to sell them, and they ain't buyin'. Now, this Belcher thing — if you can prove it, fine. But if all you got is what you got now, I'm tellin' you it's not a theory you wanna advance."

"So what do I do?"

"You find another way. Now, before you went out to this agent's house, as I understand it, you call on these two broads."

"Yeah. So?"

"You take your car?"

My eyes widened. "Are you trying to suggest . . . ?"

"If Belcher didn't frame you, someone else did."

"But he *did* frame me."

"Can you prove it? If not, you look for something else. Now, these women you called on — which one was first?"

"The granddaughter. What's her name. Amy Greenberg. So young she makes you seem senile."

"Uh-huh," MacAullif said. "And where's she live?"

"Scarsdale."

"So you took your car?"

"Sure."

"Did she have an opportunity to plant the gun?"

"Did she? Let me think. Sure. She backed her car out of the driveway so I could get out. While I was inside calling the office."

"Could she have planted the gun then?"

"Sure. I don't think my car was even locked."

"There you are," MacAullif said. "That's ten times better than Belcher."

"Why?"

"Because she can't disprove it. Plus, she isn't set up to come back at you. What about the other woman?"

"What about her?"

"Where was your car?"

"East 78th Street. Parked right in front of her building."

"She have an opportunity to go near it?"

"No."

"How do you know?"

"Because I saw her leave."

"How come?"

"She went to lunch with one of her husband's business associates. I thought that was interesting, so I tailed along."

"In the car?"

"No."

"You left it there?"

"Yeah."

"Where anyone could have got in, planted the gun?"

"Like who?"

"Like whoever killed those people. How do I know, like who? The point is, they could have."

"I suppose."

"There's no supposing about it. How about after lunch. You tail the woman home?"

"Actually, no. I went off on a job."

"In the car?"

"No, on foot. It was just down the block."

"What about after?"

"After the job?"

"Yeah."

"I went back to the restaurant, the woman was gone."

"Well, there you are," MacAullif said. "What was to stop her from going home and planting the gun?"

"She didn't know it was my car."

"No?"

"No."

"She couldn't have seen you out the window when you drove up?"

"Her apartment's on the fourteenth floor."

"Even so."

"And she didn't know I was coming."

"How about when you left?"

"That's very far-fetched."

"How about the guy she went to lunch with?"

"What about him?"

"How'd you know she was going to lunch?"

"I saw him go in."

"When?"

"When I went out."

"Did he see you?"

"I don't think so."

"Did he know you?"

"If he did, he knew me as someone else."

"What do you mean?"

"I was up in Cranston Pritchert's office once. He introduced me as a client."

"Interesting," MacAullif said. "Then seeing you would register."

"Possibly."

"So he sees you come out of the building and get into your car. So he goes up and calls on the widow, and says, Hey, what was that client of Cranston's doing coming around? She says, Client, what client? A private detective he hired was just here. Well, this guy can put two and two together, figures out who you are, and knows where your car's parked."

"And plants the gun in it?"

"Or tells her so she can. Which flies very

nicely," MacAullif said. "A guy gets killed, nine times out of ten the wife did it. Here she is with a boyfriend on the side, say they're in it together, no problem there. He tips her off to you and they say, Bingo, and plant the gun."

"But that's not what happened."

"Doesn't matter," MacAullif said. "All you need is something your lawyer can argue. So you don't go to jail."

"You think it's gonna come to that?"

"Who knows? But in case it does, you gotta prepare."

I ran my hand over my head. "Jesus Christ," I said. "What a fucked-up case. You got me trying to prove things that never happened."

"Only as a worst-case scenario. But yeah, that's exactly what you gotta do."

I shook my head. "There's gotta be a better way."

"Actually, there is," MacAullif said.

"Oh? What's that?"

"Figure out who did it."

33.

Kevin Dunbar didn't seem pleased to see me. He scrunched down in his chair as if hiding behind his desk and said, "What is it you want?"

I leaned back in my chair, crossed my legs, and smiled. "Just thought we should have a little chat."

Dunbar frowned. "This is most awkward."

"I admit the circumstances are somewhat unfortunate."

"That's not what I mean. You were introduced to me as a prospective client."

"Would it help you to continue to think of me in that way?"

"Don't be ridiculous," Dunbar said irritably. "It was in the paper. Hell, it was on the evening news. You're the one who did it."

"Well, now," I said, "fortunately our judicial system is somewhat more open-minded. But just for your own information, I didn't do it. Cranston Pritchert hired me to do a job. I did my best to do it, and, believe it or not, I'm still trying to do it."

"Oh, sure," Dunbar said.

"Hey. You're an executive vice-president and you think you're pretty shrewd. So think on this — if I killed Cranston Pritchert, what the hell am I doing here?"

"Huh?"

"Why am I here? What do I want? Let's face it, if I'm guilty there isn't a whole hell of a lot. If I'm guilty, I know exactly what happened. If I'm innocent, I have no idea, and I'm trying to find out. See what I mean?"

"Yeah, sure," Dunbar said. If he was convinced, you wouldn't know it. "Why don't you just tell me what it is you want, because, believe it or not, I have work to do."

"I want some information, and I want your opinion."

"My opinion?"

"Yes. Here's the deal. Cranston Pritchert thought someone was trying to set him up. To embarrass him and make him look foolish before the stockholders meeting so there'd be no chance of him being voted in as chairman of the board."

"There was no chance anyway," Dunbar said.

"Oh? And why is that?"

Dunbar made a face. "Shit."

"Hey, relax," I said. "It's not like you just

246

gave away trade secrets. What you said is exactly the point. If there's no chance of him becoming chairman of the board, then no one killed him to prevent that from happening. One motive that I can cross off. But I'd really like to know why."

"Because who would vote for him?" Dunbar said. "Certainly not me or Marty. And the Greenberg girl — she's a kook. Who knows how she's gonna vote. Cranston couldn't know either, unless he had her in his hip pocket. And, knowing Cranston, that's not possible. So eventually it'll all come down to the proxies. And, frankly, Cranston didn't have that many friends."

"And you did?"

"More than him. But, hey, nothing's decided yet. The race is still on."

"Uh-huh. And what happens to Cranston's shares now?"

"What do you mean?"

"In the stockholders meeting. Who votes his shares?"

"Oh. His wife. I mean, his widow."

"You happen to know her?"

"I've met her, yes."

"How do you think she'll vote?"

"That's really up to her."

"Have you spoken to her since it happened?"

"I called her, of course. Expressed my sympathy."

"And who do you think she's friendlier with, you or Marty Rothstein?"

"I would say me."

"You would?"

"Yes."

"Ever take her to lunch?"

"What's that supposed to mean?"

"Just curious as to how well you know her."

"I find the question impertinent. This is a married woman. Why would I be taking her to lunch?"

"I don't know. Just your statement that you were closer to her than Marty Rothstein."

"I think I am, but not because of anything such as you imply." Dunbar shifted in his seat. "I don't think this interview is serving any practical purpose."

I held up my hand. "I apologize for going off on a tangent. I didn't mean to be talking about Miriam Pritchert. I meant to be talking about the proxy fight. My only interest in Miriam Pritchert was how she might vote. If she were to vote for you, would that put you over?"

"Oh, not at all," Dunbar said. "As I say, there's the Greenberg girl. Her holdings are bigger, and who knows how she'll vote."

"Could *she* put you over?"

"Again, no. The four of us — her, Cranston, me, and Marty — are larger holders than anyone else, but it's still not a majority. In the end, it's the proxies will decide."

"So, Cranston was right."

"What do you mean?"

"That it could make a difference. Say none of you vote for him. You, Marty, and Cranston all vote for yourself. Who knows how the Greenberg girl votes, but say it's not him. If he had a chance of being elected — and I'm only saying if — someone could kill that by embarrassing him so the stockholders changed their proxies."

"It's conceivable, yes," Dunbar said. "But, I tell you, there's no way he had that many votes."

"But he might have *thought* he had."

"So what?" Dunbar said. "What difference would it make what *he* thought. If someone was trying to ace him out of the election, *they* must have thought he could win."

"Good point," I said. "And who might think that?"

"What?"

"Who might think Cranston had a chance to win?"

"No one," Dunbar said. "That's the whole

249

point. I knew he didn't, and so did Marty. The only one who might think that would be the Greenberg girl, and what's *she* got to do with it?"

"Oh? *Why* might she think that?"

Dunbar held up his hand. "Please. Don't put words in my mouth. I *don't* think she'd think that. I only say she *could* think that because she doesn't know any better. Me and Marty know better because we know. She knows nothing, so she could think anything she likes. But I gather she has little interest in the business at all."

"Un-huh," I said. "Are you married?"

Dunbar frowned. "What's that got to do with it?"

"I'm not sure. Are you?"

"No, I'm not."

"What about Marty Rothstein?"

"He's not married either. Why?"

"Cranston Pritchert was set up with a girl in a bar. That works in his case because he's married. But you and Marty Rothstein, same situation, no big deal. You're single. You pick up a girl in a bar and no one bats an eye."

"Yeah. So?"

"So, maybe Cranston Pritchert was set up because he was the one it works on. Not because he had more shares, or more backing, or was the most likely candidate to be elected, but simply because he's married, so in his case, it works."

Dunbar thought that over. Exhaled noisily. "Jesus Christ," he said. He squinted at me sideways, cocked his head. "You know something?"

"What's that?"

"You've almost got me convinced you didn't do it."

34.

Marty Rothstein wasn't pleased to see me either. "I thought you were in jail," he said.

"I rolled doubles."

"What?"

"That's how you do it. Roll doubles, or have a *Get out of jail free* card."

Rothstein frowned. "It isn't funny."

"No, it isn't," I said. "It's bad enough the guy's dead. Getting framed for his murder is just the icing on the cake."

"Oh, so now you were framed?"

"No, I'm guilty, Rothstein. I killed Pritchert, and I'm up here with an eye to wiping out the company."

"Why are you so hostile?"

"Am I? I hadn't noticed. I guess getting framed for murder doesn't put me in a great mood."

"Well, *I* didn't do it."

"Well, who *did?*"

"What?"

"Come on. Help me out, here. If you didn't frame me, who did?"

"Don't be absurd."

"There's nothing absurd about it. I have an edge on the cops in the fact I happen to know I didn't do it. I'm lookin' for who did. I figure whoever framed me is probably the killer. You have any ideas on that?"

Rothstein tipped back in his chair. "I could call security and have you thrown out."

"You could, but it would make you look bad. It's the type of thing my lawyer could ask you on the witness stand."

"What?"

"If the case ever went to trial, it's the type of thing my lawyer could bring out. To show bias, you know. The fact you wouldn't answer my questions and had me thrown out."

"I don't know what you're talking about."

"I'm talking about the murder of Cranston Pritchert, which is what I'm investigating. I didn't happen to kill him, and I want to find out who did. I have some questions. If you don't want to answer them, I have to assume my purpose does not please you. In light of which, I can draw my own conclusions."

Rothstein took a breath. "I'm not calling security, but I don't think I'm discussing this either."

"Oh, yeah?" I said. "How do you think she'll vote?"

"Who?"

"Miriam Pritchert. You get her vote lined

up when you took her out to lunch?"

Rothstein's eyes narrowed. "So that *was* you."

"What?"

"Coming out of her building the other day. I thought that was you."

"You saw me?"

"Sure, I did. I even asked her about it. In fact, I knew it was you because she said so. I just didn't make the connection till now. Yeah, I knew it was you. But you were leaving. How did you know I took her out to lunch?"

"How'd you know I left?"

"I saw you get into your car."

Aha. Score one for MacAullif. Except, if he thought I left, he must have thought the car was gone. And you can't hide a gun in a car that isn't there.

"So," I said. "You didn't see my car when the two of you came out."

He frowned. "What are you saying?"

"I'm saying I'm hoping you had a nice lunch, and did you happen to lock up the young widow's vote?"

"I find your questions insolent."

"Wait'll you hear my lawyer's."

"What?"

"As I say, on the stand these things will come out."

"On the stand? But I'm not going on the stand."

"You are if we slap a subpoena on you. If I go to trial, my lawyer's going to try to create reasonable doubt. I hate to tell you, but you're it. For starters, the guy was killed in your office. Then you try to tie up the widow's votes. How does that look to you?"

Rothstein blinked.

I put up both hands. "But, please. That is not why I'm here. Someone killed your business associate. I didn't do it, and I want to know who did. If you didn't do it, I would think you'd want to know who did too. I was hoping between the two of us we could come up with a lead."

Rothstein frowned. "How do you mean?"

"It all seems to hinge on this proxy fight. Whether you'd locked up Miriam Pritchert's votes or not is neither here nor there. According to what Kevin Dunbar said, it wouldn't matter anyway, it's not enough votes to swing the thing."

"*Kevin* said that?"

"No, no. Not specifically. Not those votes, and not that you'd locked them up. He said in general. That the holdings weren't big enough to swing the thing, and that it would come down to the proxies."

"Well, that's true."

"What about the girl — Amy Greenberg — what about her?"

"What do you mean?"

"Did you approach her too?"

"What are you insinuating?"

"I'm asking you if you asked her about voting her stock. It's a logical question — she's gotta vote for *someone,* you'd like it to be you — I can't imagine you *not* asking her."

"All right. So I asked her."

"What did she say?"

"Something noncommittal. Hell, practically incoherent."

"I can imagine. You ask her in person?"

"Huh?"

"You take her out to lunch?"

"I tried, but she wasn't buying."

"So you only spoke to her on the phone?"

"Uh-huh."

"What about the stockholders?"

"What about 'em?"

"You contact any of them personally?"

"What's that got to do with it?"

"I'd kind of like to know."

"I called some of the larger ones, yes."

"Get any commitments?"

"Some."

"Some waffled?"

"Some wouldn't commit. People are like that. It's nothing to do with me, you know?"

He frowned. "I don't know why I'm telling you this."

"Maybe you believe me."

"Yeah, maybe," he said dubiously.

"Tell me something," I said. "The bit about the girl in the bar — you've heard all about that, of course."

"Yes, of course."

"Had you heard anything *before* the murder?"

"What do you mean?"

"Just that. Did you know anything at all about Cranston Pritchert's problem — the girl in the bar, the fact he thought he was set up — did you have any inkling any of that was going on before the murder took place?"

"Absolutely not. Why should I?"

"I wouldn't know. I just wondered if you did."

"Well, the answer is no."

"What about the stockholders?"

"What do you mean?"

"The ones you called — to ask about their votes — did any of them mention to you about having heard anything about Cranston Pritchert?"

"Of course not."

"Why of course not?"

"Why would they?"

"I take it you made these calls before the murder?"

"Of course."

"Because after the murder it would have been a topic of conversation."

"Exactly."

"But it wasn't?"

"No."

"No one mentioned Cranston Pritchert at all?"

Rothstein hesitated.

"Yes? What is it?"

Rothstein made a face. "Nothing. It's just when you say *at all* . . . well, one of the stockholders I called was voting for Pritchert."

"Oh?"

"Which is not what you were asking. Has nothing to do with the incident. It's just his name did come up."

"Did he say why?"

Rothstein hesitated again.

"What is it?" I asked.

"Nothing. It's just . . . well, actually, it's a she."

"Oh. Did *she* say why?"

"No. She didn't."

"Is this someone you know personally?"

"Not at all," Rothstein said. "Just a stockholder. A rather large one. Not as large as any of us, but a substantial stockholder."

"And the fact is, she said she was voting for Pritchert. That must have been rather upsetting. One of your clients, voting for Pritchert."

Again, Rothstein's eyes betrayed him. Finally, it dawned on me why.

What a dope. I'd been attributing his embarrassment to the fact he must have a personal relationship with the woman. When actually it was the other way around. He had no relationship with the woman at all.

The woman was one of *Cranston Pritchert's* clients.

Aha, Rothstein.

So that's the way the wind blows.

35.

Jack Jenkins looked like a bookkeeper. I know that's a horrible thing to say, but that's how he struck me. A little man with a bald head and wire-rimmed glasses, he looked as if he spent all his time staring at books and adding up long columns of figures. Which makes no sense at all, since modern-day bookkeepers use calculators and computers and what have you, and probably don't even need to know how to add.

Anyway, Jack Jenkins, who was indeed a bookkeeper, crinkled up his nose and peered at me through his glasses. "And just what is it that you want?"

"I was hoping you could tell me about the company stock."

"Such matters are confidential."

"I'm sure they are. I wasn't referring to any particular stockholder. I meant in general."

"In general?"

"Yes. Say I was interested in buying stock in your company. What would I be buying?"

Jenkins cleared his throat. "I don't sell stock."

"I understand. But you're the bookkeeper. You keep track of it."

"Yes, of course."

"So what's a share worth? How many shares are there?"

Again Jenkins cleared his throat. "As to the worth of a share, that would fluctuate with the stock market. As to how many shares in all, I'd have to ask you what's your interest?"

"There's a stockholders meeting coming up."

"Yes. Tomorrow night."

"To elect a new chairman of the board."

"Yes. So?"

"I'm wondering how many shares it would take."

"To get elected?"

"Yes."

"It would take a majority."

"A majority?"

"That's right."

"Can you be more specific?"

"What could be more specific than that?"

"Do you mean fifty-one percent?"

"That's right."

"What if the winner got forty-nine percent?"

"Then he wouldn't be the winner."

"I beg your pardon?"

"He would have a plurality, not a majority. Which would not be enough to win."

"What would happen then?"

"There'd be another vote."

"You mean a runoff?"

"That's right."

"Between the top two candidates?"

"Yes, of course."

"What would happen with the proxies?"

"Proxies?"

"Yes. Would new proxies have to be sent in?"

"Not necessarily."

"Why not? What about all the proxies sent in for people who weren't in the runoff?"

Jenkins shook his head. "You don't understand."

"Probably not. Why don't you explain."

"A proxy isn't a vote — it delegates the *power* to vote. Say you have shares in the company. You want to see me chairman of the board. You give me your proxy to vote your shares. So I vote for me. But suppose I don't win. Suppose there's a runoff and I'm not in it. I still have your proxy and I can vote your shares for either candidate I wish."

"What if I didn't like that?"

"You could send in another proxy. Any

new proxy supersedes an old one."

"That's what I thought. Now, in the present case, have the proxies all been sent in?"

"The majority have been."

"When you say the majority, do you mean fifty-one percent?"

"No. I mean most of them. They're almost all in. There may be one or two stragglers. And, of course, there are some stockholders who never bother to turn in proxies. But of those we're going to get, they're almost all in."

"Uh-huh. And who holds the majority of the proxies?"

"That I can't tell you."

"Because it's confidential?"

"Because I don't know. And I won't know until the stockholders meeting, when the proxies are counted up."

"I would have thought that would have been your job."

"It is. And when they are counted, I will do the accounting. Until then, I merely assemble and compile them. But how they add up, frankly I don't want to know. You see, working here as I do, it would be very uncomfortable for me to know."

"Uh-huh," I said. "You have the proxies here in your office?"

"Yes, I do."

"What's to stop one of the candidates from coming in and sneaking a peek?"

He shrugged. "Ethics, I guess. That and the fact I work long hours. I'm usually the last to leave."

"What about the night Cranston was killed?"

"What about it?"

"Were you the last to leave then?"

"Yes, I was."

"So what happened?"

He shrugged. "He must have come back."

"He had a key?"

"Yes, of course."

"What about the other vice-presidents?"

"What about them?"

"Do they have keys?"

"I would imagine."

"You would imagine?"

"Yes."

"Why is that?"

"What do you mean?"

"With Cranston, it's, Yes, of course. With them, it's, I would imagine."

"In Cranston's case, I *know* he had a key because he got in. The night he was killed. If it weren't for that, I would *assume* he had a key, just like the other two."

"You're assuming now."

"What?"

"That Cranston had a key. You're assuming he had a key because he got in. But what if someone else let him in? Then he wouldn't necessarily have to have a key."

"Who would have let him in?"

"Whoever was here."

"But there was no one here."

"Someone was here."

"How do you know?"

"Because someone killed him."

"Yes, but that someone came later."

"How do you know?"

Jenkins smiled. "Because you don't have a key."

I nodded. "Nice shot."

"Thank you," Jenkins said. "See, if you are the killer, as the police contend, the theory is Cranston was here alone and let you in. Either that or the two of you arrived together. In either case, it's Cranston who had the key."

"I see you've worked this out."

"That's what I do." Jenkins shrugged. "Usually it's only money."

"I don't suppose you'd happen to know *why* I would have killed Cranston Pritchert?"

"Sorry," Jenkins said. "I deal in facts, not theories."

"Well, you could have fooled me."

"Why? I think everything I said about the key is totally logical."

"Maybe so," I said. "But —"

I broke off as Jenkins's eyes widened and I realized he was looking over my left shoulder.

I turned around.

The cops were there.

36.

"Close the door."

Uh-oh. Sergeant Belcher had dismissed the cops from his office. Without summoning a stenographer. That left me alone with the gentleman. And now he was closing the door. This did not bode well.

Belcher got up from his chair, walked around, and sat on the front of his desk. I was seated in front of it in a folding chair. Belcher towered over me, while appearing completely at ease. The effect was chilling.

Belcher tapped his fingers together, pursed his lips. "So," he said. "What am I going to do with you? Here you are, prime suspect in a murder case. Arraigned, on bail, and whaddya do? You return to the murder scene, start interviewing everyone in sight. Now, what is a poor policeman to think?"

I had no idea. When he'd closed the door, I'd expected Belcher to beat me up. The fact he wasn't was somewhat unsettling.

Don't get me wrong — I didn't *want* to get beaten up. Still, I would have liked to have had some idea what the guy was doing.

In light of what I knew about Belcher, his casual routine was somewhat nerve-wracking.

At any rate, I could think of nothing to say. I sat there, held my tongue, waiting for a question that wasn't rhetorical.

I got one. "Would you mind telling me what you were doing at the murder scene?"

"I was talking to the suspects."

Belcher held up his hand. "Oh, no. Sorry. That won't do. You see, *you're* the suspect. These other people are witnesses at best."

I shrugged. "If you say so."

"Oh, but I do. We have a very simple situation here. You've been arraigned for murder. You're lucky to be out walking around. Toward that end, I have brought you in here to offer you a bit of friendly advice."

"Oh?"

"Yes. Since obviously you need it. Let me explain the situation. You are out on bail. You know what bail is? I'll tell you. For a policeman, it is a frustrating thing. You work up a case, arrest a suspect, and what happens? The suspect is allowed to walk around free. After a while, you start saying to yourself, why did I bother? That's one reason why cops get jaded, sour on the system, you know what I mean?"

No, I didn't. And I was getting sicker by the moment. The guy was playing with me, knowing I was a friend of MacAullif. Only I didn't know what the game was. So all I could do was sit and listen.

Belcher held up his finger. "There's one saving grace. About bail, I mean. You know what that is? It's not irrevocable. A judge sets bail, a suspect walks. But . . . something happens to alter the situation, bail can be revoked. And the suspect returned to jail. See what I mean?"

Yes, I did. The picture was finally clear. There was no need for Belcher to elaborate.

He did anyway. "So here's you. Out on bail, and what do you do but go prowling around the murder scene. Talking to the witnesses. Stirring things up. Makes you stop and think. Hey, maybe this guy shouldn't be on bail after all." Belcher stopped, looked at me. "But that's just *my* opinion. What do *you* think?"

Well, that was certainly a direct question. Not one I particularly wanted to answer. Still, there was no avoiding it.

I took a breath. "I'm afraid you've got it backward. The fact is, I didn't kill Pritchert, and I'm trying to find out who did."

Belcher shook his head. "Oh, no. Sorry. Faulty premise. You killed him, all right. Just like you killed the talent agent. The only real question is, which one is it easier to prove? I thought maybe you could help me out here, analyzing this evidence. I just have to tell you, it is so rare when we get so much evidence in one particular case. Or here, in *two* particular cases. The only real question is, which one is stronger?

"Now, what's-his-name — your client — Cranston Pritchert — we got a lot there. We got the gun, but we got the gun in either case. It's unregistered — what a surprise — so we can't trace it to you that way, but it happened to be in your car.

"Aside from that, well, we got you on the scene. You discovered the body, or so you say. A convenient ruse, and not a particularly original one. Hell, practically every wife kills her husband says to the cops, Well, I came home and found him dead."

Belcher shrugged his shoulders. "Then there's the stormy relationship. The guy owed you money, tried to stiff you out of it. Of course, he lied to you up and down the line. First about the blackmail note, then about hiring the talent agent. Enough to drive anyone around the bend."

Belcher chuckled. "And that's just *your* story. That's assuming what you say is true. And who's assuming that? More than likely you and Pritchert are involved in some scam. And doing it together for the cash, which he is attempting to do you out of. It's not surprising you might shoot him."

Belcher clapped his hands together, spread them wide. "But, hey," he said. "That's just Pritchert. The way I understand it, there's a much better case for you doing in the talent agent."

"Oh, come on."

Belcher smiled. "So? Finally got a rise out of you? Good. I'm glad to see you're at least paying attention. Now, the point I'm trying to make is as the evidence mounts, if you keep messing around, there is reason for revoking bail. See that? That's my thesis. That's what I'm trying to sell to the ADA. To get the ADA to sell to the judge. Let's lock the guy up before he destroys all the evidence, so we aren't able to make a case."

Belcher shoved off the edge of the desk, stood there, towering over me. I wondered if he was going to haul off and slug me. If his whole conversational routine had been to lull me into a sense of false security, before cold-cocking me right in the chair. But no, after a moment or two he turned and walked around behind the desk.

"Now, where was I?" Belcher said. "Oh, yeah. The evidence. We were looking at the evidence. The evidence that you killed this Shelly Daniels. Granted, the motive here is not clear. But so far we have only the fairy story you've chosen to tell. Who knows what the actual scam was, and how you fit in. The way it plays best, the three of you were in it together, the other two were crossing you so you rubbed them out." He shrugged. "Too simplistic? Hey, these crimes often are."

Belcher picked up a folder from his desk. "Anyway, I pulled some cases for you, just to give you a thrill."

"Cases?"

"Yeah," Belcher said. He flipped the folder open, took out a paper. "People vs. Parker. John Parker, accused of killing Nancy Fleckstein. Both employees of the same bank. No romantic attachment. Not known to have any personal relationship. Parker clammed up, wouldn't talk. Case went to trial. No motive proven. Only real evidence against him, fact he was stupid enough to hang on to murder weapon, a bloodstained knife. Convicted of murder, sentenced to twenty-five years to life."

Belcher put down the paper, grabbed another. "People vs. Graham. Charlie Graham, accused of killing his neighbor. Again, no motive ever showed, again a conviction in the case."

Belcher grabbed another paper. "People vs. Bright. That's Judy Bright, a hooker killed her john. Why, who knows? To rob him, because he got too rough, because he tried stuff she didn't like, because she didn't like his face, your guess is as good as mine. Lady took the fall, and she's doin' the time."

Belcher flipped the folder down on the desk. "Am I makin' my point? Am I gettin' through to you?"

"I seem to catch the gist."

"Do you? Good. Then you can actually go, 'cause I got no reason to hold you. I just wanted to point out why messing around in this case was probably not an aces move." He held up one finger. "But since you're here — since you took the time to drop by — I suppose I should show you something to make the trip worthwhile."

Belcher picked up another folder, flipped it open. Inside was a stack of eight by tens. He pulled one off the top of the pile, turned it around, held it up for me. "You recognize this?"

I sure did. It was a picture of the upstairs office where Shelly Daniels' body had been found.

I said nothing, sat there, wondering what he was getting at.

"Not talkin', eh?" Belcher said. "Well, I'll

tell you. It's a crime-scene photo. Oh, it's not one of *the* crime-scene photos. They're evidence, I wouldn't have that. But it's a copy of it. A duplicate." He pointed to the stack. "So are these. And they're pretty good pictures. It's amazing what they show."

Belcher picked up another one, held it up. "For instance, here's the body. Does that refresh your memory? That's the woman you're charged with killing. Here's a closeup of the wound." He winced. "Ugly wound. And what have we here? Oh, yes. The woman's desk. Surely you recognize it. Seems to me you sat there going through several hundred resume photos."

Belcher took another photo from the stack. "What's this? Oh, it's a closeup on the desk. And why is that? Oh, I see they've dusted for fingerprints. And there's some right there. And what's this? It's a closeup of the fingerprint. Taken by the crime scene unit, to see if they get a match. And guess what?" Belcher positively beamed. "They got one." He pointed. "That fingerprint right there."

Belcher spread his hands. "And you know what's so significant about that? You claim you've never been to this woman's house before. And yet you left your fingerprint at the crime scene, right in the middle of her desk."

37.

"I can't believe he did that."

MacAullif crinkled up his nose. "What are you, a moron? Everything gotta smack you in the face?" He picked up a cigar, waved it as if it were a pointer. "If it looks like a snake, rattles like a snake, has fangs like a snake, and bites like a snake, once in a while you have to consider the possibility it might be a snake."

"I'm not disputing the fact he did it. I'm just saying it blows my mind."

"A loud fart blows your mind. Let's not go overboard."

"MacAullif —"

"You had no problem believing he planted the gun. Where's your problem believing this?"

"I don't have a problem believing this. I know he did it. Still —"

"Still what? You are the most convoluted fuck I ever met. Can't anything ever be simple and straightforward?"

"All I'm saying is, the gun was different."

"How?"

"The gun he can do himself. He finds the gun, he hides it. He questions me, he finds my car, he plants the gun inside. Hard to believe a cop would do that, but take a crooked cop with a motivation, that's exactly what he'd do. But this other thing — with the fingerprints — to have faked that."

"You can't fake a fingerprint."

"You know what I mean. If that's my fingerprint — and why would he say it was if it wasn't — unless he's just trying to spook me all over the place. But why he would pull a bluff that wouldn't pan out . . ."

"He wouldn't."

"Huh?"

"Trust me, he wouldn't. It's not in character. The guy hates to lose. Even something like that. He wouldn't put himself in the position where he'd have to eventually concede it wasn't so."

"Fine. So say that's my fingerprint. Then the only way it gets on that desk is that afternoon when I sat there going through resume photos."

"Of course."

"Which means that picture was taken some time after that."

"Right again."

"And then integrated with the crime-scene

photos. That's the part that blows my mind. Either this guy had access to the crime-scene evidence, or there are other officers involved."

MacAullif cocked his head. "That's your problem?"

"Exactly."

"Let me tell you a little story."

"Uh-oh."

"No, no. It's short."

"That's not what bothers me."

"I know. I know. But the facts are the facts. You recall me mentioning a cop named Martinez?"

"Don't tell me."

"That's right. Seems the guy got into a little bit of trouble. Hard to imagine, officer of his stature, but there you are. Anyway, I said I'd keep it short, so the short version is he got shot."

"Huh?"

"Yeah. Not that unusual. Cops sometimes get shot. But the circumstances are weird. The way I hear it, he got shot in a drug sting. Nothing strange there — happens a lot. Only thing is, rumor has it he's the one bein' stung."

"Oh, yeah?"

"Yeah. As to who shot him, big question there, still unresolved because the evidence happened to walk."

"What?"

"Yeah. Bullet pulled out of his left thigh somehow disappears between the hospital and the precinct."

"No shit."

"None."

"What's the idea?"

"The idea is they can't match up the gun that shot him."

"I know that. I mean why?"

"This is all speculation."

"Yeah. So?"

"Might have been a cop."

"Oh, yeah?"

"Yeah." MacAullif put up his hand. "You understand it didn't have to be. But the bottom line is, Martinez is involved in a drug shootout with every indication he was on the wrong side. Whether he was shot by a cop — and that's a big secret — or shot by one of his pals that he's scared enough of to want to protect —" MacAullif broke off, shrugged. "It gets pretty convoluted when you're not sure who the good guys are. I was tryin' to make this short. The bottom line is, Martinez shot in the leg, now walks with a limp, and pulls desk duty. Wanna guess where?"

My eyes widened. "Son of a bitch."

"So talk about evidence that jumps around

rings a big double bell. It reminds me that Martinez once had evidence jump around on him. And, irony of ironies, the evidence room happens to be where the son of bitch is workin' now."

I exhaled. Could think of nothing to say.

MacAullif cocked his head. Looked at me. "You don't look too good."

"I don't feel too good. Jesus Christ, Mac-Aullif, what the hell do I do?"

"Well, like I said before, you don't try to prove what you know. You don't start pointing fingers and screaming frame. Because the two of them will just pull back and lay low and you won't be able to prove a thing. Which means the evidence will stand up, leaving you in a slightly unenviable position."

I blinked. "Thanks."

"Hey, I didn't say do nothing, I said do nothing stupid. At least now you know the way the wind blows."

"Big help."

"Hey, it's something. The way you tell it, you're down at the office talkin' to the witnesses, the cops pull you in to Belcher, he hits you with the fingerprint. Is that right?"

"Yeah. So?"

"He gives you a song and dance about messin' around the crime scene. Then he slaps you with the fingerprint evidence, tells you if you keep messin' in the case, that's what you're gonna get."

"That helps me?"

"It tells you one thing."

"What's that?"

"It's not like he said. That he mocked up fingerprint evidence against you because you were messin' with the crime scene. If he had it with him, he faked the damn thing long before you went to call on those people."

"I know that. So?"

"So, it's not just cause and effect. These guys are out to frame you from the word go."

"MacAullif. You're not making my day."

"Maybe not, but it helps to have the danger defined. If it looks like a snake, you might as well know if it *is* a snake."

"It's a snake, MacAullif. Jesus, can you drop out of your lecture mode long enough to help me out here?"

"Advice? You're tellin' me you want advice?"

"I want anything I can get. Frankly, I'm very close to a nervous breakdown and I'm not thinking as clear as I should."

"Yeah, but for you that's normal." MacAullif put up his hand. "Okay, okay. Sorry about that, but the first advice I could give you is, lighten up. It's not like the charge is gonna stick. These guys are trying to hassle you, that's all."

"They're doing a good job."

"I know. And you wanna fight back, which is natural. The problem is, you can't do it. That's what I keep tellin' you, and that's why you're goin' nuts. You gotta let go of it. You gotta say, this is something I can't deal with, I gotta find something I can."

"Like what?"

"The crime. It's like what I was sayin' to you before. Belcher says, in effect, You mess around at the crime scene, I'll frame you with the fingerprints. But that's not the case. He's framin' you anyway, no matter what you do. So you don't worry about that. You wanna investigate, go ahead and investigate."

"It's not just that. He also said he'd use the fact I was messing around to get my bail revoked."

"He can't do it," MacAullif said. "He's got no clout with the judge. Best he can do is put a bug in some ADA's ear. Between you and me, there aren't that many be inclined to listen. No, you wanna investigate, you investigate."

"Investigate what, though? What more can I do?"

MacAullif made a face. "Jesus. You want

me to do all your work for you? Some detective. I'm not even involved, and I know more than you."

"I told you I'm not thinking straight."

"You're not thinkin' at all. You're wallowing in self-pity, and bitchin' about bein' framed."

"On account of you," I said. "I'm being set up and framed on account of a cop hates you."

"So, I owe you," MacAullif said. He shook his head. "It seems like I always owe you. Don't it? Okay, let's take a look at the case."

"How much do you know?"

"About as much as you do. Which isn't a whole hell of a lot. Which tells me one thing. You gotta go way back to the beginning and ask yourself why."

"Why what?"

"Exactly. Why anything? You got a guy comes to you, tells you he's bein' set up. Asks you to find out who did it. When you do, the evidence points to the fact he did it himself. Unfortunately, you cannot question him on this because he is dead. Ditto the woman he set the thing up with. The question arises, did this thing happen at all? Apparently so, because it is confirmed by the bartender, who states that your client was in the bar drinking with this girl. The girl herself confirms this, but her story is suspect. Why? Because when she told it, the principals were alive. Is that right?"

"Yes, it is."

MacAullif nodded, pursed his lips. "One wonders what she might say now that they're dead."

38.

You wanna feel really stupid some time, try ringing people's doorbells lookin' for a girl with big tits. That's not exactly how I phrased it, but that's what I was doing, and it didn't feel good. Particularly since I had it in the back of my mind that *not* finding a girl with big tits was likely to get me convicted of murder.

However, having failed to find the girl's resume photo, I had just one lead. Well, actually two. No, I don't mean her tits. Not exactly.

One lead was the topless bar. Which was a washout. The girl had been hired through the agent, she was paid through the agent, they did not have an address or phone number on her, or even a name other than Marla Melons.

Of course, she had not been to work since the murder. If she had the cops would have found her. The fact they hadn't was unsettling at best.

That left me with my other lead. She had taken a taxi to Third Avenue and 85th Street.

Presumably she was going home. And she hadn't given the taxi driver her exact address, probably a standard precaution after an unfortunate experience. Anyway, that's how I saw it. She was going home, and she told the driver 85th and Third.

I had a further clue. She'd stopped on the northeast corner of Third Avenue and 85th. The way that figured, her apartment was either right there on Third Avenue, or — and this seemed more likely — was on the north side of 85th Street between Second and Third Avenue, and closer to Third. Why? Because 85th Street is one-way going west. So she couldn't have had the cab turn onto 85th even if she'd wanted to. So, if she lived closer to Second, she'd have had the cab go around the block — up Third Avenue to 86th, across and down Second to 85th.

Anyway, from where she had the cab stop, I had to figure her apartment was on the north side of 85th, not too far from Third. So there I was, ringing bells.

Which, actually, didn't take that long.

At the fourth building from the corner, the super said, "Sure, I know her. What's this all about?"

"She may be a witness in a case," I said. I'd already shown him my ID.

The super, middle-aged, balding, and fat,

was affable on the one hand, and not about to piss off his favorite big-titted tenant on the other. "So you say," he said. "You can ring her bell, and if she wants to talk to you, fine. And if she don't, you don't. Is that okay with you?"

"Fine," I said.

There was a row of buttons inside the front door. I'd already pressed the one marked *Super*. Now I pressed the one marked *3B*.

There was no answer.

"I guess she's not at home," the super said.

"Uh-huh. You seen her lately?"

He frowned. "Now that you mention it, can't say as I have."

"Uh-huh," I said. "You got a key?"

He did, but it was no go. There was nothing I could say that was going to make him open that door.

I went to a pay phone, called MacAullif.

Who wasn't glad to hear from me. "Are you nuts?" he said. "You're bringin' this to me?"

"I gotta get in there."

"Sure you do. But with me? If it's pay dirt, we're both up shit creek. So far I got no connection to the case except I show up at the first murder scene. All that establishes is the fact I know you — which is enough to fry your ass — but it don't really involve me.

286

But we go bustin' in there, find the girl, there'll be hell to pay. Suddenly it's a fuckin' conspiracy thing, and I'm lucky if I'm not co-defendant."

"MacAullif —"

"If you think a little, you'll know you don't want me bustin' down any doors."

"So I should call Belcher?"

"Not unless you got a death wish. Try nine one one. It's impersonal, plus you don't gotta look it up."

I did, but it wasn't that easy. The cops weren't about to break down the door on my say-so. Not that they'd have to break it down, with the super having a key, but all the same. No one was going in without an explanation.

I tried, believe me I tried, to tap dance around the situation, but the long and the short of it was, ten minutes after I started talking there came a squeal of brakes and Sergeant Belcher pulled up in front. He hadn't had the same problem as the young lady's taxi — he'd come up Third Avenue and turned onto 85th despite the fact it was one-way.

Belcher was out of the car before it even stopped moving, strode across the pavement to where the cops and the super and I waited on the front steps.

"All right, asshole," he said. "This had better be good."

It was.

In a manner of speaking.

It was her.

And she was dead.

39.

The crime-scene unit got there fast. It was almost as if Belcher'd had 'em on standby the whole time. They came roaring up in their police cars, parked insolently in the middle of the street, and went in. The medical examiner, more discreet, left his car near a handy fireplug.

The police cars drew a crowd. Of course, with the cops all inside there was nothing to see. The people milled around on the sidewalk, talking to themselves, looking at the police cars, looking at the building where the cops had gone, and occasionally looking at me.

I was in the back of Belcher's car. The minute he found the girl, Belcher had dragged me out of the apartment, down the stairs, and out to his car, where he had handcuffed me in the back seat before phoning it in. The handcuff went around my right wrist, through a metal bar in the door, and around my left wrist. The cuffs were tight, the bar in the door was about an inch thick. I wasn't going anywhere.

I sat in the back seat, reflecting on what I'd just seen.

The girl had been crumpled on the floor in the living room of her apartment. She'd apparently been shot in the chest. The light yellow pullover she was wearing was stained with blood. The bullet had penetrated one enormous breast and entered her heart.

It occurred to me that was quite a feat.

A half hour later Belcher came out. He opened the door, slid in next to me on the back seat. Too bad. I'd have preferred him in the front, with the metal screen between us. Still, it didn't seem a good time to argue.

"Okay," Belcher said. "Consider yourself Mirandized. No one's taking this down, but it's no excuse to get cute. Anything you say could dork you, and probably will. On the other hand, you have the right to remain silent. Should you choose to exercise that right, I will beat the living shit out of you. You got it?"

"That seems fairly clear," I said, and wished to hell I was wearing a wire. It was the first time Belcher'd ever let the facade slip. Flat out told it like it was. After waiting so long to hear it, it was almost a relief.

"Good," Belcher said. "Now, I want a straight answer. How'd you happen to find the girl?"

"Just detective work."

Belcher's face darkened. "I said a straight answer."

"You did, and that's it. I found her through detective work. I deduced where she was. You want me to tell you how I did it?"

"I would strongly advise it."

I jerked my thumb. "The night I followed her home she took a cab to that corner. I figured she either lived on Third, or a few doors in on 85th. I figured the cab didn't turn on 85th 'cause it was one-way. I figured she lived on the north side of the street, 'cause the cab stopped on the northeast corner. I figured she had to live closer to Third, or she'd have had the cab go around to Second."

Belcher blinked. "You expect me to buy that?"

"I don't expect anything. I'm just telling you what happened."

"How come you don't remember any of this the first time you told your story?"

"Not a case of remembering. I told all the facts before. This is just what I figured out from them."

"Oh, sure," Belcher said. "Days later you make this miraculous deduction. What happened, you figure it was time we found the body?"

"I figured it was time we found the girl. I had no way of knowing she was dead."

"No, of course not," Belcher said. "Super says you asked if he'd seen her lately. You implied there was something wrong and asked him to open the door."

"He *hadn't* seen her lately. And she hadn't been to work."

"So you decided she was dead?"

"Or skipped out. In which case, she was probably involved."

"Right," Belcher said, sarcastically. "You thought she'd skipped out. You were hopin' to get into her apartment to find some signs of flight."

"Frankly, that would have been a relief. I was afraid of something like this."

"Why?"

"Because she was involved in the scam. And everyone involved in the scam is dead."

"What scam?"

"I have no idea."

"Yeah," Belcher said. "You wanna try again?"

"Huh?"

"Give it to me again. How you found the girl."

"I told you how I found the girl."

"No, you didn't. You gave me some fairy story about cabs and one-way streets. I'm askin' you point-blank, how you knew that body was there."

"I *didn't* know it was there."

"Yeah, sure," Belcher said. "How's your math?"

"Huh?"

"How's your math? You pretty good at arithmetic?"

I blinked at him. "Arithmetic?"

"Yeah. Tell me, punk, what's two plus one?"

I blinked again. "What?"

"Two plus one. Two plus one. Whatsa matter, these too hard for you? I'm tryin' to figure two plus one."

"Would three be the answer you're looking for?"

Belcher pointed at me. "Harvard man. I knew with a little prompting, you could make the grade. Well, guess what? I talked to the medical examiner, and guess what killed the broad?"

"It looked to me like she was shot."

"Good guess. She was indeed shot. Once. So says the ME. Pow. Right through the silicone goodie into the heart. Which solves my math problem for me."

"I beg your pardon?"

"Oh," Belcher said. "But you didn't know that. Because you're not indicted yet, so your lawyer isn't privy to the evidence. But that gun we found in your car — the one that killed those other two — funny thing is, there were three bullets missing from it. We could only find two, you know. No matter how hard we searched."

Belcher nodded. Grinned. "I was gettin' to think we'd never find the third."

40.

"I have a big problem."

MacAullif looked at me. "Are you kidding me? You have no problem at all. Here you are, arraigned on your third murder inside of a week, and you're out walking around."

"I have a hell of an attorney."

"That I know. But it seems to me we've had this conversation before."

"I know. And I wasn't looking forward to having it again. Only it seems your pal Belcher happens to have hit the trifecta. The lucky son of a bitch frames me with a gun, and it just so happens it killed three people. Now, what are the odds of that?"

"In this case, pretty damn good. But this time there's a saving grace."

"What's that?"

"Belcher didn't do anything."

"I beg your pardon?"

"I mean to frame you. Belcher didn't fuck around." MacAullif put up his hand. "Put aside the fact he framed you with the gun to begin with — here's another shot from it, that's fortuitous, that's something Belcher

295

couldn't have counted on. What I mean is, he planted nothing at *this* murder scene. At least, from what you say. I mean, you didn't touch anything in that apartment he's gonna be able to throw back at you later on?"

"I didn't touch a thing."

"How long were you in there?"

"No time at all. He found the body, hauled me right out."

MacAullif nodded. "So, he couldn't fake a fingerprint photo. He could still get you with a lift."

"Huh?"

"A fingerprint lift. You know, you lift the fingerprint, put it on a card, label where it's from. He could take a print from somewhere else, say it came from there."

"You think he'd do that?"

"No, I don't. It's too clumsy, too obvious. There'd be photos of everything else. Here's the one fingerprint isn't photographed in place, shows up on a lift. Even a zealous young ADA's gonna start thinkin' frame."

I waved my hand impatiently. "Fine, Mac-Aullif. What's the difference? You'll pardon me, but I'm framed for two murders, so what if I'm framed for three? If it ever got that far, the ballistics evidence would be enough to fry me. Never mind any corroborating fingerprint. If they can get any conviction of any kind, even obstructing justice, in one, they throw it in my face in the other. By the time I get to the third one, I'm convicted before it begins. Now, I happen to be having a nervous breakdown here, and I'd appreciate your help."

"It seems to me we've played this scene too."

"Yeah, we did, MacAullif. And what did you advise me to do? If you'll recall? Who did you say might shed some light on the situation?"

"I suggested you talk with the girl. At the time, it seemed like good advice. I admit, it doesn't sound so hot now."

"I'm glad you concede the point."

"Only to a degree. I mean, let's be honest here. Is the idea something happened to the girl really that new? You wanna tell me that never crossed your mind?"

"I was concerned about her, yeah. But the idea that she'd been shot with my gun hadn't really dawned on me."

"Oh, now it's *your* gun?"

"Well, it was in my car. Everyone else thinks it's my gun, why should I be different?"

"You're getting yourself all worked up here."

"I'm not getting anything. I mean, Jesus

Christ. I'm on a case here where I didn't get paid, I've been framed for murder three times over, every lead I get blows up in my face, and everyone I wanna talk to is dead. Everyone else I talk to, I get arrested. Now, you wanna tell me why I shouldn't be upset?"

"I wouldn't even wanna begin."

"Good. 'Cause there's another thing that's got me upset, and I'm not sure I understand it. I wanna run it by you. See how it goes."

MacAullif blinked. "You mean there's something *else?*"

"In a way."

"Well, you think you could figure out *what* way? Because, believe it or not, I happen to have my own case load."

"If I'm boring you, I can go."

"Don't be an asshole. I'm just tellin' you I'm pressed for time, so, whatever it is, stop dancing around and come out with it."

"Okay, but it's hard, 'cause it's just a feeling."

"Oh, Jesus."

"No, it's real, MacAullif. Christ, didn't you ever go on a feeling?"

"Don't get me started."

"Okay, here's the bit. After we find the girl, Belcher comes out and questions me. And the gloves are off and the mask is down. No pretense, he's telling me straight out I'm fucked. And that he's the one fuckin' me."

"Yeah," MacAullif said. "Well, if it's just you and him, so what?"

"Exactly," I said. "It's what I've been waiting for. For him to drop the pretense and acknowledge what's going on. Instead of playing games. So he does, and that's fine."

"And that bothers you?"

"No, like I say, it's what I was waiting for. But *after* he does, he starts grilling me about the girl. And everything he's saying is like I killed her."

"Yes, of course. If it's the same gun, now he's framing you for that too."

"Yeah, I know. But that's not it. The thing is — and this is what blew my mind — he's questioning me like he really thought I did it. You see what I mean?"

MacAullif frowned. "Not exactly. What are you trying to say?"

"Just that. I got the impression, when Belcher was questioning me about the girl, that he thought I really might have done it. Which doesn't compute somehow. Not with him framing me." I shrugged my shoulders, spread my arms. "I mean, if he's framing me, he *knows* I'm innocent because he knows I'm being framed."

MacAullif thought that over. "Yes and no."

I groaned. "Oh, great. You wanna elaborate on that?"

"Yes, he knows he's framin' you," Mac-Aullif said. "But that don't mean you didn't do it. I mean, try the concept. Belcher shows up at the crime scene. Finds the murder weapon, shoves it in his pocket. When you show up, he plants it in your car. He does that to frame you. But he has no idea who actually committed the crime. So, it could be you just as well as anybody else. In his own mind, the fact he's framed you doesn't make you any less likely a suspect. You see what I mean?"

"I suppose so."

"Hey, you don't have to *like* these theories. I just throw them out for what they're worth. But you want an explanation for him grillin' you about the girl. The way I see it, that's it."

"You think he seriously considers me a suspect? A real suspect, I mean?"

"I don't think he did when he framed you. But the way things stand now? Think about it. Ever since he framed you, all you've done is run around meddling in the case. Granted, it's a no-win situation — you're framed, so you gotta meddle, and meddling makes you look guilty. With all your runnin' around talking to witnesses. And then you lead him right to the girl and she's dead. Well, hell, you'd start lookin' like a pretty good suspect to me too."

"Thanks a lot."

"You can see that, can't you?"

"I suppose so. It just bothers me."

"Hell, everything bothers you. You're an analyst's dream. If I were a shrink, I'd make a fortune off you, retire to the Bahamas."

"I haven't got a fortune."

"Too bad. Is that it now? Or you got another homicide you'd like to throw at me?"

"I was hoping for some help with this one."

"You were hopin' that yesterday. I give you the girl, and this is the thanks I get."

"She wasn't in the best condition."

"There are no guarantees."

"You don't have another suggestion?"

"What, I'm supposed to solve this case? You don't have any theories of your own?"

"I got theories. It's just the more people dead, the harder they are to confirm."

"So, what's your theory?"

"I go back to square one. Cranston Pritchert claims he's being set up. Apparently, that's a lie. But what if it's not? What if at least part of what he told me is true?"

"What if it is?"

"Then what was the original scam? That's

the question I need answered. That's what I hoped the girl would know. With her dead, it gets tough."

"You were talkin' theory."

"Right. Cranston Pritchert claimed he was being set up to make him lose the proxy fight. It seems far-fetched to me, but I got nothing else to play with. So I had my wife buy a share of stock."

"Why?"

"So I could attend the stockholders meeting."

"When's the meeting?"

"Last night."

"You didn't go?"

"I was in court. Bein' arraigned on my third homicide."

"Oh. Right. So, what happened?"

"I don't know. I was gonna go down, check it out. Only the last time I went by there I got arrested."

"Yeah. So?"

"I figured if I did it again, you'd tell me I was a total moron."

"You *are* a total moron."

"See what I mean."

"I assume you're going to do this whether I advise you to or not?"

"Unless you got a better idea."

"Oh, great," MacAullif said. "I either solve

the case for you, or endorse your line of action."

"Hey. That sounds pretty good. I couldn't have said it better myself."

"At least you're in a better mood."

"I'm *not* in a better mood. I'm losing it and getting giddy. If I should start laughing hysterically, it would not mean I was happy."

"I'll bear that in mind. On the other hand, if I should tell you to get the fuck out of my office, it would not mean I was angry. It would just mean I was through with the conversation, and had business back on planet earth."

I got up. "You want me to let you know how this goes?"

"Don't bother." MacAullif winced. "I got a feeling I'll hear."

41.

"The first time I talked to you, I got arrested."

"That was not my fault."

"Oh, really?"

Jack Jenkins put up his hands. "It wasn't me. I mean, come on. You were here. Did I call anyone? Or leave the room at any time while you were here?"

"No."

"There you are."

"But you knew I was in the office. Calling on the other two."

"How would I know that?"

"How would you know anything? It's not that large a suite of offices. Are you telling me you *didn't* know?"

"I really don't recall."

"Oh, come on. A precise guy like you. I bet you recall perfectly well."

Jenkins smiled, put his hands on the desk. "This is silly. Did you really come in here with a chip on your shoulder trying to find out if I turned you in? Is that why you're here?"

"Actually, it isn't."

"I didn't think so." Jenkins took a manila folder off his desk, flipped it open. Took out a piece of paper. "This came in yesterday. Certificate of stock. In the name of Stanley Hastings. I'm wondering if that might be you."

"My name is Stanley Hastings."

"I'm aware that it is. Are you the Stanley Hastings who purchased this stock?"

"Actually, it was my wife who purchased the stock. I believe she did it through a broker."

"I'm sure she did. So, this stock is yours. I thought it was. I rather expected to see you at the stockholders meeting."

"Something came up."

"So I understand. You got arrested again. Without the slightest help from me."

"Now, there's a thought."

Jenkins frowned. "What?"

"I hadn't really considered you a suspect until you said that. I guess it's just my nature. You tell me you had nothing to do with it, so I immediately think you did. It's the self-serving declaration — it always sets me off."

Jenkins frowned, cocked his head. "Are you all right? You're not making a lot of sense."

"I found another body yesterday, got charged with my third homicide. All in all, it's been a rather bad week."

"The girl you found — was she the one?"

"The one?"

"You know. The one Cranston was looking for. Was it her?"

"It was her, all right. What do you know about it?"

He shrugged. "Only what I've heard. From you and from the cops. Cranston himself never let on. Secretive type. Pain in the ass. Well, I guess you know."

"Yeah. So, you wanna tell me about it?"

"What?"

"The stockholders meeting. The one I couldn't go to."

"Oh. So you don't know."

"What?"

"What happened."

"I don't know a damn thing. So, who won? Rothstein or Dunbar?"

"Neither one."

"What?"

"That's right."

"So who's the new chairman of the board?"

"Amy Greenberg."

I looked at him. Blinked. "I beg your pardon?"

"Amy Greenberg is the chairman of the board."

"Whoa. Time out. Flag on the play. You mind telling me how that happened?"

"Simplest thing in the world. And the fact is, I never saw it coming." He shook his head. "Asleep at the switch. All of us were. The next thing you know, disaster."

"Help me out here," I said. "I wasn't there. How'd the meeting go?"

"Fine, at first. No hint of trouble. Just like any other stockholders meeting. Except that Cranston and Philip weren't there."

"Who was?"

"Me, Marty, and Kevin. Miriam Pritchert, there to vote Cranston's shares. And Amy Greenberg there to vote Philip's."

"What happened?"

"Well, we're about to start the meeting when Amy Greenberg comes in. All bubbly and schoolgirlish. I mean, from her attitude you wouldn't know her grandfather'd died. Let alone a board member'd been murdered. But no, she's all, This is a stockholders meeting, what am I supposed to do?" He grimaced. "Damn. See, she's even got me talking like her. That girl screws up your head. Anyway, I wasn't sure whether to expect her. I had talked to her on the phone, of course, advised her how things were. I knew the other two were courting her votes, but she was being coy. I told her she had to either show up herself and vote the stock, or give someone her proxy. Well, like I say, she wasn't giving up her proxy, so I said she should come. So she said she would, but that didn't mean anything, because she's so ditsy she wasn't even clear on the day. So I don't know whether to expect her or not. Actually, she's late and we're about to start the meeting. And then she shows up like a bolt out of the blue."

"And what happened?" I said, somewhat impatiently.

"So, we start the meeting and I count out the proxies."

"You hadn't counted them before?"

"No. I thought I told you. I don't like to do that. It puts too much pressure on me, knowing who's got what. I always add 'em up right there on the spot. So that's what I did."

"So, what happened?"

He shrugged. "What happened was totally unexpected, on the one hand. On the other hand, if I thought about it, it was perfectly natural. See, you got stockholders all over the country. And they're not really involved. You know how it is. Half the business reports they get, they throw 'em away. So the people sending the proxies in, a lot of 'em don't even know Philip Greenberg is dead. They just fill in his name as a matter of course. He's the chairman of the board, they always give him their proxy. So they give it to him again. Not all of 'em, but a lot."

"Do you mean . . . ?"

"Sure I do. Amy Greenberg is there, voting Philip Greenberg's stock. Philip Greenberg gets a shitload of proxies. Enough that, coupled with his personal holdings, constitutes a majority. Suddenly Amy Greenberg's in the driver's seat, voting over fifty percent of the stock."

Jenkins threw up his hands. "So what does she do? She giggles, she says something idiotic, like her grandfather would have liked her to keep it in the family, and she votes herself in as chairman of the board."

"Good lord."

"Good lord is right. Now, just between you and me, I don't know if it makes any difference. Too soon to tell. I mean, is she going to be personally involved in the business, or is she just going to go off and play golf? If she wants to just run around being a playgirl, fine. On the other hand, it's like having an infant in charge. A superbaby with unlimited powers. I mean, if she wants to start firing people, changing things, making policy, she can. She's the goddamn chairman of the board."

"What a mess." I jerked my thumb. "Is she here now?"

"No. Thank goodness for small favors. She breezed in first thing this morning, took a look around Philip's office, and breezed out again, saying she'd be back next week with an interior decorator. As if all there was to running a business was how your office looked."

"That doesn't exactly inspire confidence."

"No kidding. So, if I seem a little indifferent to your problems, it happens I have problems of my own." Jenkins picked up a sheet of paper from his desk. "You know what I've been working on this morning? My resume. I don't know which way the wind blows, but I'm not taking any chances. First sign of trouble, I'm bailing out."

I exhaled. "Jesus Christ. Look, I know this is a disaster, and it's hard for you to think of anything else, but try this on for size. If this hadn't happened — if the proxies hadn't come in for Philip Greenberg . . ."

"Yeah?"

"Who would have won?"

"What?"

"Look, Mr. Jenkins. Aside from thinkin' I'm a murderer, you seem like a decent enough guy. So try this concept on. Say I didn't kill Cranston Pritchert. Say he got killed because of the proxy fight, because someone was setting him up to lose. And say things didn't work out the way they did — people sending in their proxies for Philip Greenberg. Which of the two would have won?"

"Between Marty and Kevin?"

"Right."

He frowned. "That's hard to say. I mean, the people who gave proxies for Greenberg, who knows who they would have supported. There's really no way to tell."

"Fine," I said. "Never mind the Greenberg proxies. What about everything else?"

"What about it?"

"Well, let's put it this way. Who came in second?"

He cocked his head. "I'm not sure I should tell you that."

"Hey, I'm a stockholder. If I'd made the meeting, would I have known?"

"It wasn't a secret ballot."

"There you are."

Jenkins frowned. He thought a moment. "Marty Rothstein."

"Oh?"

He nodded. "Rothstein came in second. By a fairly wide margin. Miriam Pritchert went for him. Not that it made any difference, what with Amy having over fifty percent of the vote. But for what it's worth, Rothstein was second."

"So Miriam Pritchert went for Rothstein, huh?"

"Yes, she did. Why?"

"I dunno." I shrugged. "I just had a hunch she might."

42.

"You gonna call the cops again?"

Marty Rothstein frowned. "What do you mean again?"

"It wasn't you who called them last time?"

"Why would I do that?"

"I dunno. But I find people who answer a question with a question are often attempting to evade."

Rothstein frowned again. "This is getting nowhere. I have little patience this morning, and I don't really feel like talking."

"That's understandable, after the stockholders meeting last night."

His head came up. "Who you been talking to?"

"Hey, I'm a stockholder. These things affect me too."

"You're what?"

"I'm a stockholder. I own stock. I was going to the meeting, but something came up. Cranston's topless dancer turned up dead. Or hadn't you heard?"

"Yeah. I heard. I also heard you were involved."

I waved it away. "Oh, no. That's the type of line the cops put out to keep the real killer from knowing what they're doing." I crossed my fingers, held them up. "Actually, the cops and me are like that."

He frowned, squinted at me. "You're acting kind of strange."

"You know, you're the third person today who's told me that. I'm going to start to get a complex."

"Uh-huh," Rothstein said. He stood up. "Would you excuse me a moment? If this is going to take time, I have some instructions for my secretary."

"Aw, sit down, Rothstein," I said. "You wanna call the cops, call the cops. You don't have to pussyfoot around about it. Just call the cops and say I'm here." I leaned back in my chair, crossed my legs. "They probably know I'm here anyway. They're probably following me around. I seem to be the best source of information they've got. I led 'em to Cranston. I led 'em to the girl. Now I'm leadin' 'em to you. Call 'em up and get 'em down here. Maybe we can all have a little chat."

Rothstein looked at me a moment. Blinked. Sat down.

Well. There was something to be said for acting slighty manic.

I smiled. "See? Much better, just you and me. Now, let's talk about what happened last night. The way I hear it, a little girl comes in and steals your job."

Rothstein's face darkened. "You don't understand."

"I know. It's a business matter, and business matters leave me cold. That's why I need all the help I can get. So, you wanna explain it to me in simple, layman's terms, well, maybe I got a chance. The way I see it, you bet on the wrong horse. You locked up the widow Pritchert, and the Greenberg girl did you in."

"It wasn't like that."

"Wasn't like what?"

"The way you make it sound."

"Well, how was it then?"

"She had to vote her stock for someone. I personally think I was the best choice."

"Oh, sure," I said. "Were you having an affair with her *before* her husband died?"

Rothstein came out of his chair again. "You son of a bitch!"

I held up my hand. "I admit, a very rude thing to say. But being a murder suspect has robbed me of some of the social graces. If I go to trial, your relationship with the widow Pritchert may be material to my defense. Just thought you should be prepared."

Rothstein sat down again. When he stood up, his face had been flushed. Now it looked decidedly pale.

"You'd go after me?" he said. "You'd actually go after me?"

I shrugged. "A case like this, they look for reasonable doubt. You're about as reasonable as they come." I put up my hand again. "But I have no intention of letting this go to trial. That's why I'm here. That's why I'm asking questions. I didn't do it, and I'm trying to find out who did. If I can, I'll nail 'em. If I can't, I might have to frame you."

Rothstein blinked. "What?"

"In a manner of speaking. Someone framed me, I have to fight back. But, please don't get upset. It's not like I'd plant any clues, tell any lies. Still, your relationship with Miriam Pritchert could be misconstrued. You see what I mean?"

He blinked again. "You're threatening me?"

"Heaven forbid. I'm asking for help. I'm telling you what I *don't* want to do. So you can help me not to do it."

Rothstein couldn't seem to think of a thing to say.

"Let's start over," I said. "No threats one way or another. No one calling the cops, no one embarrassing you. Just you and me, a

316

couple of stockholders, takin' it easy and shootin' the shit. So, what'd you think of the meeting last night?"

Rothstein gulped. "Jesus Christ."

I nodded. "Good assessment. Now, here's the thing. What do you think Amy Greenberg's game is — she vote herself in for a lark, or does she mean to make trouble?"

"I have no idea."

"Me, either. As a stockholder, I'm rather concerned. But at least I don't work here. You sending resumes out?"

Rothstein looked guarded. "As you say, it's too soon to know."

"Uh-huh," I said. "A bit of a problem. A babe in charge who's immune to your charms. I can't think of anything worse. So, tell me something. Did it surprise you?"

"What?"

"The way the proxies went."

Rothstein exhaled. "I'll say. It never occurred to me. And yet, it makes sense. People used to writing in Greenberg do it as a matter of course. Still, who would have thought that so many would."

"And there's nothing to be done?" I said. "I mean, if these people really didn't know. Assuming they wouldn't have given *her* the vote — is there a way to let them vote again?"

The guarded look came into Rothstein's eyes again.

"Oh," I said. "Of course. There *is*, and you've considered it. You're considering it now. But you don't want anyone to know it."

Rothstein exhaled. "Jesus," he said.

I nodded. "Of course. Because you're afraid Amy Greenberg might find out. And if she found out, she'd fire you. Which would be a pretty effective answer to your demand for a recount."

Rothstein said nothing.

"On the other hand," I went on, "if you just shut up, and work quietly behind her back, you can line up enough stockholders to take control of the next meeting and vote her out." I looked at him. "How'm I doin' so far?"

Rothstein ran his hand through his hair. Somehow, it seemed thinner than when the conversation had started. "I thought you knew nothing about business."

"I don't. I happen to know a little bit about human nature. Well, now. We've talked about everything else. Let's try the sixty-four-thousand-dollar question. You happen to shoot Cranston Pritchert?"

"No, I did not."

"I'm glad to hear it," I said. I looked him up and down. Cocked my head. "If that happens to be true, it might just be the only thing that you and I have in common."

43.

I found Amy Greenberg lounging in her front yard in a bikini bathing suit. She didn't look bad.

"So," I said. "This is what being chairman of the board is like."

She sprang up when she saw me, took a few steps toward the front door. "You stay away from me," she said. "You come any closer, I'll call the cops."

"Sure, why should you be different?" I said. "Ask for Sergeant Belcher. He's the one handling the case."

She crinkled up her nose. "What?"

"I realize since the last time I talked to you I've become a bit of a persona non grata. That's the problem with being a murder suspect. People snub you. Dinner invitations fall off. You just get no respect."

She cocked her head. "Are you all right? You're acting kind of weird."

Well, that made it unanimous.

"Sorry," I said. "I'm not having one of my better days. So let me tell you what I wanted to talk about. I happen to be a stockholder in Philip Greenberg Investments."

She blinked. "What?"

"Yeah. I was going to the meeting last night, but I got held up. Too bad. I understand it was a honey."

"What do you want?"

"I was going to ask you the same thing. What is it you want? I mean, chairman of the board — why do you want to be chairman of the board? Do you want to run the company, or is it just for fun?"

Her face darkened. "Why is it, when I want to do something, everyone's all, Why do you want to do that? Grampa was the same way. I go to see him, I'm like, Tell me about your business. And he's like, Why would you want to know that? It's like, you're a girl, you don't need to know."

Oh, great. Here I was, once again, tiptoeing on dangerous sexist ground.

"I admit that attitude is wrong," I said. "But speaking of you, personally — do you have an interest in the company? Were you planning on running it yourself? I mean, what's the deal?"

"Why shouldn't I run it myself?"

"I didn't say you shouldn't. I was just asking if you intended to."

"That's none of your business."

"Oh, but it is. Like I said, I'm a stockholder. I'm deeply concerned in the interests of Philip Greenberg Investments."

Amy Greenberg didn't seem convinced. "I'm warning you," she said. "You get out of here."

I took a step backward, spread my arms. "I am unarmed and not dangerous. I am the least threatening person imaginable. I seek only conversation. If you want, I'll go call you from a pay phone on the corner. Though I don't happen to see one, and that would be rather stupid. Now, is it *me* you're afraid of, or what I might say?"

Her eyes flashed. "You want to tell me, like, I'm not smart enough to run the company, I don't have to listen to that."

"That's not what I want to tell you."

"Yeah? Well, what then?"

"I understand Miriam Pritchert was at the meeting."

"Yeah. So?"

"Do you know her?"

"No. Why should I?"

"What about Marty Rothstein?"

"What about him?"

"Do you know him?"

"Don't be silly. He works for the company."

"I thought you took no interest in the company until your grandfather died."

"Yeah, but I told you, they were all after me, trying to get me to vote my stock."

"Un-huh. And what did you think of Miriam Pritchert?"

Amy made a face. "Are you kidding? She voted for Marty Rothstein. Like, we women ought to stick together. But no, she's all, I think Cranston would have wanted it this way. Like hell. Like he would have liked what's going on."

"What's going on?"

"I'm not saying anything. But she shouldn't have voted for Marty Rothstein."

"Uh-huh. You ticked off enough at Rothstein to fire him?"

She frowned. "Who told you that?"

"Is it true?"

"Hey, like, where do you get these ideas?"

"I'm trying to figure out the case."

"Case? What case?" Reminded, she backed away again. "That's right. You're a killer. I'm standing here, talking to a killer."

"Not at all."

She held up her hand. "You stay there. Stay right there. No, like, what am I saying? You *don't* stay there. You get in your car and you go. Asking me questions. Saying you're a stockholder. All, What are you going to do now, little girl. Well, I'll tell you what I'm going to do now. I'm going to go inside my house. And I'm going to lock my door and I'm going to look out my window. And if you're not gone, I'm going to call the police. Now, how do you like that?"

I didn't like that.

I got the hell out of there.

44.

Mary Mason beeped me on my way back from Scarsdale, and when I called in she had a message from Sergeant MacAullif. That was a switch — the guy actually wanted to talk to me. I hung up on Mary, made the call.

"Better get in here," MacAullif said. "Shit's hit the fan."

And hung up.

Nice guy. I had to either call him back — and probably have him hang up again — or drive all the way to Manhattan to find out. Not that I really wanted to find out. I mean, I'm on the hook for three murders, now what's the *bad* news?

I drove downtown, got a meter in the municipal lot. My lucky day. I went up to MacAullif's office to see just how lucky.

MacAullif was seated at his desk looking gloomy. Actually, he was looking the way he always looked — it was just that today it translated as gloom.

"What's up?" I said.

MacAullif looked at me, cocked his head.

"You have a bad memory for faces, don't you?"

I gawked at him. "Hey, what is it, shit on Stanley Hastings day? I don't have enough troubles, you gotta point out my shortcomings?"

"That *is* your trouble," MacAullif said. "Your eye's none too good."

"Yeah? So what?"

MacAullif picked up an eight by ten from his desk, passed it over to me. "You recognize this?"

I turned the picture around, took a look.

It was a head shot of a young woman. Black and white. High contrast. Dramatic. An attractive woman, with straight dark hair, high cheekbones, bright eyes. An excellent resume photo.

"Well?" MacAullif said.

I shook my head. "Can't place it."

MacAullif exhaled disgustedly. "I'm not surprised. Well, the cops can. They can place it just fine. And just wait till you hear *where* they place it."

I grimaced, put up both hands. "MacAullif. Please. What the hell's going on?"

"What's going on is you're taking it on the chin again, and this time it's partly your fault."

"My fault?"

"Yeah. For bein' such an unobservant, dumb schmuck." MacAullif pointed. "You know who this is? You might if the picture was full figure and you could see the boobs."

My eyes widened. "Are you telling me . . ."

MacAullif grimaced. "Schmuck. What a schmuck. Yeah, it's her. Who the hell would you think it would be? But, yes, that happens to be a resume photo of the late Laura Martin."

"Laura Martin?"

"What, they didn't get her right name at the arraignment? Gee, maybe you can get it thrown out for that. But, what, you think her real name was Marla Melons? Well, it ain't. It ain't the other name she gave you either — what was it? — Lucy Blaine? No, her name's Laura Martin and, believe it or not, that is her."

"What's the punch line, MacAullif? You said the shit hit the fan."

"It did. And this is it. This photo didn't recognize. But the fact is, you've seen it before."

"Where?"

MacAullif held up one finger. "Ah. There's the whole ball game. According to the cops, you saw it in her apartment about the same time you popped her."

"What!"

"See the problem?" MacAullif said. "Let me show you how it is." He picked up another picture from his desk. "Take a look at this."

That one I recognized. It was a picture of the young woman — Marla Melons, Lucy Blaine, Laura Martin, or whatever her name was — lying in her living room in a pool of blood, just as Sergeant Belcher and I had found her.

"See that?" MacAullif said. "Crime-scene unit photo, right? Now, never mind the body, look at the bookcase in the back."

I looked at the picture again. The body was lying in front of a couch. To the left of the couch was a bookcase.

"So what?" I said.

"Second shelf from the bottom. Left side. What do you see there?"

I looked. My eyes widened.

"Resume photos?"

"Bingo, right on the button," MacAullif said. He handed me another picture. "Here's a closeup on the bookcase. If you look there, you can see they're not only resume photos, they're *this* resume photo."

"Yeah, well, so what?" I said. "I told you I didn't see it."

"Yeah, but you told me wrong," MacAullif said.

I looked at him. "What?"

"Guess whose fingerprint is on the resume photo on the top of that pile?"

My mouth dropped open. I blinked. My head felt very light.

"No way," I said.

"Oh, yeah," MacAullif said. "You want me to tell you the way? It's pretty fuckin' easy when you stop to think about it."

"MacAullif . . ."

"You want me to tell you how it is? It starts with, you don't know your ass from a hole in the ground. You look at this picture, you don't know it's the girl. And that's the key — if you don't know it now, you didn't know it then. I know that for sure. Sergeant Belcher must have figured it was a good bet."

"What are you saying?"

"I'm telling you how it happened. I'm telling you the only way it works. Your fingerprint is on that photo, which means you've seen it before. Remember when we were sayin' Belcher couldn't frame you on this one, because you hadn't touched anything, and how could he frame you with a fingerprint lift? Well, this is better than a lift. You take an identical piece of evidence from one place and drop it in another."

"You mean . . . ?"

"Sure. You're at the talent agent's going over resume photos. And guess what? When you look at photos, you touch 'em. You saw this at the talent agent's, but you're a moron, it don't mean nothin' to you, so you leave it there with the rest. Then you find this dead girl. Belcher looks at the crime scene, sees the stack of resume photos, and, bingo, light bulb goes on. A photo like that, why wouldn't her talent agent have it? Well, what if she did and the photo was different enough from the girl to have been overlooked." MacAullif snapped his fingers. "Bingo. Jackpot. Perfect frame."

"Wait a minute, wait a minute," I said. "Even if Belcher made that leap of logic, it took me hours to go through those photos. How would he have the time?"

"Easy," MacAullif said. "You didn't know what you were lookin' for. He did. Laura Martin. I don't know about the photos at her home, but weren't the files in her office alphabetical?"

I sighed. "Christ, yes."

"There you are. He goes to her office, looks under *M*. Ten minutes later he's lookin' at this. He dusts it for fingerprints, lookin' for yours. Bingo, he gets a match."

I rubbed my head. "I'm starting to feel sick."

"I don't blame you," MacAullif said. "You know how I got this stuff? You know how it came to me? Well, I know this ADA, good guy, who happens to know the ADA handling this. Belcher came in with the shit after your arraignment went down, saying new evidence had come in and they should push to rescind bail. Same old song. Old news, and not gonna happen, but there you are. Belcher would like nothing better than to go out and drag you back in handcuffs again. Because I'm stickin' up for you, so gettin' you would humiliate me. That's the way he sees it, that's the way he'll play it, that's the way it's gonna be. Meanwhile, he's runnin' around manufacturing evidence like there was no tomorrow."

"Jesus Christ."

"Yeah. So how'd it go?"

"What?"

MacAullif jerked his thumb. "You and them. The boys at the company. Did you get arrested or what?"

"No, I didn't."

"Well, that's something. But you went up there?"

"I sure did."

I filled MacAullif in on the events of the

afternoon. As he listened, the frown lines on his forehead grew deeper and deeper.

"So," he said. "The babe gets it all. Interesting."

"Yeah. But not what I was looking for."

"How do you know it's not? She could be the answer just fine. You look at the thing, you say, who gained the most?"

"Yeah. But not from his death. The shares went to the widow, who voted the other way."

"Yeah, but could she know that?"

"She doesn't have to know that. She'd have to think some way they'd come to her."

"Maybe she did."

"Unlikely. Plus, if it's her, what's the original scam?"

"How should I know?"

I made a face. "Well, it's your damn theory, MacAullif. I mean, you wanna throw these things out, you can at least defend them. But if it's her, how does setting up Cranston Pritchert make sense? What, does she think he's her most likely rival? How does she know that? She knows nothing about the company. Of course, that would explain how she could get such a wrong idea. But even so. Of all people, why the hell hustle him?"

MacAullif spread his arms. "Once again,

we have no facts from which to make deductions. You have a brand-new development here to check out. Which is good. This morning you were upset 'cause all you had was a dead girl. Now you got a live one."

"It's not the same thing."

"You're hard to please. So anyway, you did all that and didn't get arrested?"

"That's right."

"Interesting. You talk to the same people as last time?"

"Actually, no. I talked to Rothstein — that's the one made the play for the widow — and Jenkins — he's the bookkeeper. I didn't talk to Kevin Dunbar."

"Why not?"

"I dunno. When this thing came up about the girl, Amy Greenberg, I wanted to talk to her."

"Uh-huh. And how was she?"

"Hostile. She kept backing away and threatening to call the cops."

MacAullif shook his head. "Tough being a murder suspect."

"You wouldn't believe. Anyway, that's why I didn't talk to Dunbar. Besides, I heard the story twice already. I couldn't think of a question to ask him I hadn't asked the others."

MacAullif nodded. "In other words, you fucked up."

"Hey."

"Anyway, it's interesting. You talked to everyone but him and didn't get arrested. Can we conclude it was him who called the cops the first time?"

"I dunno. Can we?"

"Well, it's something you can ask him, if you ever decide to talk to the guy. Ordinarily, it would be a good deduction. Only in this case . . ." MacAullif chuckled. "It's perfectly possible someone called the cops, but Belcher was too busy framin' you with the fingerprint evidence to show up."

"That's not funny."

"No, it's not. That's why you gotta start laughing if you wanna stay sane."

I put up my hand. "Don't. Don't do it, MacAullif. I passed punchy one whole murder ago. I'm at the state now, everyone I talk to asks me what's wrong."

"There's nothing wrong with you solvin' a murder or two wouldn't cure."

"How about three?"

"Now you're talkin'."

"Yeah," I said. "Solving the crimes would be fine. Would go a long way toward restoring my mental health. Only I really think I'm at the point that wouldn't quite do it."

MacAullif frowned. "What do you mean?"

"It wouldn't quite be enough, just getting off the hook." I took a breath, blew it out again. Held up my hand for emphasis. "I'm at the point with this son of a bitch Belcher, where getting even with the motherfucker seems more important than getting off."

MacAullif nodded his head, raised his eyebrows.

"Now you're *really* talkin'."

45.

"Interesting," Richard said.

I wanted to kill him. I just *knew* he was gonna say that.

"Oh, is that right, Richard? You find it interesting that I'm being framed?"

"Yes, I do."

"I find it more upsetting than interesting, Richard. If you must know, it pisses me off."

"I'm glad to hear it."

"It also scares the shit out of me."

"I see. It's big on bodily functions. Does it also make you want to throw up?"

"Richard."

"You have to admit, it's skillful," Richard said. "I mean, to take a piece of evidence from one crime scene and insert it into another."

"It wasn't necessarily from a crime scene."

Richard waved it away. "Right, right. It might have been from her New York office rather than where she was killed. No matter, the principle is the same. Well, what a neat idea. You have a serial killer committing a series of crimes. A cop wants to frame you for it. So he invites you to one crime scene, lets you handle some evidence. And it's something there happens to be an identical copy of at another crime scene. So he switches the two pieces of evidence, making it look as if you'd been there."

"I'm glad it pleases you so much."

"Well, why not? It's artistic as hell. This is some cop, this sergeant what's-his-face. And an ex-partner in the evidence room — these guys are gonna go far."

"Can you prove it?"

Richard looked at me, cocked his head. "Oh, dear."

"What?"

"Is that why you're bringing me this? Is that what you're looking for now?"

"Richard."

"You expect me to prove these cops are framing you?"

I gawked at him. "Of course not," I said, sarcastically. "I'm just going to sit back and be framed."

Richard put up his hand. "Temper, temper. Did I say that? I didn't say that at all. All I said was, that wouldn't be our line of defense."

"Why not? Attorneys do it all the time — my client was framed, the evidence was fabricated by the cops. They use it all the time."

"Sure they do. And you know why?" Richard held up one finger. "Their clients are guilty. That's the bottom line. They're defending some miserable motherfucker that the cops got dead to rights. So, what do they do? They claim their client was framed by corrupt cops. If he's black, he was framed by *racist* cops. If the client's a woman, she was framed by *sexist* cops. It doesn't matter, it's the same old song."

"Yeah, but it works."

"Sure it does. You know why?" Richard smiled. "Because it isn't true. It's a lie. The lawyers made it up. There *are* no such corrupt, racist, sexist cops who framed whoever the hell it was. A fabrication of the evidence did not take place. The lawyers can rant and rave, point fingers, make allegations of all kinds, and there's not anything anyone can do about it, because it's all a crock of shit. The cops can't disprove it because it has no foundation whatsoever — it's very hard to prove a negative. 'I didn't take this piece of evidence.' 'Oh, yeah? Prove it.' It works very well in those cases. Nothing's proven either way, but the point has been raised. And in some asshole juror's mind, that constitutes reasonable doubt. So some scumbag miserable son of a bitch who ought to rot in jail, walks the streets."

"This, from a defense attorney?"

"Hey, I'm a negligence lawyer. Think of me arguing damages against the State of New York when some punk freed by the system harms a client."

"Fine, Richard," I said, impatiently. "How about the fact I'm being framed?"

"I was trying to explain," Richard said. "The main problem with that defense is the fact that it's true."

"What?"

"Yeah. Like I said, if it isn't true, you make the allegation, no big whoop, and the odds are you get off. In this case the allegation's true, which is another matter entirely."

"Why?"

"Think about it. You start yelling corrupt cop, well, here's the corrupt cop you're yelling about, sitting there and hearing you yelling it. He doesn't like that, so he does two things. One, he covers up. Two, he strikes back."

"How?"

"I don't know how. But I know this. The guy is an expert at pulling a frame. You think the evidence looks bad right now, check out what the guy can do if you piss him off."

I blinked. "You're scared of him?"

"Scared is the wrong word," Richard said.

"I'm not the one going to jail. I would think you would want me, as your attorney, to be prudent regarding the length of your stay."

"Stay?"

"Just a figure of speech," Richard said. "Anyway, that's the situation. If you cry wolf and there's no wolf, no harm done. But if you cry wolf and the wolf is there, you piss the wolf off. Which puts you in a very vulnerable position if you can't prove the wolf's a wolf."

"Jesus, Richard."

"Hey, no reason to get upset. We are months away from trial, and you're out walking around. You are in no immediate danger, unless they rescind bail, which hasn't happened or we would have heard."

"Belcher's pushing for it. He brought it to the ADA."

"How do you know?"

"From MacAullif. That's how he heard about it."

"What about the ADA?"

"From what I hear, he's not buyin'."

"There you are," Richard said. "Your bail's set, there's no problem, we got plenty of time."

"Time for what?"

"Figure a scheme by which you can beat the rap." Richard shrugged. "Either that or prove who did it. No matter how good the frame is, an ADA will have a tough time convicting you with the actual killer in jail."

"No shit. Any suggestions who that might be?"

"The field's wide open. Pick a killer, any killer. There's so little to go on, who could prove you wrong?"

"Unless I happen to pick the right one, in which case I'll piss them off?"

"I'm glad you haven't lost your sense of humor."

"I *have*, Richard. I'm just way beyond punchy. You planning on solving this case for me, or do I have to do it myself?"

"What, it's not enough I should keep you out of jail?"

"That's what I thought. But if I'm gonna do it myself, you have any suggestions? I'm going slightly batshit and I can't think straight."

"I'm not sure thinking straight would help."

I groaned. "Please. I'm in enough pain without you going cryptic. You got something to say, say it."

"An analysis of all the facts we know so far yields absolutely nothing. This is significant — it indicates the facts are wrong. Knowing that, this shouldn't be that hard to figure out. Complicating the issue is getting framed by a crooked cop."

"I'll say."

"No, no. You don't understand. Yes, of course, it complicates your life and makes it hard for you to think. But that's not what I mean. I mean when you try to figure out what happened here, the solution is, a cop framed you. That's the solution you arrive at — not who committed the crime, but who committed the frame. Seeing that as your solution blinds you to seeing the true solution."

"True solution?"

Richard waved his hand again. "No, no, no. I'm not saying the cop didn't frame you. That could be perfectly true without being the true solution to the crime. The solution to the crime is, never mind the cop framed you, who killed these people?" Richard looked at me. "Unless you think he did that too?"

"Don't be silly."

"Silly? Isn't that the solution in some of those books you read? In some of those murder mysteries? The policeman did it — isn't that a popular unexpected dramatic surprise solution?"

"Richard, the cop didn't do it. This all started way before he was involved."

"How do you know?"

I blinked. "Are you kidding me?"

"Not at all. You just told me flat out the cop wasn't involved — I just want to know how you know."

"Look when he entered the case. It wasn't until Cranston Pritchert was dead."

"So? Maybe he knows him from way back. Or maybe he knows the topless dancer or the talent agent. You happen to know that isn't true?"

"Richard, this isn't helping."

"Oh? Sorry. I thought you *asked* for my opinion."

"I did. I didn't think this was it."

"It isn't. It's merely one possibility. I have no knowledge, all I can do is throw out possibilities."

"Yeah, well throw out that one. You got anything else?"

Richard didn't appear ruffled. He put his elbows on his desk, put his fingers together, pursed his lips. "Well," he said, "from the beginning I am struck with how convenient everything is."

I frowned. "What do you mean?"

"From the minute you're given the case, up until Cranston Pritchert is dead, nothing is a problem. For instance, he brings you an extortion note. Piece of cake. In no time at all, you manage to prove that he sent it to himself. Then there's the girl. Is she hard to find? Not at all. You find her by going to just that one bar. She isn't tough to find at all."

"Sure," I said. "If Cranston Pritchert's the one who hired her, it's just like the extortion note. He asks me to find her, makes her easy to find."

"And why does he do that?"

"I have no idea."

"And what is the original scam?"

"I don't know."

"No, you don't. You also don't know who is being scammed, although you suspect it might be you."

"Is there a point to this, Richard?"

"I don't know. We're talking it through. But go back to the idea it was easy to find the girl because Cranston Pritchert set her up and Cranston Pritchert wanted you to find her."

"What about it?"

"How did he do that?"

"What do you mean?"

"How did he make it easy for you to find her?"

"He didn't have to. It turned out the bartender knew her."

"How did he know that?"

"He didn't know that. It just happened."

"So the girl being easy to find was not his doing. Suppose the bartender hadn't known her. What would have happened then?"

"I don't know," I said. "I assume he would have found some way to tip me off."

"Makes sense," Richard said.

He cocked his head.

"What if he did?"

46.

Sandy was shaking up a mixed drink when I walked in. It was happy hour, and the joint was jumping. I stepped up to the bar, slid in between two attractive young business-women, and said, "Take a break, would you, we gotta talk."

Sandy dipped two glasses in salt, poured the young ladies margaritas, and said, "It's a bad time."

"I know," I said. "I'm afraid there aren't gonna be any good ones."

"What's that supposed to mean?"

"Five minutes, Sandy. I think you owe me that."

Sandy read my face, didn't like what he saw. He called to the other bartender, "Sam, cover for me." He went down to the end of the bar, moved two glasses, flipped the hinged part up, and came out.

"There's a table in the back," he said.

I shook my head. "Outside."

His face drained of color. "Look here," he said. "It wasn't me."

"It wasn't you what?"

"Snitched to the cops. I don't know where they get their ideas. If they think you did it, that's their fault. It's got nothing to do with me."

"Oh, is that right?"

"What do you mean?"

We'd been standing close and shouting at each other. Now I took him by the shoulder. "I can't hear myself think in here, Sandy. Outside."

He wasn't happy, but he came.

Out on the sidewalk in the clear light of day, Sandy didn't look too good. A little pasty in the face. Almost a sickly color. Of course, standing face to face with a cold-blooded killer might have something to do with that. Though he was bigger than me, you wouldn't have known it. It occurred to me I could play off it.

"All right, Sandy," I said. "Here's the deal. I want you to talk, and I want you to talk straight. If you do that, you and I have no problem. If you don't, we have a problem in a big way. Someone set me up to take a fall, and I'd like to think it wasn't you."

Sandy looked ready to pee in his pants. "No, no," he said. "It wasn't me."

"Now, let's be careful here. Like I said, you gotta talk straight. Maybe it wasn't *all* you, but maybe just a little bit."

"Oh, sweet Jesus," Sandy said.

"Hey, no one's gonna hurt you, Sandy," I said. "But I got a little problem here. Let me tell you what it is. To begin with, I know where you live."

Sandy's knees buckled. "Oh, my god!"

"Hey, don't freak out on me. This is just conversational. You happen to live on the Upper West Side. 88th and Columbus. You live there, you work here. And that's my problem."

He blinked at me. "What?"

"What are you doin' in a topless bar on 20th Street and Eighth Avenue? It's not near where you live. It's not near where you work. It's not one of the big-name joints. Why, of all the places you could pick, did you happen to hang out there?"

"I don't understand."

"Sure you do, Sandy. You understand just fine. I wasn't findin' the girl fast enough, so you had to give me a hand. Only thing I don't know is who put you up to it. But that's what you're gonna tell me. And you're gonna tell me straight."

"Oh, shit."

"Hey, Sandy. Look at the position you're in. You've already given your story to the cops. And you didn't happen to mention this at all. Cops don't like that. They'll be pissed off. They'll be pissed off at *you*." I pointed my finger. "But they won't get nearly as pissed off as I will if you don't tell it and tell it fast."

"It was her," Sandy said.

"Huh?"

"It was the girl."

"You were in it together?"

"No, no, I swear," Sandy said. He looked like he was gonna cry. "I had no idea. No idea. I still don't."

"Careful, Sandy."

"No, no. I'll tell you what I know. It's just not much."

"Whatever it is, let's have it."

He took a breath. "When you came in the bar. The first time. Lookin' for the girl. I remembered her and him, just like I said."

"Yeah. So?"

"But I had no idea who she was. Swear to god. It was the first time she'd been in, and I'd never seen her before."

"What about the topless bar?"

"I made it up."

"You didn't make it up. She worked there."

"Yeah, but I didn't know it. I'd never seen her there. I'd never been there."

It was all I could do to keep my hands off him, and I think he sensed it. "Go on," I said. "Tell me what happened."

"You're not gone half an hour when she walks in the door large as life."

"You're kidding."

"Not at all. Swear to god. Straight stuff. She comes walkin' up to the bar, sits down at a stool, bats her eyes, says, How'd you like to make some cash?"

My mouth fell open. "What?"

"Yeah," he said. "Well, I recognize her, of course. And I just got through talking to you. So, I'm wondering what's the deal. When she tells me, it floors me."

"What?" I said. "What's the deal?"

"She wants me to tip you off."

"What?"

"That's right."

"Tip me off to her?"

"That's the ticket."

"Hold on. Hold on," I said. "The girl wants *you* to tell *me* where to find *her?*"

"Sure. She's the one tells me the whole thing. She works in this topless bar. I'm to tell you I recognize her from there, bring you there, and point her out. I do that, I make some cash."

"How much?"

He made a face. "That's where she's cagy. She tells me I'll get it from you."

"What?"

"Right. She says you'll be happy to pay. Turned out she was right. If not, well, I knew where she worked."

I blinked. "So, she wanted to be found."

"Yeah. I don't know why."

"So you say. But you've said a lot of things."

"No, no, no. It's the truth. I swear."

"Oh, yeah?" I said. "You'd never seen this girl before?"

"No. Not before the night she was in here."

"And you'd never seen her again after that, and then out of the blue she walks in here and asks you to tip me off to her?"

"Essentially, yes."

"Why *essentially?*"

"I don't know. Forget *essentially*. The answer is yes."

I put up my hand. "Sandy, you're very nervous and you're not taking time to think. I want you to take time to think. To make sure you tell it right. Is it *essentially* yes, or is that *exactly* what happened?"

"That's exactly what happened."

"And the time she was in here with my client — you didn't notice anything else special then?"

"Well . . ."

"*Well*, Sandy? Now there's a *well?*"

"I might have seen them leave."

The guy was getting so tied up in knots I was afraid to jump on that as hard as it deserved. "Uh-huh," I said. "And when they did, was there anything special about the *way* they left? Anything worth commenting on?"

"It seemed to me the guy was rather drunk and leaning on her a bit."

"Oh, really?"

"That's just how it seemed. I didn't really have a good look. I mean if the guy was just trying to paw her, it would have looked the same way. You see what I'm saying?"

"I see what you're saying, Sandy. You seem to be saying a lot of stuff to try to make me think you weren't involved. That you and the girl weren't in this thing together."

"No, no, I swear."

"I'm trying to believe you, Sandy. It's hard because I'm so desperate for information. So the more you tell me, the more I believe."

And if he bought that, the guy was more freaked out than I thought. I mean, hell, the reality was, the more he knew to tell me, the more it looked like he was involved.

"I'm trying to help you all I can," Sandy said. "I just don't really know anything."

"Well, you knew about them leaving together. That's something. But what I really want to know is why. Why this girl came to him, why this girl came to you, and why this girl wanted to get to me. Now, did she say anything at all when she walked into the bar that would give you a clue?"

"Not really."

"Not really, Sandy?"

"Aw, please," Sandy said. "You're picking on every word."

"Because I really need this information. Now, if there was anything she said that gave you a clue, I wanna hear it."

"Well, she did say it wasn't just the money."

"What wasn't just the money?"

"Why she wanted me to do this."

"You mean tell me?"

"Yeah."

"Whaddya mean it wasn't just the money?"

"That's what she said. She said it wasn't just the money, there was a lot of pressure on her."

"Pressure?"

"Yeah."

"From who?"

"From her agent."

"You mean her talent agent? The dead woman?"

"Yeah."

Damn.

"Was there anything else? Anything about who was putting the pressure on? Or why?"

"No. I can't remember exactly what she said, but that was all I got. That there was pressure on her to do this, and it came from the agent. If someone was pressuring the agent, that's something I wouldn't know."

"And the only one who might know is dead."

Sandy blinked.

If I were any less involved, I might not have caught it. But I was so tuned in to the guy, looking for anything, that that's all it took. One blink.

"What is it, Sandy?" I said.

And the guy dissolved.

"Look," he said, "you gotta understand. I don't want to get in trouble. I'm in bad enough already. I mean, do the cops have to know?"

"Know what, Sandy?"

"All of this. What I'm telling you. That I didn't tell 'em before."

"That remains to be seen, Sandy. Right now I don't know. What I *do* know is you're stalling. I just got through saying there was no way to find out what the girl and the talent agent knew. And it flashed in your mind that there *was*. When that happened, you blinked. When I noticed it, you panicked. And now, you're covering up. So, we can do this the easy way or the hard way. You ask me if the cops have to know. Well, if they do, that's the hard way. You wanna try the easy way first, you try talking to me. But you try pulling the song and dance again, we'll try talking to them. Your call. What's it gonna be?"

He put up his hand. "No, no. We can work this out."

"Let's work it out now, Sandy. What is it you're not telling me?"

It was as if I could see the resistance actually drain out of him.

He sighed, said, "Well, that afternoon — when she walked into the bar . . ."

"Yeah?"

"She wasn't alone."

47.

Though it was almost noon, the young man who opened the door gave every indication of having been sound asleep. He was rubbing his eyes, his hair was matted, and there was a pattern from a pillow on his cheek.

"What is it?" he mumbled.

"Jamie Pollack?" I said.

"Yeah?"

I flashed my ID. "Private investigator. I have some questions for you."

If the guy had been more alert, he might have slammed the door. As it was, I lowered my shoulder, pushed my way in.

"Hey, what the hell?" Jamie Pollack said.

I found myself in a dark, cluttered studio apartment. It was dark because the shades were down, and cluttered because the fold-out couch had been pulled out into a bed. This left very little room to stand. I squeezed between the bed and the dresser, which left me practically on one foot. I tried not to look ridiculous, and addressed Jamie Pollack.

"It's about Laura Martin."

That woke him up. His mouth fell open.

After a few seconds he said, "Who?"

I waggled my finger at him. "No, no, Jamie. Nice try. But bad reaction time. You gotta come right in with the *Who?* Otherwise I can see you thinking it up."

He blinked. Frowned. Gradually waking up. "Who the hell are you?"

"I told you. I'm investigating the murder."

"No, you're not. I've seen you. You were on TV. Jesus Christ, you're the one who did it!"

"No, I'm not, and you got nothing to fear. If you did, you'd be dead already."

His mouth fell open again, and he took a step back and wound up sitting on the bed. That really panicked him, and he scuttled to his feet.

"Hey, hey," I said. "Don't hurt yourself. I'm not a killer, I just wanna talk. You probably don't wanna, but that's good too. 'Cause I figure, most of all, you don't wanna talk to the cops. And if you talk to me, there's a chance you won't have to talk to them. But if you *don't* talk to me, you *do*."

Jamie blinked. Gawked at me. "I don't understand."

"I know you don't. So here's the deal. I'll explain it to you, and then you explain it to me."

"Explain what? I don't understand. How'd

you even find me?"

I had found him the same way I hadn't found her. The minute Actors' Equity had opened this morning, Sandy and I had started going through stacks of resume photos. Luck had been with us — it had only taken an hour and a half.

The resume photo Sandy had identified had shown a slightly cleaner-cut, wider-awake version of Jamie Pollack. The address on the resume was the grungy, one-room affair in which we stood.

I didn't feel like boring Jamie with all of that, though. I just said, "The bartender fingered you."

"The bartender?"

"Yeah. From when you came in with her that day."

"What day?"

"Hey, Jamie," I said. "I know all about it. We're talkin' about the bar where she met Cranston Pritchert. She went back there to tell the bartender to tip me off how to find her. You were with her. The bartender can identify you. Not that I want him to. Right now I'd be happy to keep this between us. But that's the situation, that's what we're talking about. Why don't we take it from there?"

"What do you mean?"

"I'm wondering how much you know."

He put up his hands. "Hey, hey. I didn't do anything."

"I'm not saying you did. In fact, if you had, I'd be mighty surprised. But you might know something that could help me. Maybe even shed some light on who killed her. Because, believe me, it sure wasn't me."

"But you had the gun."

"Grow up. The gun was a plant. It's a clumsy, amateurish plant, and it's not going to stand up in court. But it sure is fucking things up right now. I can't talk to anybody in this damn case, they don't look like they're gettin' ready to duck."

He blinked. "The gun was a plant?"

"Yeah, I know, that's what they all say, but this time it's true. I mean, come on, use your head. Cranston Pritchert hired me to find this girl. What, I'm such an over-zealous detective, as soon as I find her, I decide to kill them both? You're an actor, right? Well, like, hey, man, what's my motivation?"

That jarred him. He'd probably asked some director that in exactly those words.

"So, anyway," I said, "just pretend for a moment I'm telling the truth. Now, the girl knew something I needed to know."

"Stop calling her *the girl*," he said. "You didn't even know her, you're talking about her like that."

Good. He'd gotten over being afraid of me and was comfortable enough to get pissed off. Now if I could just get him talking.

"Exactly," I said. "You knew her. I didn't. And someone killed her, and he shouldn't get away with it. That's why I need your help. For her sake. Help me. Please."

He blinked at me uncertainly.

"Okay," I said. "Here's the thing. You were with her in the bar. When she came and told the bartender what she wanted. About leading me to her. Now, I know she did that, but I don't know why. Well, I sorta know why. She was gonna make some money doing it, and her agent was putting pressure on her. But beyond that I need help. She can't help me. You can."

He blinked again. "Why should I trust you?"

Great. He knew something.

"You rather trust the cops?"

"No."

"Then help me out. What do you know?"

"I don't want to get in trouble."

"Who does? You think I'm runnin' to the cops? Every time they see me, they

360

arrest me. It's getting to be a real fuckin' drag."

He drew back again. "You're acting kind of funny."

Jesus. Another one.

I exhaled loudly, shook my head. "Yeah, I know. I'm really stressed out and I'm not takin' it well. Help me out. Please. Whaddya know about this?"

He furrowed his brow, seemed to be making up his mind. "That night in the bar. With the guy — what's his name?"

"Cranston Pritchert."

"Yeah. The dead guy. Well, she was supposed to tell you what happened so she'd get her bonus."

I blinked. "What?"

" 'Cause that was the deal. She did the job, she got paid. But then, if anyone came poking around asking questions — well, if she told them the right story, she got a bonus."

"Wait a minute, wait a minute. What she told me was a story?"

"Of course."

"How is it a story? All she told me was she had drinks with the guy in the bar."

"Right."

"What do you mean, *right?* That's exactly what she did. How is that a story?"

"Oh," he said. " 'Cause that isn't all she did. The story was to tell you that's all that happened."

"But it wasn't."

"No."

"What else happened?"

"I don't want to get in trouble."

"We've been through all that. What happened?"

He hesitated. Looked around the room. On one wall was a poster of Marlon Brando on his motorcycle from *The Wild One*. He stared at it a moment, as if trying to get inspiration. He must have got it, because he turned back to me.

"She put something in his drink."

"What?"

He nodded. "That was the deal. That's what she got paid for. To drug his drink."

"Are you kidding me?"

"Hey, this is what you asked for. Now you're not gonna believe me?"

"No. I believe you. It's just . . . well, what was the idea?"

"That I don't know. All she was told was to drug the drink and get him out of there."

"Get him out of there?"

"That's right."

"Get him out of the bar?"

"Sure thing."

"And she did?"

"Of course. Didn't anyone see them go?"

I sighed. "Actually, the bartender did. But the first I heard of it was yesterday. And even he wasn't entirely sure."

"Yeah, well, that's what happened. She brought him out to her."

"To *her?*"

"Yeah. To her agent."

"Her agent? Her agent was there?"

"Yes, of course. But you don't know that. That's part of what she wasn't supposed to tell."

"Wait a minute, wait a minute. What did her agent do?"

"Took the keys."

"What?"

"She took the guy's keys, went off with them. Came back a half hour later."

"She took Cranston Pritchert's keys?"

"Right. And then she brought them back."

"And what was . . ." I groped for the name so I wouldn't have to say *the girl.* "What was Laura doing then?"

"Staying with the guy. On the doorstep. You know, the front steps of a brownstone. Like the guy had had too much to drink, and she was helpin' him out. Or like they were sweethearts, or something. Anything at all, so a cop wouldn't see 'em."

"What happened then?"

"The agent came back with the keys, put 'em back in his pocket, and they took off."

"And that's it?"

He looked at me. "That's not enough? You want more?"

"No. I mean, that's everything that happened. She drugged him and got him out of the bar so the agent could take his keys for half an hour and then put 'em back?"

"That's it."

"And the story she was supposed to tell me to get a bonus was simply that she was hired to have drinks in a bar with a guy for two hours, and that was it?"

"Yeah. That's right."

"Why was it so important that she tell me that?"

"So she wouldn't tell you what I just did."

I exhaled. Exactly. That had to be exactly right. So I wouldn't know about them taking Cranston Pritchert's keys.

"Okay," I said. "So why did they take the keys?"

"I have no idea."

"Did Laura know?"

"No. She only did what she was told."

"By her agent."

"Right."

"And her agent never told her why?"

"That's what she said."

"Or who it was that hired her?"

He shook his head. "No."

Damn.

48.

MacAullif made a face. "Why do you bring me this?"

"Are you kidding? This could crack the case."

"This could crack my nuts. You know what you got here? You got two witnesses withholding evidence from the cops. You come here to make me a party to that, well, thanks a lot."

"Who's withholding evidence from the cops? You're a cop, I brought it to you."

"Don't be a dickhead. I got a very short fuse on this one, and you know why. Belcher would love to nail me if he could, and you just came up with all the ammunition he'd need. If he could prove I knew what I know now and I didn't tell him, it's my ass. Good Christ, you couldn't do a better job of fuckin' me up if you were workin' for the guy."

"Hey, MacAullif, you wanna calm down and look at what we got?"

"I see what we got. Withholding evidence, obstruction of justice, tampering with a witness, and conspiring to conceal a crime."

"Conceal a crime?"

"Sure. The bartender lied in his signed statement. We know it, we're coverin' it up."

"Sorry to piss you off, MacAullif, but I happen to be facing three murder counts. This obstruction of justice shit is just chicken feed."

"Yeah, but it's true," MacAullif said. "You didn't kill anyone. You didn't commit the murders. But obstruction of justice, you're doing just fine. And you can go to jail for that, in case you didn't know."

"You mean if Belcher found out?"

"Of course."

"Then let's not tell him."

MacAullif scowled. "What a wiseass. God save me from a wiseass."

"Uh-huh," I said. "Any time you're ready."

"Huh?"

"Any time you'd like to stop beating me up and look at what we got."

"You got jack shit."

"Come on. I know the girl wanted me to find her. And I know she drugged the guy's drink to steal his keys."

"You just think you know that."

"What do you mean?"

"Are you never gonna think like a cop?

Just 'cause someone tells you something don't make it true. This bartender, whom we *know* has lied once already, now tells a different story. You buy it as gospel, but does it have to be true? Not necessarily. I know this is a hard concept for you to handle, but people who tell lies don't always tell the truth."

"The part about the boyfriend was true."

"Huh?"

"This Jamie Pollack. Her boyfriend. That was true."

"Right," MacAullif said. "And that's where you make your big mistake. He told you there was a boyfriend. There *was* a boyfriend. You figure that confirms his story. All it confirms is that there was a boyfriend. The rest of what he told you could be total bullshit."

"I don't think so."

"You don't know. I mean, what do you know about this bartender, anyway? How well did he know Cranston Pritchert? How well did he know this girl? Did he know the talent agent? I mean, for all you know, this guy was mixed up in it right up to his eyebrows."

I put up my hand. "Okay," I said. "I'm not letting him off the hook. I just happen to have spent the morning with him looking at resume photos and he seemed sincere to me. I concede my judgment is not perfect and I should not wash him out. Now could we move on to something else?"

"I'd love to move on to something else. I happen to have two homicides of my own pending."

"I know, MacAullif. But first you have to clear yourself of this obstruction of justice charge."

That stopped him dead. MacAullif couldn't quite believe I'd said that. I could see his brain going, trying to come up with the ultimate rejoinder. Before he did, I said, "Sorry. I'll get out of your office. I was just hoping you could put a spin on these new facts. The fact she wanted to be found, and the fact she took the keys."

"We know why she wanted to be found," MacAullif said. "She got a bonus for tellin' her story."

"Yeah, but why?"

"So you wouldn't know about the keys."

"Why is that so important?"

"Because if you knew about the keys, you could figure it out."

"But I *can't* figure it out."

"Sure, but you're a moron. The person who set this up was concerned with a *bright* person stumbling on the facts."

"Fine. If you're so smart, tell me what the keys mean."

"I have no idea."

"Then how do you get off slamming me for not knowing?"

"Oh, you want fair? I'll come find *you* in *your* office, make *you* guilty of conspiring to conceal a crime."

"Come on, MacAullif. What's the dope on the keys?"

"You know as much as I do."

"Yeah, but what's it mean?"

MacAullif took out a cigar, drummed it on the desk. "A person wants a key to unlock a door. In your client's case, it could be the keys to the office, it could be the keys to his home. The first consideration is the keys to his home."

"Why?"

"Because it's him. All these guys had keys to the office, right? But he's the only one's got keys to his home. If the target was the office key, then it's random — I mean, the fact that it's him. If it's his apartment key, then it's specific. It's him and him alone. In that case, you got one suspect loomin' larger than the rest. The guy from the company makin' a play for the wife."

"How does that make sense? He and she were thick as thieves."

"So they appeared. It doesn't make it true. What did you actually see? As I recall, the guy called on her, took her out to lunch. She, in return, voted her stock for him. But it doesn't necessarily mean they were in it together, or even that they were having an affair."

MacAullif leveled the cigar. "There's another thing. All this happened before your client was dead. Obviously. Suppose this guy — the one hitting on his wife — what's his name?"

"Marty Rothstein."

"Right. Suppose this Marty Rothstein is your man. Suppose it's him all along. He wants the keys to your client's apartment. Why? To get in there and get something on him. He does that, but it backfires in his face, because your client calls him on it, and he has to kill him."

I frowned. "How the hell does that make any sense?"

"I don't know. I'm coming up with theories from brand-new facts. *Assuming* they're facts. Assuming they're not a bunch of lies you've been fed. Taken at face value, we're speculating who stole the keys and why. The most obvious answer is this Marty Rothstein, to get into your client's apartment. I know you don't like that, because your storybook mentality says the most obvious answer can't be true. The thing you lose sight of is, every once in a while it is."

"Fine, MacAullif," I said. "Can I point out a flaw?"

"Be my guest."

"If Marty Rothstein stole Cranston Pritchert's keys to get into his apartment, it seems to me the most likely scenario is he does that, Cranston Pritchert comes home unexpectedly and surprises him, and he shoots Cranston Pritchert dead. But Cranston Pritchert wasn't killed in his own apartment, he was killed at work."

"Not a big flaw," MacAullif said. "How's about this? Your client comes home, finds someone's been through his study. Perhaps something's missing. I don't know what, maybe a list of friendly stockholders. But whatever it is, the guy goes batshit. He rushes up to the office, and who does he find but what's-his-name, this Rothstein, going over whatever it is he just filched. Say it *was* a list of stockholders, and Rothstein's now on the phone calling everyone on the list. Your client goes ballistic, and Rothstein has to shoot him."

"What about the others?"

"What others?"

"The talent agent and the girl — why does he kill them?"

"Because he killed *him*. These murders were never intentional. Not from the beginning. But once he kills your client, he has to cover up. Who can link him to the crime? The talent agent and the girl. So they gotta go."

"Wait a minute. How do you mean, the crimes weren't intentional?"

"I mean from the beginning. That's obvious. If the story you got was true. Because the girl and the talent agent were paid off to tell phony stories. *That's* the way they're being hushed up. And if your client isn't murdered, that's enough. But once *he's* dead, they can link the killer, not to the scam, but to the murder. Which is a brand-new ball game. They can convict him of murder on the one hand, or blackmail the shit out of him on the other. Either way, they gotta go."

"And what *was* the original scam?"

"We still don't know. If the story's true, there *was* no scam. The guy was not being set up, he was essentially bein' mugged. Ripped off for his keys. Only thing is, you don't know if this is a story someone paid the *bartender* and the *boyfriend* to tell."

"Oh, come on, MacAullif."

"That's so far-fetched? That's no worse

than what I've just heard. In fact, it's better, because if it's bullshit, maybe the obstruction of justice goes away. I'm not a lawyer. Is it a crime to willfully withhold *false* information from the police?"

"I think it would depend on whether you knew at the time it was false."

MacAullif made a face. "Count on the dickhead to come up with a definition that dorks him." He exhaled. "Look, you wanted a spin on the facts and that's it. I don't think there's anything more I could tell you."

"What about an autopsy report?"

"What about it?"

"You happen to get the time of death?"

"Yeah, not that it's gonna do you any good. She'd been dead for too long. Hard to be accurate. She was killed in the neighborhood of when your client got killed. But the parameters are loose enough she could have been killed before, or she could have been killed after. It makes no sense she was killed before, but it's medically possible. For my money, you can wash it out."

"Yeah. Except . . ."

"Except what?"

"What if it's the other way around? What if someone's closing up the pipeline, starting from the end? Goes from the girl to the agent to the guy."

MacAullif groaned. "Oh, please. What is that, James Bond? Closing up the pipeline? We got enough problems without you going off the deep end."

"I wouldn't reject it out of hand."

"Fine, but come up with a theory that makes sense. The one you got there doesn't fit with these people were bribed to tell a story."

"Yeah, well, you said that didn't have to be true."

"Granted. But *something* has to be true. You throw out everything and start from scratch, well, where do you start? See?"

"Yeah, I see. So what should I do about these two witnesses?"

"Are you kidding me? If you have knowledge of any material witnesses in a murder case, you should give the information to the officer in charge. And that's my official advice on the subject."

MacAullif pointed with his cigar. "In the event you should choose not to do that, you should get the fuck out of my office before someone sees you not doing it."

49.

I rode uptown with my head spinning. I was straphanging on the Broadway Number One. That's a local train making all local stops. And I do mean all. The ride seemed to last forever. Meanwhile, my mind was turning cartwheels.

Talking to MacAullif had been frustrating. Talking to MacAullif usually was. The guy was so sharp on the one hand, yet so stubborn on the other, that he could be thoroughly exasperating. It seemed like time and again he would take some stupid concept that I knew couldn't be true, and try to ram it down my throat.

Like the bartender bit. I knew Sandy wasn't lying now. What I had was the straight goods. Sandy had lied before, sure, but he had a reason to. That reason made perfect sense. So did the fact he was telling the truth now. It was all perfectly logical, perfectly straightforward. Why the hell did MacAullif have to suggest it wasn't so?

Same thing for the boyfriend — was his story false? It sure struck me as the real

McCoy. I mean, why should he lie? Unless *he* was the killer. But why *would* he be?

Unless. . . .

Unless the whole thing was the other way around. Like I said to MacAullif, with the shutting down the pipeline bit. Well, never mind the pipeline, but what if the other part was true? The medical report couldn't tell who died first. So what if it was her? What if the boyfriend killed her, and it was because of that the others had to die?

In that case, how did I get the gun?

Wait a minute. Maybe that works. He kills the girl. To cover up, he has to kill Pritchert. Then he has to knock off the agent. She's the last to die, and he leaves the gun there. For Belcher to find and frame me. Hey, that works just fine.

Small problem with motivation. Well, you can't have everything.

But then, MacAullif always tells me you kill the one you love. Husband-wife thing, girlfriend-boyfriend, it's always the other one that did it. There you are. Maybe the guy just goes bonkers that she's dancing in a topless bar. Surely men have snapped for less.

Damn.

Maybe I should turn around, take the subway back down to MacAullif. Maybe I got this figured out.

It suddenly hit me, good god, I must be desperate if I'm grasping at straws like that.

My beeper went off, filled the car. I switched it off as all heads turned toward me.

Good. Just what I need. A nice assignment from Richard to get my mind off the case. A bit of busy work, routine, easy, something I could handle on automatic pilot. A gentleman with a broken leg who would be thrilled to see me. I'd pick up my car from the municipal lot, drive out to wherever it was, sign the guy up, and that would be that. Probably just what I needed to clear my head. Sometimes things work out.

I came out of the subway, headed for the nearest pay phone. It occurred to me things couldn't be better. Ordinarily I would be faced with Wendy/Janet, and would have to suffer the anxiety over whether I could actually *find* my client, due to the uncertainty of whether the information she gave me would be true. But with Mary Mason on the job, that wasn't a consideration. The information would be one hundred percent accurate and nothing could go wrong.

Better still, unlike the Wendy/Janet situation, I'd know who I was talking to. A small satisfaction, but one's own. I actually felt a sense of well-being as I punched in the number.

"Rosenberg and Stone," Mary Mason said.

"Hi, Mary," I said. "It's Stanley."

"Maggie," she said.

I blinked. "What?"

"I changed my name to Maggie."

"I beg your pardon?"

"I'm using the name Maggie Mason now."

I don't know how to describe it. It was as if the top of my head had been ripped off, and my brains were drifting away. I mean, there I was, teetering on the verge of insanity. Facing three murder counts. Not to mention an obstruction of justice. Not to mention a vindictive cop with a personal grudge who was out to get me.

All of that somehow paled into insignificance compared to what I was facing now.

Maggie Mason?

I suddenly have to deal with Maggie Mason?

The concept crowded everything out of my mind. All I could think of was why? Why? What earthly reason could cause an otherwise sensible, capable, intelligent woman to change her name from Mary to Maggie? Clearly, the only reason she had done it was to deprive me of what was left of my rapidly depleting wits.

And, oh god, how it worked. The one constant, the one thing I had been able to cling to, as realities changed all around me, as Sandy's lies were replaced by Sandy's truths (if they were indeed true), as hitherto unknown boyfriends suddenly emerged from the woodwork, as fingerprints jumped from one crime scene to another, that one tiny corner of reality had just been ripped away. And in one fell swoop, the super-competent Mary Mason had transformed herself into Mary/Maggie, the moral equivalent of Wendy/Janet — good god, could I even trust her information anymore? Or was it, too, subject to change?

I stood there on the corner of Broadway and 50th Street, holding the phone to my ear. It was midday, and the sidewalk was jammed with people on their way to lunch. I was surrounded by a mass of humanity.

And I'd never felt more alone.

50.

"Maybe he's right," Alice said.

I didn't want to hear it. I'd have rather been in the living room playing Nintendo with my son, Tommie. But it's hard to brush off your wife when you're facing a murder rap or two. With three, it's practically impossible.

"Right about what?" I said.

There was a pause before Alice answered because she had switched on the Cuisinart. Alice was making pesto, and reggiano cheese, garlic, basil, and pignoli nuts were being ground to bits. She switched off the machine and, as if there had been no interruption, said, "About the bartender."

"Huh?"

"Maybe he's right about the bartender."

"What do you mean?"

"Just what I said. You said MacAullif thinks the bartender's still not telling the truth. Well, what if he's right?"

"I gave you my opinion on that."

"Yeah. And now I'm giving you mine. What good would it be talking to me if all I did was parrot back your opinion?"

"Yes, of course," I said. "I'm just telling you you happen to have picked one that doesn't thrill me."

"Of course not," Alice said. "If it did, it would be *your* opinion. Which wouldn't be worth talking about."

"Thanks a lot."

"You know what I mean. I mean if you already *have* that opinion, it's no help to suggest it."

"Alice —"

"You wanna hear *my* opinion, or you just wanna complain about the fact that I'm giving it?"

I know better than to argue with Alice. At least, I always *tell myself* I know better than to argue with Alice. And I certainly *try* never to argue with Alice.

"By all means," I said. "What's your opinion?"

"Well, then," Alice said, "what if MacAullif's right and the bartender's lying still? Take it another step further, and what if the bartender's guilty?"

"Oh, come on."

"You want to hear this opinion or not?"

I took a breath. "I most certainly do."

"Fine. Then here it is, for what it's worth. Say the bartender's guilty. Not that big a stretch. We already know he was in league with the girl, at least in terms of setting you up. So what if he was in league with her in terms of setting your client up? What if he was in league with her from the beginning? What if this scam — and you still don't know what it was — but what if this scam was something the two of them were pulling on Cranston Pritchert? And by association were pulling on you? And what if something went wrong and he had to kill?"

"Who?"

"What?" Alice said.

"Who did he have to kill? Cranston Pritchert? The girl? The talent agent? When the scam went wrong, who died first?"

"How should I know?" Alice said.

That's the problem with Alice's theories. The fact they're not entirely thought out in no way diminishes her ability to argue them.

"But that's the whole point, you see," I said. "If he's pulling a scam and something goes wrong and he has to kill somebody, then he either has to kill his confederate or the person he's scamming."

"Yes, of course."

"And it makes a big difference which."

"Maybe so. But since we don't know the answer, why don't we move on?"

"To what?"

"To what happens next."

"Which is?"

I was not to know immediately, for olive oil had joined the cheese, basil, pignoli nuts, and garlic, and the Cuisinart was switched on again. When the mixture had been blended to perfection, Alice switched the Cuisinart off and said, "What happens next is, whoever he killed first, now he's gotta kill two more. He does that and hangs on to the gun, which he later plants on you."

I blinked. "Wait a minute, wait a minute. That didn't happen. The cop planted the gun on me."

"Yeah, but what if he didn't? What if it was actually the bartender that did it?"

I grimaced. Sighed. "Alice. I don't want to hear the if-my-theories-were-your-theories bit again, but that particular theory is in contradiction of known facts. This cop Belcher happens to be framing me. I can't get away from that."

Alice nodded. "That's your problem. You take something as a given and you can't get away from it. Well, fine. Take that as a fact. Now, set it aside and say, if it wasn't true. Because that's what I'm doing here. I'm playing what-if. Now say, if it wasn't true that the cop was framing me, would it be possible that this bartender planted the gun?"

"Are you serious?"

Alice looked like the next thing to go in the Cuisinart might be my head. "How many times do I have to say it?" she said. "Play what-if. I thought that's what detectives were supposed to do to begin with. Consider what-if. Well, the what-if I want you to consider is, if this bartender was the killer, could he have planted the gun?"

"No. How could he?"

"I don't know. I'm asking you. I'm just curious how you're so sure. It seems to me, from what I remember, this guy showed up practically every place you were."

I blinked. Considered.

"I mean," Alice went on, "weren't you and he constantly going over resume pictures together? At the talent agent's office and then at her home?"

"Yeah. That's right."

"Well, there you are. You tell me the police can't pin down the time of death, so no one's sure who was killed first. But both those times — they were after *your client* was killed. So we could assume by then all three were dead. So either of those times — at the talent agent's office or at the talent agent's house — could the guy have planted the gun?"

I took a breath. Blew it out loudly. "I'm not sure."

"There you are," Alice said. "Not five minutes from your answer of an automatic *no*."

"Okay, fine," I said. "I grant the possibility. But it's like if an elephant had fins would he be a fish?"

Alice stared at me. "What?"

"I *know* the cop's framing me. So to say, *if* the cop *wasn't* framing me does the theory make sense? — well, maybe so, but so what?"

"*That* I got," Alice said. "I just never heard the expression about the elephant and the fish."

"I may have just made it up."

"You may have?"

"Alice, I'm stressed out. I don't know where that came from. The point is, valid as that thought might be, it doesn't help me. Frankly, right now it's more input than I can handle."

"I know. Go play Nintendo."

"Huh?"

"Hey. Don't pretend. I know you wanna go play Nintendo with Tommie. Go on. Do you some good."

I'll say that for Alice, she was pretty understanding. On the other hand, it occurred to me, she was awfully unconcerned about her husband being on the hook for three homicides. She had explained it away in almost the same terms as MacAullif — I was innocent, there was nothing to it, the whole thing was absurd and would eventually go away.

I knew in voicing that opinion Alice was being a brick. She knew my own state of mental health was precarious, and was taking the pressure off in letting me know I didn't have to worry about her. That was kind, considerate, and thoughtful.

Still, it occurred to me she might have appeared just the *least* bit concerned.

Anyway, I happily escaped to the living room, where Tommie was playing *Zelda: Link's Awakening* on Super NES. That was something in itself. *Link's Awakening* was a Game Boy game. But Nintendo's latest wrinkle, the Super Game Boy adaptor, allowed you to play Game Boy games on your Super NES system.

I couldn't have been happier. The Zelda games were my favorite, and I could now play this one, which had been too small for my ancient eyes on the tiny Game Boy screen.

I went into the living room to help Tommie, who was coping with Level Five.

And also with a moral and ethical dilemma.

One of the items Link uses is a bow. It's an important item, because there are certain enemies that you can't beat without it. In the original Zelda game, you find the bow in one of the levels. In this game, you have to buy it. And it cost 980 rupies.

Believe me, that's a lot. Even if you're close to it by the time you get to Level Five, you'd hate to blow all the loot you spent the whole game saving up just on one item.

Which is where the moral and ethical dilemma comes in. In addition to making games, Nintendo publishes its own magazine, *Nintendo Power*, which gives you tips on how to play the games. Tommie of course subscribes. And one of the tips they give you is called "Grabbing Goods." It tells you how to get around paying for the bow. You go into the shop that sells it, you take it, and instead of paying the shopkeeper for it, you run with it out the door. If you do that, you will have the bow. But for the rest of the game, all the people you meet will point at you and yell, "Thief!"

But that's not the moral and ethical dilemma. That's just the beginning. If you don't *want* people to point at you and yell "Thief!" but you still don't want to pay for the bow, in another *Nintendo Power* magazine there's another tip called "Free Bow." The catch here is, to get the free bow, you must *have* the 980 rupies. Here's how it works. You go into the shop, pick up the bow, go to the shopkeeper, and when he asks if you want to buy it, say, "Yes." Before he can take the rupies from you, you push A, B, Start, Select, and save your game. When you return to the game, you will have the bow and the rupies too.

And no one will yell at you.

Tommie accepted this cheerfully, but it totally blew my mind. What are we teaching the young of today? Well, we're teaching them if you don't have any money, you can get stuff by stealing. But if you do, you'll be despised as a thief. On the other hand, if you have money, you can get stuff without paying for it. Which is a sort of corporate, white-collar crime that is not the same as stealing, and no one will say boo.

As I watched Tommie run around with his new bow, my mind wandered.

Something was bothering me. No real surprise there — with everything that had happened, something *should* be bothering me. But more than that. It was like there was something neglected. Something that I'd missed. I don't know why, but in the back of my mind was the feeling there was something that I'd heard today that was important. I just couldn't put my finger on it.

Which again was not surprising. It had been a long day. Filled with revelations. First there was Sandy and the resume photos at Actors' Equity. Segue into the topless dancer's boyfriend and his story of stealing the keys. Then wrap it all up and kick it around with MacAullif. Who, in his typical irritating manner, points out it might not be true. And hands me Marty Rothstein as one suspect, and the bartender as the other. Dangles them at me tantalizingly, as if saying, *Here they are, pick one.*

And then there's Alice, who *does* pick one. The bartender. My least-favorite suspect. And then compounds the insult by arguing something I *know* isn't true — that the guy might have framed me with the gun. And then points out with annoying logic that the guy was at the talent agent's office and at the talent agent's house. Which would have allowed him to do it if he had done it, only the fact was, he hadn't done it.

Yeah: pretty long, exasperating day. Ironically, about the only bright spot was the sign-up Mary/Maggie Mason had given me. And even then I'd had the irritation of the changing name. But the sign-up itself had been a piece of cake. A nice seventy-five-cents-an-hour ride out to Far Rockaway to sign up a woman who had fallen down in Sloan's. I'd even managed to slip into the offending supermarket and snap off a few location-of-accident photos when no one happened to be looking. The client, one Rosita Velez, had slipped on an icy floor. In a case like that, you don't expect much, but, sure enough, in the seafood section they had a bunch of fish on ice, and a lot of the cubes had actually fallen on the floor. Of course, they weren't the same ones that had tripped Rosita Velez, but an ice cube is an ice cube, and I shot 'em for all I was worth.

I thought all that as I watched my little corporate crook running around slaying monsters with his free bow. And it occurred to me, maybe I was a white-collar criminal myself, photographing ice cubes that had nothing to do with anything.

It also occurred to me that was one crime they would never convict me of, even though I'd done it. Whereas murder was a crime they might convict me of, even though I had never done it and never would.

I pushed all such thoughts from my mind, tried to concentrate on Zelda. It was hard, because I still had the feeling I'd missed something.

Come on. Concentrate. Level Five's a tough level. We found the hookshot, yeah, the special grappling hook that let us cross chasms too wide to jump, but we still hadn't found the Nightmare Key. And you can't get to the big boss without the Nightmare Key.

The Nightmare Key — was that it? Had someone drugged Cranston Pritchert to get the Nightmare Key? What would be the point? And who was the big boss?

And what was it that I couldn't remember that was driving me crazy?

My mind did a backflip and suddenly I had it.

Mary/Maggie Mason.

51.

"It's not a snake."

MacAullif looked up from his desk, frowned. "What?"

"I know who killed Cranston Pritchert. I know everything."

"Oh, you do?"

"Yes, I do. I know the whole thing, and I think I can prove it. I'm gonna need your help, but it shouldn't be hard."

"Oh, is that so?"

"Yes, it is. But that's not important right now."

"Not important?"

"No. The important thing is Belcher. I wanna nail that son of a bitch. Everything else is secondary."

MacAullif leaned back in his chair, cocked his head. "I'm not going to interrupt you and ask you to make sense. I'm gonna assume when you get good and ready you're gonna tell me what this is all about. In the meantime, have your little fun."

"This isn't fun. This has been one of the worst experiences of my life. If you think acting manic is a sign of having fun, I suggest you take a refresher course in psychology."

"Uh-huh," MacAullif said. "You were saying you solved the crime, but the most important thing is to get Belcher?"

"Right, and I think I know how to do it."

"Oh?"

"My wife has a friend whose husband works for Channel 2. He's an on-camera reporter, does AAA interviews."

"AAA?"

"Ask any asshole. That's how they pad the news reports. You got a two-minute time slot for a one-minute story, how do you fill the other minute? Turn on the camera, point the microphone, and ask any asshole in the street what he thinks of the story. That's why local news is so bad. It's all padded with AAA interviews."

"That's really interesting," MacAullif said. "How does this help us?"

"He'll help us nail Belcher. Whenever we're set, whatever we need. I think the guy's getting a kick out of it."

MacAullif exhaled loudly. Grimaced. "Now I *am* going to urge you to the point. This is coming out worse than I thought. You say you solved the crime?"

"Yes, I did, and, believe it or not, you helped."

"I'm glad to hear it."

"But the real key was Mary/Maggie Mason."

"Who?"

"Richard Rosenberg's switchboard girl."

"You'll pardon me if that doesn't help."

"You know Richard Rosenberg's regular switchboard girls are Wendy and Janet and I can't tell 'em apart?"

I was not restoring MacAullif's faith in my sanity. "I've seem 'em," he said. "They don't look anything alike."

"No, no. It's their *voices* I can't tell apart. Never mind that. The point is, they're on vacation and he replaced them with this other girl Mary Mason."

"So?"

"She changed her name to Maggie. And that's what put me on the right track."

"The right track?"

"Yeah. Actually, you had me on it already. With what you said yesterday about the keys."

"What about 'em?"

"What you said about it must be the keys to his home because why would anyone want the keys to his office when everybody had 'em."

"That was important?"

"Right. It was dead wrong, but it was an

important idea to state. The other thing you gave me was my chief suspect. Marty Rothstein. That got me thinking. Well, actually it was my wife Alice got me thinking. But, anyway, wherever the credit is due, the point is, if Marty Rothstein did the crime, then Marty Rothstein had the gun. So what did he do with it, after the three people were dead?"

"Is there a point to this?"

"There sure is. The point is, who died last? We know who died first. Cranston Pritchert. But the real question is, who died last? A bit hard to determine from the medical evidence, as we discussed, but logically it's the girl. Last to die, I mean. At least the way we doped it out. Killer kills Pritchert. Killer says, Oops, gotta get rid of the people can connect me to this crime. Killer goes does 'em in. Logically, the killer doesn't know where the girl is any more than I did. So the killer finds the girl through the talent agent. Which makes the talent agent die second."

"So what?"

"The girl was killed with the same gun. Big stumbling block. If the gun was used to kill the girl, how does it wind up in my car?"

MacAullif frowned. "What do you mean?"

"It's like you said yesterday. Just because the bartender changed his story once, he doesn't have to be telling the truth now. And Alice says what if he planted the gun? So, I'm thinking about that. And it occurs to me — when I'm out at the talent agent's house — when the gun winds up in my car — when I get framed with the gun — well, what happens just before that? Sandy the bartender arrives to look at the resume photos. I'm there at the talent agent's house, suddenly he walks in the front door, looking for the cops. And all the time my car is parked out front."

I frowned, hit my forehead. "Then it occurs to me, how would he *know* it's my car? And, lo and behold, I have the answer. The day before. At the talent agent's office in the city. When we went through resume photos there. When we were done, I go out, get in my car, and drive off. Sandy's right there, sees me go. So he'd know it was my car."

MacAullif was staring at me, open-mouthed. "Are you telling me *the bartender* killed these people?"

I waved it away. "No, no, no. That's all bullshit. The bartender had nothing to do with it."

"Then what the hell are you talking about?"

I raised one finger, scowled. "I'm talking about Belcher. That son of a bitch Belcher.

The guy I wanna nail. The guy caused me more problems than you could believe."

"I understand the sentiment. Could you be more explicit?"

"Belcher's the reason I couldn't solve this case to begin with. All along it's been Belcher fucking everything up."

"We *knew* that."

"Yes and no."

MacAullif raised one eyebrow. "I'm getting ready to strangle you. I don't care how stressed out you are. You better start making sense, or I'm coming around the desk."

"Okay," I said. "The big stumbling block here has always been Belcher framing me. Because it's hard to get past. The solution is Belcher framed me. The fact it's not the solution to the crime gets swept away."

"We've been through all that."

"Yeah, but there's a wrinkle. And that's what did it for me. I spent the whole morning with the bookkeeper for Philip Greenberg Investments, so I know that I'm right."

"About what, for Christ's sake? Right about what?"

"About the snake."

"What?"

"I'm right about the snake. See, that was the problem all along. That goddamn Belcher. That's what screwed everything up."

I ticked them off on my fingers. "It looks like a snake. It has rattles like a snake. It has fangs like a snake."

I raised my finger in the air. "And . . . *it even bit me!*"

I spread my arms, shrugged, smiled.

"But it's not a snake."

52.

"Get out of here or I'll call the police."

"That's what you said the last time."

Amy Greenberg's eyes blazed. "Hey, like, I mean it. Barging in here like that."

"You really shouldn't have opened the door. It's the suburban life sucks you in. In New York City you'd open that door on a safety chain."

Amy Greenberg blinked. "Are you retarded or what? I said to get the hell out of here."

"And I heard you. I believe you also said you would call the police."

"That's right. I will."

"If you must, you must. Remember to ask for Sergeant Belcher. He knows me. He's the one arrested me before."

She backed away. "What is it with you? You get weirder every time you come."

I shook my head. "No. Not weirder. Just another day older and deeper in debt."

She frowned. "Huh?"

"Sorry," I said. "Way before your time. The thing is, I keep learning more and more.

I have more information now. And it's information I might want to share."

She looked at me suspiciously. "What does that mean?"

I shrugged. "Well, that's the thing. I could share it with you. On the other hand, if you call the police, I'd have to share it with them."

"Share what? What are you talking about?"

"My theory of the case."

"Oh, you have a theory?"

"What, you think my theory is I killed those people? No, my theory is I didn't. My theory is someone else did."

She looked at me mockingly. "What a great defense. I bet no one's ever thought of that before."

"Oh, I'm sure they have. Only in this case it happens to be true."

"Yeah, right. If you didn't kill those people, who did?"

"You did."

She looked at me a minute. Blinked. "Now I *know* you're nuts."

"No, I'm actually rather sane. In fact, compared to the last few days, I got both feet on the ground."

"I'm gonna call the cops now."

"If you do, I'll have to tell 'em what I know."

She hesitated. I could see her eyes move from me to the phone. She looked back at me. "Just what do you know?"

"Just about everything. Which is remarkable, because yesterday I knew just about nothing. But suddenly it all fell into place.

"From the beginning the thing that stymied me was *What's the scam?* A guy gets set up in a bar with a topless dancer, there's gotta be a scam. It was a real shock to find out that there wasn't."

"What are you talking about?"

"You know perfectly well. You're the one who set it up. You're the one who went to the talent agent to hire the dancer to make the play. Pretty stupid in retrospect, but only in retrospect. After all, you didn't know you were going to have to kill anyone. So you hired the girl to drug Cranston Pritchert and steal his keys. That's where you blew it — that's where you made the bad move. And, ironically, you did it just when you thought you were being so smart. That's because you're young — you didn't take account of human nature."

"I don't know what you're talking about."

"I know you don't. Which is just my point. I'll try to explain. In case Cranston Pritchert should try to figure out what happened, you didn't want the trail to lead back to you. So you thought you would insure against that happening. So, here's what you did. In addition to paying the talent agent and the girl for doing the job, you told 'em if anyone should come snooping around, you'd pay them a bonus not to tell 'em the truth, but to feed 'em a bullshit story. The girl's story was that she'd been hired to have drinks in the bar with the guy, but nothing else happened — basically not to tell about drugging the drink and stealing the keys.

"The talent agent's story was different. She was the only one who had supposedly had personal contact with the person who hired her. Her story was to describe that person as six foot six. So any detective Cranston Pritchert hired would think his client was giving him the runaround. Which, I must admit, was pretty neat."

I held up one finger. "Except for one thing. Human nature. You saw these bonuses as a contingency — *if* a detective comes around, here's what you have to say. But that wasn't the way the talent agent and the girl saw it at all. They looked at it as, There's the money, how do we get it? If the detective wasn't finding them, they'd go out of their way to find him."

I shrugged. "See what I mean? So, instead of being hard to find, which is what you intended, by offering them a bonus, you *guarantee* the fact they'll be found. Once found, they tell the stories you wanted told. Which, again, might have been okay if no one died."

"I don't see what any of this has to do with me."

"You don't? Well, let me spell it out for you. This started out as white-collar crime. Little bit of corporate greed. Granddaughter playgirl of company head, dismissed as young, flaky, and, dare I say it, female — because I'm sure gender bias had something to do with all this. Well, I'm sure none of that sits too well with a headstrong young lady, sick to death of never being taken seriously, and when Grandpa dies she sees a chance to do something about it. She's inherited his stock, she's gonna have an interest in the company and be a force on the board.

"But what happens? Before you can say boo, all the guys in the company are swooping down on her, feeding her a line of patronizing bullshit, trying to line up her stock.

"Not if she can help it. That's when she gets the plan.

"The guys have asked for her proxy. She has it there in her hands. A proxy which, if she wanted to, she could fill out in their favor.

"But she doesn't want to. She has her own shares of stock. And she has Philip Greenberg's shares. Plus any proxies that have come in in his name.

"Which is when it occurs to her, what if *a lot* of proxies came in in his name?"

"You're full of shit."

"I'm right on target. See, the tip-off was the key. Cranston Pritchert was set up to get his keys. That meant someone either wanted the keys to his home or the keys to his office. My first thought was it had to be the keys to his home, because why would anyone want the keys to the office, they all had them? Well, that's true, they did. Marty Rothstein, Kevin Dunbar, and Jack Jenkins all had keys to the office.

"But not you. The little granddaughter *visited* the office, but the little granddaughter didn't have the keys. She needed the keys to get into the office. Why?" I stopped. Smiled. "Mary/Maggie Mason."

She gawked at me. "Huh?"

"That's what gave it to me. A girl by the name of Mary Mason changed her name. That bothered me, and I didn't know why. But it was the concept. Changed the name. Changed the name. Changed the name. You had to get into the office to change the name on the proxies.

"Here's how you did it. You went into the office at night, you found the proxies, you xeroxed them. You had your own blank copy you were supposed to send in. You xeroxed a bunch of blanks from that. Then, working from the copies you made, you forged a whole bunch of new proxies, filling in Philip Greenberg's name. Not on all of them, of course, but on enough to give you over fifty percent.

"You did a careful job. It took you several days. When you were done, you went back to the office to replace the real proxies with the set of forgeries you'd made.

"One small problem. Cranston Pritchert showed up, caught you doing it, and you had to kill him."

I broke off, shook my head. "See, I feel sorry for you, except for one thing. Well, a couple of things, actually, but one thing here. Up until that point in time, you got a white-collar crime. Corporate theft. No one's gonna despise you. No one's gonna point at you and yell thief. You're a corporate crook, no better, no worse than all the rest."

I pointed my finger. "Except you had a gun. Had it with you all the time. As a contingency, you could say, just in case something went wrong. But the fact is, that contingency was planned. If something went wrong, you had a gun.

"You see what I mean? That's where I stop feeling sorry. Because, any way you slice it, you were ready, willing, and able to kill."

I shrugged. "But you probably haven't admitted that, even to yourself. You probably still think it just happened."

She said nothing, just looked at me.

"But no matter how you want to justify it, the fact is you did it. You're up there in the accountant's office, making the switch. You hear Cranston Pritchert come in. You can't afford to be caught there. You try to get out. But there's no time. You're trapped, and you hide in Marty Rothstein's office. Only he sees you and he finds you. Bad news. You got no excuse for being there. Even if he doesn't see the proxies, once you win the election, he'll know. The way you see it, you've got no choice. You pull your gun and you shoot him."

She looked at me sideways. "What are you doing? You're trying to get a rise out of me, aren't you? Trying to get me to say something. What's the idea?" Her eyes narrowed. "What's that?"

"What?"

"There. In your shirt pocket."

"Nothing."

She stepped forward, wrenched my jacket

aside. "Oh, yeah?" She reached in, jerked the microcassette out of my shirt pocket. "And what do we have here? A pocket dictaphone. Switched on and recording. Well, what a surprise."

She clicked it off, flipped it open, popped out the cassette. "How stupid do you think I am? You come in here, talking nonsense. You're all, I know all about you. Trying to goad me into saying something. Probably thought you were being subtle too. Now, let's us just have a little talk with the recorder off, okay?"

Amy Greenberg set the dictaphone and cassette down on the coffee table. She straightened up, said, "You come in telling me this story. You know what? I think you made it up. I don't think you have shit."

"Oh, yeah? Then how'd I know about drugging the drink? No one knew that. Just you, the agent, and the girl. The agent and the girl are dead, so how did I know?"

"How the hell should I know? Maybe your client told you way back when — I was out with some girl who drugged my drink. Is that what the guy said to you?"

I shook my head. "No. He had no idea. I didn't find out till yesterday."

"Who told you?"

"Sorry. I'm not going to tip you off to

someone else you need to kill. Even if you don't have the gun anymore."

I held up my finger. "And that's the second reason I can't feel sorry for you. Because you're the one got me into this whole mess."

"And how did I do that?"

"By giving me the gun. The first time I was out here. You slipped it under the seat of my car."

"The hell I did."

"The hell you didn't," I said. "I gotta admit, it was a pretty nifty move. I come out, talk to you, you realize I'm the private detective Cranston Pritchert hired. You know I met the talent agent and the girl, because you had to pay 'em the bonuses for lying to me. So there I am, perfect patsy. Even without the murder weapon, the police can tie me in to all three victims. Give me the gun and I'm dead.

"So, that's exactly what you did. The office beeped me, I had to make a phone call. When I get off the phone, I go out and find you in your car. You've backed out of your driveway to let me get out. Perfectly natural. Only, you know, it's just like you opening your door just now — sucked in by the suburbs, I left my car unlocked. You figured I had, and you figured right. So when you moved your car, you gave me the gun."

"Oh, sure," she said. "You remember what I was wearing? Like I really had a gun on me."

"Don't be silly," I said. "The gun was in your car. You took it out of your car, you put it in mine. You figured eventually the cops would find it. If they hadn't, I guess they would have got an anonymous tip.

"They found it just fine. In fact, it couldn't have been better. Because where should they find it, but at the talent agent's house."

I stopped, shook my head. "Which is what screwed me up from the start. I knew the gun had been planted. I just didn't know by who. With my car being out at the crime scene, I figured it was planted there. Which is one of the reasons it has taken me so long to get to you."

"Uh-huh," she said. "You got a real nice story there. But that's all it is. A story. It's all theories. You haven't got one fact. There's not a single thing you can prove."

"I don't think you've been paying attention," I said. "Which is understandable. There's been a lot of information you've had to assimilate very fast. You remember the proxies? The forged proxies? Well, that can be proven. A handwriting expert can prove that just fine. He can prove that they're forged. *And* he can prove that it's your forgery. There's no way to get away from that."

"So what? What if I did? You said it yourself, that's corporate crime. Nobody gives a damn."

"Like I say, you're a little slow on the uptake. It's understandable, but make the effort. Cranston Pritchert was killed in the office. He surprised the forger, and the forger killed him. If you're the forger, it's not good. That is not the part in which one would wish to be cast."

I could see her eyes moving, calculating. "Who knows this?" she said.

"I beg your pardon?"

"You say this is your theory. I'm wondering who you've told."

"And now I'm wondering why you're wondering. I know you've gotten rid of your gun, but you just might have another. Just as a point of information, were you thinking of killing me or bribing me?"

She stared at me. "God, you're weird."

"Thank you. I'll consider the source."

"Huh?"

"But as I was saying, I don't know how much this company is worth. And I don't know how much it's worth to you to remain

411

the chairman of the board."

Her eyes narrowed. "You mean for keeping quiet about the proxies?"

"That's the only way you're going to remain chairman."

She looked at me a moment, then said, "Wait a minute. Who you trying to kid? There's not just money involved. You shut up about the proxies, maybe, but, what, you're gonna shut up about the gun? You'd take money to take the fall? You can't have one without the other. You either shut up or you talk."

"You're telling me we have no deal?"

"Deal? How could we have a deal? Look, could you give me a moment? I gotta think this over."

"I would very much prefer it if you didn't leave this room."

"Huh?"

"You might come back with a gun."

"Oh, sure. I'm gonna shoot you in my living room."

"Actually, it would be your safest move. And having killed three people, the fourth couldn't be that hard. Plus, this one you could acknowledge. It would be a piece of cake. After all, I'm the murder suspect. I barged into your house and you had to shoot me dead. It wasn't murder, it was self-defense. You were in fear for your life. Hell, if you play your cards right, you'll wind up a hero."

"Why are you telling me this?"

"Because I'm tired of not knowing which end's up. I figure if you're gonna shoot me, you're gonna shoot me. I also figure if you got a gun, it's in the other room. If you go to get it, I'm out that door. Even if you should catch me, it's hard to claim self-defense when you shoot someone who's running away."

I spread my arms. "So, we seem to have a bit of a stalemate here. I suggest we work something out."

"What do you propose?"

"Believe it or not, I'd like to get off the hook for murder. The problem is, how to do that without getting you on it."

"You have any ideas on that?"

"Actually, I don't. You're like Rome. Every solution leads to you."

"How about whoever tipped you off?"

"What do you mean?"

"You come in here and you know all this — about the bonuses and drugging the drink. So, whoever it was, they're involved, and that's someone we could frame."

"Frame?"

"Or someone you could claim framed *you*.

Come on. That's the basic question. If you didn't do it and I didn't do it, who did?"

"If I tell you who, do you promise not to kill him?"

"Don't be stupid."

"That's not stupid. All the other principals are dead. If I tell you this, frame him, fine, kill him, no. Do I have your word?"

"Give me a break."

"I'm giving you a big break by talking to you instead of the cops. Considering what you did to me, that's a hell of a concession. Now, my patience is wearing thin. You start talking turkey, or I'm out the door."

"Fine, for Christ's sake. I won't hurt him. Jesus Christ, just show me a way out of this mess."

There came a pounding at the door, and a loud voice. "Open up! Police!"

Amy Greenberg turned on me. "You son of a bitch!"

"Hey, I didn't call 'em. You've been with me all the time."

"Hey! Open up in there!"

"I think you better open the door."

She waggled a finger at me. "If you tell them anything."

"It'll be my word against yours. I know. Right now, you'd better open the door."

She did, and Sergeant Belcher came

through it like a linebacker on a blitz. He pushed by Amy Greenberg, grabbed me by the arm, and spun me around. I felt the metal dig into my wrist, heard the click of the handcuffs snapping shut.

"All right, you son of a bitch," he said. "Let's see you make bail now."

"What the hell," I said.

I barely got the words out of my mouth.

I caught a glimpse of Amy Greenberg's face as Sergeant Belcher jerked me sideways.

The last thing I saw was my microcassette recorder lying on Amy Greenberg's coffee table as Belcher dragged me out the door.

53.

There were TV crews everywhere. Sergeant Belcher could hardly get a parking space. He pulled up behind one of the mobile units, jerked me out of the car.

The news crews descended on us. In the forefront, holding a Channel 2 microphone, was Chris Harris — the husband of Alice's friend.

"Sergeant Belcher," he said. "Chris Harris, Channel 2 News. Could I have a statement?"

Belcher was baffled. "Statement? What statement? What's going on here?"

"We just got the word. There's been a break in the Cranston Pritchert case."

"Where'd you hear that?"

"High-ranking sources. Word is the police have a suspect in custody." He pointed to me. "Is that him?"

I could see Belcher's mind going. He hadn't been prepared for any publicity at this juncture. On the other hand, if anyone was taking credit for my arrest, it might as well be him.

"This is Stanley Hastings. A suspect in the crimes. I've placed him under arrest."

"Hasn't he already been charged with the crimes?"

"He has. He's currently out on bail."

"Then why have you arrested him again?"

"Because new evidence has come to light which will probably result in revoking bail."

The TV reporters all began shouting questions at once.

"Evidence?"

"What new evidence?"

"Did he confess?"

"What have you got?"

Belcher raised his hand. "All I can say is he had the murder weapon, and his fingerprints have been found at all three murder sites, two of which he claims he was never at."

"That's old news, sergeant," Chris Harris said. "The word is there's been a break in the case."

"There has. The suspect has been apprehended in an attempt to influence witnesses in the case through bribes and intimidation."

The reporters again began shouting at once, and once again my buddy cut through.

"Bribing and intimidating who, sergeant? What's the story here?"

Belcher took a breath. "He's been attempting to influence the testimony of members of Cranston Pritchert's firm. Just now, he was arrested in an alleged attempt to intimidate Amy Greenberg, granddaughter of the late Philip Greenberg and newly elected chairman of the board. He was in the process of doing so when I made the arrest."

"So, Sergeant Belcher," Chris Harris said. "You claim you have the defendant dead to rights on three murder counts?"

"Yes, I do."

He shoved the microphone at me. "Mr. Hastings. Do you have any comment at this time?"

"Yes," I said. "I'm innocent. This cop doesn't know what he's talking about."

Belcher's eyes blazed, but he wasn't about to hit me on camera.

At that moment, a car screeched to a stop. Sergeant MacAullif got out and pulled Amy Greenberg from the back seat.

"There's Ms. Greenberg now," I said. "Why don't you ask her?"

As the reporters turned to look, Sergeant MacAullif pushed Amy Greenberg through the crowd to where Sergeant Belcher and I were standing.

Once again, Chris Harris took charge. "Ms. Greenberg," he said. "Chris Harris, Channel 2 News. Are you pressing charges against the suspect Stanley Hastings? We understand he attempted to threaten and bribe you. Is that true?"

"Not exactly," MacAullif said.

"And who are you?"

"Sergeant MacAullif. NYPD. I have a suspect under arrest for the murders of Cranston Pritchert, Shelly Daniels, and Laura Martin."

"I beg your pardon, sergeant, but I believe it's Sergeant Belcher who has the suspect under arrest."

"Who, him?" MacAullif smiled. "Well, yes, he does, but he has the wrong man. Stanley Hastings didn't kill anyone." He raised Amy Greenberg's arms to show the handcuffs on her wrists. "I have *Amy Greenberg* under arrest."

"Amy Greenberg?"

"That's right. Only in her case, I happen to have a full confession." MacAullif reached into his jacket pocket, pulled out a microcassette. "I have it on tape. A conversation between her and Mr. Hastings. He pretended to record it with a pocket dictaphone. She didn't say much until after she found it and switched it off. Then she said a whole bunch. Only that dictaphone was really a radio mike, it broadcast the whole conversation, and I recorded it outside in my car. I have it right here. Fascinating stuff, like how she killed three people, then planted the gun on him." MacAullif shrugged. "Which is the only reason he was ever a suspect to begin with. That, and some rather embarrassingly bad police work, both from the crime-scene units and the evidence room. Mishandling of evidence. Mislabeling of evidence." He turned to me. "All of which resulted in Mr. Hastings's arrest."

My buddy, Chris Harris from Channel 2, shoved the microphone back in front of Belcher. "Sergeant Belcher," he said. "What do you have to say to that? How is it you happened to arrest the wrong man?"

Sergeant Belcher looked totally baffled. He stood there, gawking at the television cameras. His eyes were wide, his mouth was open.

He said, "Huh?"

I loved it.

54.

It was on every evening newscast. Every single channel. We called a bunch of friends, got 'em to tape the broadcasts for us, so I know.

And every channel had it. The news deals in sound bites. And by far the best sound bite going was Sergeant Belcher saying, "Huh?"

The rest of the story they handled differently. Some led with me and Belcher, then had MacAullif bring Amy Greenberg in. Some of them started off with her — "Greenberg Arrested" — then ran it back from there.

It all added up to the same thing. Sergeant MacAullif had the right killer, Sergeant Belcher had the wrong one, and Sergeant Belcher looked like a schmuck.

And, boy, did that feel good. He deserved to look like a schmuck. True, he wasn't a snake — that is to say, he didn't frame me with the gun, Amy Greenberg did that — but he sure looked like a snake. And he sure acted like a snake, messing with the fingerprint evidence, so it sure was nice to nail him on TV.

And in terms of revenge, that was enough. Since he hadn't framed me like I thought. He'd planted evidence against me, sure. But, you see, he thought I was guilty. He thought that it was my gun, he thought I'd done it all along. These little assists with the evidence weren't to frame an innocent man, merely to nail a guilty one.

Am I excusing him? No, no. Please. The man is a nasty, rotten son of a bitch, a bad cop, I hope he burns in hell. I mean, Jesus Christ, if it weren't for the fact he did such a good job looking like a snake, the case would have been a whole lot easier to figure out. Because, aside from him, who could have planted the gun?

Well, Sandy the bartender could have, but he didn't. He did have the opportunity, as Alice pointed out, but he didn't really have the motive. I mean, when you examine what people got, Sandy got a hundred dollars cash, and Amy Greenberg got control of a corporation. In terms of motivation, she stood out like a sore thumb. So, subtract Sergeant Belcher, and I solve the case like that. The moment the gun's in my car, her ass is grass.

But it's never that simple. There's always

some schmuck stirring things up. At least, I always find it to be the case. I'm sure other PI's solve their murders just like that — they always seem to on television.

Speaking of television.

Boy, did we stick it to Belcher. I know I've already said this, but you'll pardon me if I say it again. If you've never been arraigned on a triple homicide, you probably can't know how I feel. But, boy, was that a beautiful thing. Sticking it to Belcher, and MacAullif holding the knife.

Yeah, that was a nice touch too. He was out to get me because of MacAullif, so it was only fair MacAullif get him.

I asked MacAullif, by the way, before it went down, whether he would mind. Nailing Belcher on TV, giving him a reason to hate his guts. MacAullif couldn't have cared less. His opinion was, Belcher already hated him and was out to get him for no good reason, what difference would it make if he actually had one?

I suppose that's true. Still, I told MacAullif to watch his back. And he looked at me as if to say, "Gee, what a bright idea, I never would have thought of it," which was about par for the course.

As for Amy Greenberg, it's just like I said. I sympathized with her to a point. As a young woman, dismissed and abused by the men in the company, I could root for her to win. But the minute she starts killing people, I don't care how politically correct her cause, she happens to have lost my support. If that sounds overly sarcastic, it's only because there are people who wouldn't agree, indeed, who would be angry at me for exposing the killer and damaging her cause. Just as I would have damaged someone's cause had the killer been black or gay.

Sorry, gang. Call it as you see it, play it as it lays.

Anyway, that's the wrap-up for Amy Greenberg. She was all, "I didn't do it," and MacAullif was all, "Oh, yes, you did." And with what he has on tape, there's no way she isn't going down.

As for Sergeant Belcher, he's already gone. In a manner of speaking. Last I heard, he'd been transferred off homicide, pending investigation by Internal Affairs.

And his buddy, Martinez, has been transferred out of the evidence room. There's something for you. I more or less made that happen, and the fact is, I never met the man. Don't even know what he looks like. I could bump into him on the street tomorrow and I wouldn't have a clue. A somewhat unsettling thought, considering how he must feel about me. Unless I want to spend the rest of my life flinching every time I see a Hispanic man with a limp, perhaps I'd better ask Mac-Aullif if he has a photo on file.

Aside from that, I'm feeling fine. And getting off the hook for murder is just part of it. I also might get paid. Richard Rosenberg says I do indeed have a claim against the widow Pritchert for the money her husband owed me, and has offered to facilitate my collecting it, just for the fun of bopping her attorneys around.

As for Miriam Pritchert, last I heard she and Marty Rothstein had become an item. So maybe it always was more than just stock.

Speaking of stock, there's another stockholders meeting coming up. I know because I got a proxy in the mail. I can't decide if I should send it in, or show up in person to vote my one share. Hell, maybe I could swing the meeting, wind up chairman of the board.

Yeah, I'm in a pretty good mood.

But the main thing I'm happy about is Sergeant Belcher. TV star extraordinaire. Ask any asshole, indeed. Boy, how he fell for the bait. All it took was one phone call from Chris Harris from Channel 2 News. And what yeoman work Chris did. Aside from the phone call, he was responsible for all the TV crews being there. Which was pretty damn nice of him, giving up the exclusive in order to give us bigger play. Anyway, he was the one who made the anonymous phone call, tipping the cops off that I was bribing and intimidating witnesses and was out at Amy Greenberg's house.

And Belcher did the rest. Nice bit of irony there. Because that's why Cranston Pritchert came to me in the first place. He thought he was the victim of a scam. Only he wasn't. As it turned out, no one pulled a scam on him at all. No, the only scam in the case was the one I pulled on Belcher.

And he never suspected. Never had a clue. Poor guy. Should have been a bit more like Cranston Pritchert. Just a little more suspicious.

But he never stopped to consider.

Never once did the thought occur to him.

I'm being set up.

The employees of Thorndike Press hope you have enjoyed this Large Print book. All our Large Print titles are designed for easy reading, and all our books are made to last. Other Thorndike Press Large Print books are available at your library, through selected bookstores, or directly from us.

For information about titles, please call:

(800) 223-2336

To share your comments, please write:

Publisher
Thorndike Press
P.O. Box 159
Thorndike, Maine 04986